DAD BOD
—DRILLED—

Jasinda Wilder

DRILLED

ONE

I OPEN MY EYES, GROGGY AND DISORIENTED. WHERE AM I?
Oh, right. It's all coming back to me. I'm at the
Marriot, just off the freeway, some three or four miles
from the Waverley jobsite Franco is working on.

As I come fully awake, the next thing I realize
is that I'm sore, if you know what I mean. It's not as
if I've never woken up with a sore hoo-ha before—I
do have some experience with this. Actually, it's happened quite a few times, and all of them were memo-
rable to say the least. But this time? Holy Moses, I'm
so sore. I feel like I've been fucked into next week.

Ah, yes…Franco…

I roll over, tugging the sheet up past my shoulder, and slide up against him from behind. He's facing
away, breathing evenly and slowly. I don't think he's
totally asleep, though—I don't know him well enough
to be able to say, one way or the other, considering
we only met the previous evening, and have spent the

intervening ten hours having sex, calling room service, and sleeping. But I'm fairly certain I can tell—he snores ever so slightly, a subtle rasp of his breath in his throat on the inhale, and a gentle huff on the exhale.

Pretending, perhaps.

I'm all too familiar with pretending to be asleep, so I recognize the signs. I normally fake being asleep to let the guy I just hooked up with leave first. I have a feeling that's the same game Franco is playing right now.

Joke's on him, though, because I have another plan: one more round of epic sex for the road.

I snuggle up behind him, rest my cheek between his shoulder blades, nudging my core up against his taut, firm butt. God, that ass is a work of art. I feel the hard globes against my thighs and pubis, his warm skin, and his faint dusting of body hair.

Casually, as if by accident, I toss my arm over his waist, letting it rest for a moment. And then, less accidentally, I place my hand on his body and find his abs, grooved and ridged and rock hard. Gently, I slide my palm against his skin, carving a path downward. His breathing doesn't catch, but his core tenses. I smile against his back, knowing for certain he's awake. He doesn't move, doesn't give anything else away. I run my hand down his thigh and back up, and then over his abs repeating the pattern, daring to go lower and lower on each pass over his stomach. The lower my hand travels, the harder his abs tense.

Finally, I clasp his erection in my fist and stroke it gently. Even though I've had this incredible organ inside me four—no, five—times already, I'm still marveling at its size and perfection. It's just glorious and breathtaking. Eight inches long if it's an inch, thick as a goddamn kielbasa sausage, and curved just enough toward the tip to hit my G-spot when he drives in at a certain angle...and believe me, he found that angle last night. And used it to scream-inducing effect. In fact, we got a call from the front desk at two-nineteen in the morning asking us to please quiet down, as there had been several noise complaints from other guests. Meaning, me. I'm loud—I'm a screamer and, when I'm coming hard enough I can't stop myself from shrieking like a banshee, and last night, Franco made damn sure I couldn't help myself.

Even my throat is sore from screaming.

And despite my sore throat and aching lady bits, I still want more. Five rounds of epic sex in less than twelve hours, at age forty, and I'm still ready for more from this guy.

I texted my girlfriend Imogen earlier last evening to tell her that Franco has a magical dick and, not only that, I'm scared because he makes me *feel* things. And I hate feeling things—at least, things other than orgasms.

Franco is still pretending to be sleeping, even as I slowly caress his shaft with one hand. The soft flesh stutters against my palm and fingers, all those inches sliding and gliding through my fist. I rub my thumb against the tip, stroke down to the base and back up, rub the tip—repeating until I feel pre-cum smearing against my thumb. Yet still, he remains motionless, breathing evenly.

Damn, he's good.

I move my hand lower, cupping his balls, using my middle finger to massage his taint, and then return my touch to his iron-hard, yet velvet-soft erection. This time, I increase the speed of my strokes incrementally, sliding my fist up and down faster and faster in gradual degrees, until I'm pumping him rapidly.

He holds out admirably, remaining still until the last possible moment. And then, at last, he snarls wordlessly and knocks my hand away, rolling up onto his knees. Levered upright over me, he stares down at me with pale, icy-blue eyes flickering like twin flames. His chest rises and falls rapidly, his abs tense, muscles bunched, fists clenched.

"Dammit, woman," he breathes. "I was trying to sleep."

I quirk an eyebrow up at him. "Bullshit. You were awake."

He just stares balefully down at me. "Yeah— when you started messing with me."

I reach for him, grasp him in my fist, and lazily stroke him. "Like you're complaining."

He glances at the alarm clock on the nightstand beside the hotel bed. "Coulda waited until at least six in the damn morning."

I shrug. "Eh, I wake up at five thirty or so every morning without an alarm clock, just out of long habit. I couldn't sleep in past six even if I wanted to."

His eyes watch the movement of my hand as I slowly caress his length. "You want me to come everywhere, Audra? Because that's what's about to happen if you don't quit for a damn second."

I shrug again, the movement causing my admittedly overly generous breasts to sway. "I wouldn't mind seeing that. Could be kinda hot."

"Maybe, but it wouldn't get you an orgasm."

"You have ten fingers and a tongue, don't you?" I reply, not stopping. "You could use those."

He narrows his eyes as he looks at me. "I could." He pulls out of my reach, pinions my wrists in one of his hands, and then leans over me, stretching across me to snag a condom from off the table beside the bed. "But I have other ideas."

I fake a confused expression. "You've already fucked me missionary, bent over the bed, doggy style, and with my feet on your shoulders. What's next, some weird *Kama Sutra* position?"

He doesn't respond, just keeps hold of my hands with one of his, rips the condom wrapper open with his teeth, spits the strip of wrapper aside, holds the wrapper in his teeth and withdraws the ring, then rolls it onto himself in a single, smooth motion.

"You're good at that," I remark, grinning up at him.

"Lots of practice." He doesn't grin back.

"Ooh, so serious," I say, in a mocking tone of voice. "You know, I can put that on you with just my mouth."

He pauses, staring down at me in surprise and skepticism. "Really?"

I nod, struggling to break his hold on my wrists. "Oh yeah. I'm really good with my mouth."

"Why didn't you say so earlier?"

I laugh. "Sorry, I was too busy screaming."

He smirks. "Never made a girl scream so loud that we got a call from the front desk. I've had neighbors pound on the walls, but never got an actual noise complaint before."

"Yeah, well, I'm not exactly the most inhibited lady you'll ever meet." I struggle harder to break free.

"Now let me go, dammit."

He's back to super serious Franco again. "I don't think so."

"Let me go and I'll show you what I can do with my mouth."

"You know you're gonna show me anyway." He shoves my hands up over my head and bends over me to nuzzle my breasts. "I told you, I have different plans."

"Like what?"

He reaches between my thighs, two fingers circling my clit, still pinning my hands over my head. He watches me as he touches me, bringing me expertly and swiftly to the cusp of climax in a matter of a minute or two, and then pushing me inexorably over the edge—this first one doesn't make me scream, just moan and whimper and thrash underneath him, but he doesn't stop even when I've finished my orgasm—instead, he just keeps touching, this time slipping those same two fingers inside me, curling them and stiffening them, using them to massage deep inside me, slicking them in and out, in and out, faster and faster, always striking that one particular little spot just right, again and again, tirelessly. This one isn't as fast to overtake me, but when it does start to rise within me, it's a hot, expanding balloon of pressure and frenzied energy and desperation, a deep, throbbing vaginal orgasm pulsing through me in a tidal wave of ramping intensity.

Again, he doesn't tease or draw it out, just throws me mercilessly over the edge—and this time I do scream, just a small breathless shriek as I'm racked by the waves of climax. My whole body is tensed and I thrash, kicking and bucking, but he has an iron grip on my wrists, and just lets me thrash and shriek underneath him, fingers driving in and out of me through the entirety of the climax.

Next, he transfers his grip on my wrists to his other hand, and I feel my sticky juices dripping down his fingers onto my wrists. Using his now-free hand, he slides two fingers inside me and presses a thumb against my clit.

I'm gasping, shaking, limp, and I rock my head side to side, no longer struggling. "Oh god, Franco, not another one. Jesus. I'll die."

He just snorts derisively. "You came at least half a dozen times last night. You'll survive a few more."

His combined touch, in me and on me, is almost too much, stimulating my now-hypersensitive flesh. I groan raggedly, bucking under him as he guides me unerringly to the cusp of yet another climax.

"You brute," I mumble, "you're trying to kill me. Death by orgasm."

"There are worse ways to go."

"I'll get you back for this," I vow, my eyes on his as I hold back the writhing pressure of the most powerful orgasm yet. "I'll tie to you a bed and have my way with you until you beg me to stop."

"You're welcome to try," he says with a smirk. "But I'm forty-five, sweetheart. My refractory period isn't what it used to be, so that may take a while."

"You—oh, *oh*-Jesus-have-mercy—you have the refractory period of a twenty-one-year-old porn star, so don't play coy with me, Franco." I was in the grip of it, now, still trying to hold it off, draw it out, get the most out of it.

He's relentless, not allowing me to hold out for very long. This time, though, he stops when I'm riding the edge, just when I feel a scream starting to bubble up inside me. He doesn't stop for long—just slips his hand away from me, lets go of my wrists, grabs me by the waist and tosses me onto my belly in a single effortless flip. He immediately pounces, snatching my wrists up again and pinning them behind my back with one hand. He nudges his knees between my thighs, forcing me to spread apart, and then his other hand dives between my belly and the bed and tugs my hips upward in a quick jerk, leaving my the upper half of my body pressed down against the mattress and my ass in the air.

Seconds have passed since his fingers were

pushing me to the edge of climax, and in those seconds I've drawn away from the cusp, but now I'm right there again as he thrusts in, his massive organ splitting me apart with a sudden stinging ache that sears a breathless gasp out of me. His hips slap against my ass as he pounds deep, and I'm filled and throbbing, the climax ramping up inside me hotter and harder and huger than anything yet. I'm helpless, my breasts smashed against the bed, my butt in the air, my hands pinned behind my back in a firm, unbreakable, yet gentle grip.

A scream rips through me as he drives against me, suddenly hard and fast, each stroke striking the tip of his cock against my G-spot until I'm wild with the furious climax shattering me like a porcelain vase dropped on a marble floor.

He doesn't slow as I come, but his thrusts aren't as hard, just fast and deep, his hips smacking against me loudly.

I can't stop myself from screaming, each stroke sending further piercing pangs of pleasure spearing through me, driving me past orgasm into something else unquantifiable as a mere climax.

God, oh god—this is why I've spent the last many hours in bed with this man, because it's like this every time.

Shit, shit, shit—just when I think he's nearly

done, he's going to come and it'll be over, just when I think it's impossible for me to come anymore, he pauses in his thrusting and lets go of my wrists. He lifts me upright so we're both up on our knees, him behind me, still inside me, our breathing matched in ragged synch. He guides one of my hands down to where we're joined, leaving the other one free.

"Touch yourself," he orders. "One more."

"I can't—I can't."

"I need to feel you come once more, with me." He powers up into me, his breath and voice in my ear, hot and intense. "Touch yourself, Audra."

I wrench my hand free of his grip and reach up to tangle both my hands in his long, loose blond hair, clutching at it behind his head, arching my back as I lift up and sink down on him. I hope he doesn't think orders will work on me. I'll let him toss me around, because that's hot AF, but I don't do orders. He'll learn.

Or, maybe he won't, because this is probably it for us.

I don't need to touch myself, anyway. Just him, like this, is enough. Which is crazy, because it usually takes a hell of a lot more than that to make me come, especially when I'm on my fourth in less than twenty minutes.

Oh, holy fuck, here we go…

He grasps at my breasts with both hands, using them as leverage to drive into me, holding them in place, rough palms scratching my hardened nipples. Harder, harder, his breath in my ear, his grunts ragged and increasingly breathless.

I rise and fall, reaching up and back to hold on to the back of his head, feeling him slide through me, splitting me apart and slamming into me loudly, wetly. A scream escapes from me as the first tremors of my next climax shear through me, this one nuclear in comparison to the ones that preceded it. He's tireless, a feral tiger, snarling in my ear, and my ability to hold to the rise-and-fall rhythm of our union stutters, and his grip on my breasts is all that holds me upright.

Finally, I feel him lose the rhythm as well; here comes my favorite part.

I feel his head move, dipping down, and then his teeth sink sudden and hard into my shoulder, and he growls past a mouthful of my flesh, his hands gripping my boobs with an almost painful force, his hips driving madly, wildly, his shaft singing through my spasming channel, my scream shivering the room as I come in unison with him—something I've only had happen one other time in my life.

His yell is wordless, a strained, primal roar as he slams into me once—twice—three times—harder for one last drive, and then he goes limp, his grip on my tits releasing to wrap his arms around me, face buried in my neck, my hands knotted in his hair so tightly I'm not sure I'll be able to loosen them.

We're both gasping brokenly, the only sound in the room.

Something wiggles and niggles and nips inside me—not a physical sensation, but an emotional one. Something odd and frightening centered on the way his arms feel wrapped around me like this—suspiciously hug-like. An embrace.

He lets go abruptly, and I'm so limp I fall bonelessly forward, moaning as I flop onto the mattress. Franco hits the bed beside me, and we lie there, breathing into the silence.

After a long while, he speaks. "You want the bathroom first?"

I moan again, and then find my voice. "Yeah—yes. I'll take the bathroom first. Gotta pee."

He rolls to his back, tossing an arm over his eyes. "Okay, cool. Go for it." He reaches out with his other hand and squeezes my ass cheek once, and then pats it.

I snicker as I roll away. "What was that?"

"What?" he asks, not removing his arm from his eyes.

"The thing with my butt?"

He just chuckles. "Eh...I don't know. I just

appreciate your ass." His voice drops an octave deeper and takes on a tone that indicates he's quoting something. "'I don't normally do this, but I feel compelled to tell you something. You have…the most breathtaking…hiney. I mean it is *good*. I wanna be friends with it.'"

I cackle as I traipse to the bathroom. "First time anyone's quoted *Anchorman* to me post-coitus." I pause in the doorway. "But thank you. And…I think you already *are* friends with it."

He lifts his arm up slightly to smirk sidelong at me. "Better friends, then. Much, *much* better."

"Yeah, well, we'll see. Maybe I'll let you make better friends with my ass after I take a quick shower."

He lays his arm back down. "Take your time. I need to recover anyway."

"Don't tell me I've worn you out, already, old man."

He just flips me off. "I won't dignify that with a response."

I laugh again and close the door. I turn the shower on and pee as the water heats, and then spend several wonderful minutes luxuriating in the hot water, stretching under the spray and enjoying the deep, delicious ache of a well-sated hoo-ha.

Once I'm clean, I step out, dry off, twist a towel around my hair and wrap another around my body, and then yank the door open as I wipe steam off the mirror.

"Hey, Franco—have you ordered breakfast yet?" I call. "Because I'll need at least six cups of coffee to make it through the rest of today, so order two pots."

Silence.

My stomach drops as I peek out, and find an empty bedroom. His clothes are gone, his wallet, his phone. Not even a note.

"You ass," I mutter. "Could've at least ordered me room service before you ghosted on me."

TWO

I DRESS AND DO MY HAIR AS BEST I CAN WITH THE complimentary hotel toiletry products and no brush—the nice thing about having a pixie cut is that in a pinch I can blow-dry it and finger comb it and get by. I feel yucky putting on my clothes from yesterday, but I didn't exactly preplan this little rendezvous with Franco.

I think about ordering room service for myself, but decide against it—I have a client for a personal training session in less than an hour, followed by my own scheduled workout, and I'd rather stay fasted until after my workout. Plus, eating room service by myself just feels lame.

I try not to think too much about anything as I snag my purse and stuff my feet into my shoes. Don't think about Franco. Don't think about last night—or this morning…or any of the time in between. Don't think about his dick; don't think about his hands, or his fingers, or his mouth, or his ass. Certainly don't think about those rippling, eight-pack abs that turn me on like a damn light switch.

Really, really, *really* don't think about the way he bolted without even saying goodbye.

I refuse to think about any of it as I head to the elevator and the front desk to check out. The desk clerk is a decently attractive man several years older than me—nearing fifty, maybe—with a polite smile that tightens as he takes in my push-up sports bra and tiny white Lycra booty shorts.

"May I help you, ma'am?" he asks, his voice barely masking his disapproval, even as his eyes suggest something else.

"Yeah, checking out of room six-nineteen." I toss the little envelope with the keycard onto the marble counter and dig my wallet out of my purse, preparing to pay for the room.

He taps at his keyboard with two fingers, spinning a Mont Blanc pen in the fingers of his other hand—his name tag says his name is Michael and that he's the General Manager. Under different circumstances, I'd be interested. As it is, at the moment, it takes all my concentration not to think about stupid Franco and his stupid David Copperfield vanishing impression.

"Ah…okay, you're all checked out. Thank you for

choosing Marriott hotels, ma'am." His smile is, once again, polite and tightly disapproving even as his eyes flick up and down.

I frown. "What about the room charge?"

He taps again. "It's been paid, ma'am. At…seven-oh-four this morning, charged to the card on file from check-in last night."

I blink. "Oh. Okay, cool. Thanks."

"My pleasure, ma'am. Have a wonderful morning."

"Yeah, you too." As I exit the hotel, I remember that Franco had put his card down to reserve the room, but I suppose my disquiet at his vanishing act made me assume he'd stick me with the hotel bill, too.

Less of an asshole, but still an asshole.

I get into my car, start it, wait for Bluetooth to connect, and turn on 80s pop in an attempt to distract myself. I sing along to ABBA's "Super Trouper" before punching the radio off in disgust.

"Damn you, Franco! I can't even enjoy ABBA!" I shout.

In desperation, I call Imogen, putting it on hands-free while I drive.

It rings four times, and then I hear her pick up the call, followed by shuffling and rustling as she tries to get the phone to her ear. For a lifelong nurse, she's not really a morning person. "Hunh—hello?"

"This is bad, Imogen, really, really bad."

"Whassit? Audra? What's—what's bad?"

"Why is she calling this early?" I hear Jesse's voice rumble in the background.

"It's seven thirty!" I say, "so not really that early."

"Yeah, but it's Saturday," Imogen mumbles. "And we both have the day off."

"Sorry, sorry. But I just—bad things, Imogen, bad things. I need you to talk me off the ledge."

"What ledge?" Her voice echoes as she goes into the bathroom; I hear the toilet seat slam down, and the sound of her peeing—we've been friends for so long that such things don't faze either of us. "Is this about Franco?"

"Yes, it's about Franco."

"And his magical dick?"

"It's the most magical. You don't even understand." I sigh. "The thing has unicorn magic *and* fairy magic, and I swear I heard angels singing on numerous occasions throughout the night."

"So, that's…good, right?" She puts the phone on speaker as she washes her hands and then takes it off again as I hear her moving throughout her house, probably to the coffeemaker. "Or is this about *feeling* things?"

"We were only a few hours in when I sent you

that text. It only got better, by which I mean worse, from there."

"I'm lost."

"Hands down the best sex of my life. Legit, it was—I have no words for how amazing."

"Still not understanding the negative."

I sigh. "It was *too* good, that's the negative."

She laughs, and I hear a coffee grinder whirring in the background. "The sex was *too* good. Are you hearing yourself? You know how many times you've called me to complain about lackluster sex from the night before? Now you're complaining it was too *good*?"

I groan as I pull up to a red light. "Yes! But the sex itself isn't the problem—surely you see that. The sex itself was...how do I even put it? I just had sex with a god, an actual god, like from Greek mythology or something. I'm probably pregnant with a demigod right now."

Imogen laughs harder. "You're crazy, you know that?" She goes serious, then. "You *did* use protection, right?"

"Duh, of course I did. I'm forty, not twenty. You think I want to pop out an accidental kid at my age? Hell no. I have a six-pack and my hoo-ha is as tight as a goddamn djembe, and I plan on keeping it that way, thank you very much."

Imogen snorts. "A lot of moms out there would take exception to that, you know. Moms can have six-packs and a tight hoo-ha too."

I groan. "I know, I know. You're missing my point, dammit."

"Okay, what's your point, then?" I hear her coffeemaker gurgling and the sound of cabinets opening and closing, the distant rumble of Jesse's voice, and her voice answering, muffled, the asides of a couple starting their morning.

"My point is, the sex was so good I'm worried I'm not gonna be able to resist wanting more. Hell, I already do want more and I'm still sore from this time! Plus, he snuck out on me while I was taking a shower! No note, nothing, just left. I mean, sure, he paid for the hotel room, but shit, he could've said goodbye. It's not like I was going to fucking propose or something." I merge onto the freeway for the short jaunt to the gym.

"If you want to bang him again, then bang him again. What's the issue?"

"Do not sully the majesty of such glorious intercourse with such derogatory terminology, dammit! It wasn't mere *banging*, Imogen—it was…a godly union of ecstasy and wonder. I had no less than eight orgasms. Eight! I was counting! And there were several times one ran right into the next, so it was hard to tell if it was one or two or, like, seven, all in quick succession."

"Jesus." She sounds suitably stunned.

"Yes, exactly. If I were Catholic I'd be in confession from now till doomsday."

"I'm still lost, Audra." She takes a sip of coffee, and then continues. "If you want more of the...how did you put it? Godly union of ecstasy and wonder or whatever, go see him again. It's not like he'll be hard to find. His best friend is my boyfriend, and they work together."

"Yes, I know all that." I sigh again. "You don't do casual sex like I do, so I guess you wouldn't understand. I *can't* see him again. It'll stop being a hookup and become something else if we fuck again, and because it was as good as it was, there's a high probability I'll develop actual feelings for him, and that would be an absolute disaster on an epic scale. You know I don't do commitment, Imogen."

"Or maybe it wouldn't be a disaster at all."

"It *would*." I pause as I change lanes and exit the freeway, make the turn, and head for the gym. "And you know why."

"That was a long time ago, Audra. Maybe it's time to—"

"Nope, nope, nope, *nope!*" I say over her in a sing-song. "It would be a disaster. The way he left suggests to me that he's been down this road before, and many times. Plus, he's just too good at sex to not be as much of a player as I am."

"So?"

"So, I can't see him again. Either it wouldn't live up to last night and I'd lose the memory of the best sex ever, or it'd be just as good if not better, and I'd get hooked, and then I'd start *liking* him." I blew a raspberry. "Shit, I already *do* like him. I was gonna slip out while *he* was taking a shower, but he beat me to it, damn the man. It's not often a guy gets the drop on me."

"Are you mad or impressed?"

"Both."

"Why are you mad?"

"Because I want to fuck him again! I'm telling you—he's dangerous. I'm basically a nympho at this point."

"You *are* a nympho, Audra, and you can't blame it on Franco."

"No, I'm not really a nympho. I knew an actual nymphomaniac in college, and it's not as funny or as hot as it sounds. It was a difficult condition for her to live with."

I hear Imogen sipping coffee again. "So—he left before you did, and you're mad about it because you wanted more sex, but also because he got the drop on you, but you're also impressed because of the afore-mentioned, and also scared because you're worried you'll end up actually liking him, which for some stupid reason you're convinced would be a bad thing. Do I have that right?"

"Yes, exactly."

"You're giving me a headache." She let out a slow breath, and I heard a spoon tinkling against her mug. "What if you just tried letting yourself like him?"

"NO!" I shout immediately. "Do you NOT remember The Incident?"

"Yes, Audra, I remember The Incident. But, again, that was almost twenty years ago."

"Doesn't matter. Men are for looking at and having sex with. Not friendships, not romance, and certainly not allowing yourself to *like* them."

Imogen sighs. This is an old argument and one that we stopped having several years ago, because it always threatened to turn into an actual fight, and neither of us wanted to risk that. "Audra, I..." Another sigh, a sip of coffee, and she starts again. "What do you want me to say? You know how I feel about this. I want you to be happy. If you're happier never letting yourself like a guy or fall in love, then okay, fine, I get it, I love you, and I support you, even if I disagree with you. But, I'm just saying, Franco seems like a great guy. What if he's different from—?"

"They're *never* different," I hiss, cutting her off before she can say the dreaded name. "Not when it comes right down to it."

"Jesse is," she says, very quietly.

"Congratulations, Imogen—you found the *one* decent man on the planet." I know I sound snarky as hell—or even downright nasty. But I can't help it. I signal my turn into the gym parking lot while letting out a long, slow breath. "I'm sorry. I'm happy for you, I really am. But that's never gonna happen to me. I won't let it."

"I'm sorry I can't be more help in this situation, Audra."

I laugh. "Funny thing is, you actually have been helpful. You've reminded me why I need to stay away from him."

"Are you actually going to do that?" she asks. "Stay away from him, I mean?"

I groan, laughing. "Probably not. I'm still pissed at him for vanishing on me. Only I get to pull that move. And yes, I'm fully aware of the hypocrisy of that statement."

"Well, I'm here if you need me." A pause. "Actually, why don't you come over for dinner tonight?"

I consider. "Yeah, maybe that's a good idea." I laugh. "Just keep your wine rack stocked, babe, because I foresee this getting interesting."

"No kidding. It already is, and you've only just met him."

"Exactly." I park and shut off the car, taking the phone and putting it to my ear. "I have to go, I've got a client in twenty minutes and I haven't had any coffee yet, and I think I got a total of four hours sleep divided into, like, six segments."

She's silent a moment. "You were seriously having sex the whole night?"

"Pretty much, yeah. We had some room service and watched an HBO comedy special, but other than that, yeah. The whole night."

"Can you even walk?"

I burst out laughing. "Not really. Remember that summer we spent riding horses all day every day at your great-uncle's ranch in Wyoming?"

She cackles. "We were both bowlegged for the first month. We walked like we had a barrel between our legs."

"That's pretty much how I'm walking right now."

"That sore?"

"You have *no* idea," I say, getting out of the car and leaning against the driver's side door. "The man is hung like a goddamn rhinoceros. You could seriously club baby seals with his cock."

"Too much information, Audra—WAY too much information."

"Well, you asked."

"I did *not* ask for penis dimensions, as a matter of fact."

"At *least* eight inches long, almost as thick as my wrist, with just the perfect amount of curve. It's legitimately the most perfect dick I've ever held in my slutty little hands."

"AUDRA ROSLYN DONOVAN!"

"What? It's the truth!"

"He's my boyfriend's best friend, Audra! I don't want, need, or care to know the details of what his penis looks like."

"You should. It's a unicorn dick."

"A what?"

"A dick so perfect and rare that it's a unicorn."

"Oh." She sighs. "Audra, can you maybe think beyond his penis for a minute?"

"Can you stop calling it a *penis*? That's weird and clinical and icky. Nobody calls it a penis. Do you refer to Jesse's as a penis?"

"I—no. But that's different."

"What do you call it, then? His glorious manhood?"

"Oh my *god*, Audra! No! That's so stupid. God, you're impossible."

"What do you call it, then?"

"That's private!"

"Oh, come on, don't be a prude! It's not like I'm asking for a picture of it, just what you call it. His magical thunder-hammer? His wee-wee? What?"

"Magical…thunder-hammer? Wee-wee? *How* do you come up with this crap?" She can't help laughing, I notice. "We don't often actually refer to it or talk about it. When we do, we tend to say cock, okay? Does that satisfy your curiosity?"

"So why do you keep saying 'penis' with me, then?"

"Because the other term is…" she trails off awkwardly.

"Your version of dirty talk?"

"Yeah, basically."

I laugh. "Fine, fine. Just stop saying penis, for the love of god. I'd honestly rather you say ding-dong or johnson or willy or something. Anything but penis." Another trainer was exiting her car nearby, and burst out cackling when she heard my statement; I shot her the finger, and she replied in kind—we were friendly, so this was all meant as joking banter. "Look, I really have to go."

"What are you going to do, though?"

"I honestly don't know," I say. "I'll probably confront him and yell at him for ditching me."

"Even though you're fully aware you were about to do the same thing?"

I push away from my car and head for the gym entrance. "Yep. I'm fine with holding a few double standards."

"It's going to backfire on you, Audra," Imogen says, noisily stirring her coffee. "Consider yourself warned."

"You know what's going to backfire, Imogen? All the cream and sugar you put in your coffee. Switch to black. If you want to trim down like you say you do, you *have* to cut out sugar and carbs."

"Blah, blah, blah. There's no sugar in my coffee, just half-and-half, and I only use about a quarter of what I used to use. I'm working my up way to drinking it black."

"I'm just trying to help you reach your goals," I say, entering the gym and heading for the employee break room where I know there will be fresh coffee. "What about your sodas and prepackaged carbage snacks?"

"Carbage?" she asks.

"Yeah, you know, garbage carbs—pretty much everything you'd buy from the middle of the grocery store."

"Oh...um..." I hear her say, around a mouthful of food.

"Imogen—what are you eating?"

"Nuh-hing." Her tone, however, screams *guilty*.

"Imogen." I pour myself coffee into a Styrofoam cup while checking the time—still ten minutes before my first client.

"A pastry," she says, swallowing noisily.

"A pastry?" I turn the question into a doubting scold.

"Fine. A donut."

"Imogen!"

"It's Saturday! I'm off! Jesse is off! He went and got us donuts and they're delicious and I'M NOT SORRY."

I sigh, knowing I can't push her too hard. "Sugar and bleached flour still go straight to your ass on Saturdays, even when you're both off."

"I know, I know." She groans. "I'll just do some extra crunches and squats or something."

"It doesn't work like that, babe, sorry. You can't spot-reduce fat, and also, crunches aren't just useless—they're bad for your back and neck. Do some in-and-outs, or vee-ups. Squats are good though—you can never do too many squats."

"Won't it make my butt bigger if I do too many?"

"Nope. Firmer, rounder, and more toned, but not bigger, exactly. Just...an athletic butt versus a jiggly donuts-and-soda butt."

"So, the difference between your butt and my butt."

"Yeah, pretty much. Although I didn't mean *you* have a jiggly donuts-and-soda butt, just that—"

"My butt *is* pretty jiggly," she interrupted.

"Your ass is perfect," Jesse's voice rumbles distantly.

"I know *you* think so, but it could be tighter and firmer," Imogen replies.

"Sure, and I'd love that," I hear Jesse say. "My point is, I'll enjoy spanking your beautiful ass till it's pink either way, baby."

"OKAY," I cut in, loudly. "On that note I really seriously, truly have to hang up now. Bye, Imogen. No more donuts."

"Yes, Evil Diet Overlord."

"It's not about dieting, it's about changing your lifestyle," I say. "And I'm not an evil diet overlord, I just want you to be the best version of you."

"I thought you had to go?" Imogen says.

"I do, I do. Bye!" I hang up and drink my coffee—it's hot, and I burn my mouth, but that's a small price to pay for the caffeine hit which, at the moment, is my lifeblood and my sanity.

Right on the dot, I toss back the last of my coffee and leave the break room, finding my client by the squat rack, loading plates onto the bar in preparation for our workout of the day—which, she correctly assumes, will include heavy barbell back squats

because, if anyone needs to squat away a jiggly donuts-and-soda ass, it's this client. The workout will
also include high volume HIIT work: burpees, high
knees, band-assisted chin-ups, and mountain climb-
ers. Oh yeah, she'll hate me by the end of the session,
but I figure if my client can breathe without wheez-
ing, and doesn't hate me at the end of our hour together, I haven't done my job right.

The hour goes fast, and my client requires my
full, undivided attention to keep her motivated to
make it through the workout without giving up, especially when we get to the burpees. I'm grateful for
this distraction, because it means I'm not thinking
about anything or anyone else.

When I get to my own scheduled hour of workout, I go heavy on the upper body and light on the
legs because I'm so sore that certain movements
would be torture. I refuse to think about anything but
my workout, using the movements as a kind of moving meditation, a way of focusing on just my workout, just the push and pull of my breath. The rest of
my day goes just as fast, thankfully, since I'm totally
booked through five thirty.

After my five thirty client, I'm mentally fried,
physically exhausted, and cranky as hell. I also feel
crusty and gross because I've been wearing the same
outfit for two days, which is just icky even though I

did take a shower in between. I know, rationally, that I just need to go home and take another shower and put on my PJs and binge-watch Netflix until I fall asleep, but that's not where I end up.

I end up at Imogen's house. Because she promised me dinner, and she's a better cook than I am, and I'm way too done-for to even think of making real food. Plus, if I'm with Imogen, I'm less likely to obsess and overthink myself into a tizzy.

I enter without knocking—she has Debbie Gibson playing so loud you can hear it from the street, and I hear her singing along in the kitchen. I watch from the doorway into the kitchen as my best friend dances like a lunatic, bopping her head and shaking her butt as she chops something on a cutting board. I wait until she's done chopping to announce my presence, because knowing Imogen, if I were to startle her now there's a good chance she'll lop off a finger or something.

She swipes the garlic she minced into a bowl and sets the knife down.

"Imogen!" I shout over the music.

She jumps a foot into the air, and I'm glad I waited until she put down the knife, because she'd have stabbed herself in the eye.

"Holy shit, Audra! You scared the crap out of me!" Imogen lowers the volume on the sound system installed under a cabinet—we are now able to hear each other without shouting, which is nice. "I wasn't expecting you till later."

"I was going to go home and shower and change, but if I did that I'd never leave the house again, so I came right here." I indicate the food. "Can I help?"

Imogen laughs. "Oh no, no way. I remember what happened the last time you tried to help me cook."

"That was an accident!"

"You almost burned my house down!"

I huff. "It could've happened to anyone."

She laughs, eyeing me skeptically. "You set my oven on fire."

"I don't bake my chicken, I grill it on my George Foreman. I forgot it was in there. Sue me."

She waves a hand. "Fine, whatever. Just pour us some wine and tell me about Franco."

I uncork a bottle and pour us each a glass. "Nope, not talking about that. I'm here to NOT think about or talk about that situation."

Imogen takes a sip of her wine and goes back to cooking—she's making something fancy and Italian, it looks like, and the minced garlic goes into a pan filled with tomato sauce. "A-*void*-ing!" she says in a singsong, stirring the sauce.

"Yes. Yes, I am."

"Which is unhealthy."

I roll my eyes, taking a seat at the kitchen table. "Whatever. You eat donuts, I avoid things. We all have our vices."

Imogen laughs. "Well, if avoidance is the emotional version of carbohydrates, then you have the biggest ass on the planet."

I flip her off. "You can go to hell."

Imogen stirs the sauce and then checks on the pasta. "You're just mad because you know I'm right."

I'm about to clap back with something biting and witty when Jesse clomps in through the front door.

"FOOD," he growls. "Donger need food."

Imogen turns from the stove with a red sauce-smeared wooden spoon. "Hi, babe," she says. "Yeah, my day was great, how about you?" She answers herself in a funny impersonation of Jesse's growl. "My day was awesome too, I spent it thinking about how much I love my girlfriend."

Jesse is dressed for work in dusty, faded blue jeans, heavy work boots, and a Metallica concert T-shirt with the sleeves cut off; he grabs her wrist, tastes the sauce on the spoon, and then curls his arm around her waist, yanking her up against him. "Don't be petulant. I did spend my day thinking about much I love my girlfriend, but I'm fucking hungry and it smells good in here."

"I'm not petulant," Imogen says, between kisses. "I'm just irritated that you went to work when you were supposed to be off."

"Hey, if the boss calls, I go."

"Your boss is also your best friend, and you haven't had a full day off like, ever." She wiggles out of his arms. "I was just looking forward to spending the day with you watching Netflix."

"Yeah," I say, sarcastically, "Netflix and chill, heavy on the chill."

Jesse's gaze slides over to me. "Hey, Audra."

"Hi, Jesse." I nudge the bottle of wine. "Want a glass?"

He shakes his head. "I drink wine with her when that's what she wants, but if it's up to me, I'll opt for beer or whiskey every time." He goes into the fridge and pulls out a bottle of something locally brewed. "So I'll leave that for you two."

"Yay, more for us." I want to ask about Franco, but I don't.

"By the way, Jesse, Audra is joining us for dinner," Imogen says.

Jesse laughs into the bottle. "I figured. Fine by me." He slumps tiredly into the chair across from me, setting the bottle onto the table and unlacing his boots. "The bastard owes me," he says, groaning.

"Who, James?" Imogen asks. "Yeah, he does. He

swore you'd have at least today off."

Jesse thumbs off his socks, stuffs them into his boots, and then tosses the boots out into the back patio. "Nah, not James, Franco." He sighs, wiggling his toes as he sits back down and swigs from the bottle of beer. "James is paying me overtime and a half for today, so I'm fine with that, and you and I can make up for lost time tomorrow."

"What does Franco owe you for?" Imogen asks, eying me warily.

I sit and keep quiet and hope this doesn't come back to me.

"He was a real tool at work today," Jesse says. "He was cranky all damn day. Barely said two words, and when he did speak, he was a dick. By the time we were ready to knock off for the day, he was dragging ass. I tried to haul him out for a quick beer before coming home, but he pussed out and wouldn't go."

"Huh," Imogen says. "That doesn't sound like him."

Jesse's eyes slide to me—he knows Franco and I left together last night. "Yeah, well, I think someone kept him up past his bedtime."

"Who, me?" I say, and then try to look busy drinking too much wine too fast.

"Yeah, you." He quirks an eyebrow. "You guys hooked up last night, yeah?"

I shrug. "Um. We hung out for a while."

He snorts. "Hung out. Right. Which is why he had circles under his eyes and was wearing the same thing as yesterday, and was acting like someone pissed in his Wheaties."

I frown. "I can cop to us staying up late, but the rest is on him."

"Staying up late, or not going to bed at all?" Jesse says.

I sigh. "I'm not sure I'm comfortable having this conversation with you, Jesse."

"Well, if hooking up with you is gonna make him act like this all the time, I'm not sure I'm down with it."

I roll my eyes at that. "We don't need your permission, Jesse." I shrug again. "But it's a moot point. We won't be seeing each other again."

"Why not? Didn't go well?"

"Actually, according to the emergency call this morning, it went *too* well," Imogen says, in a betrayal of my confidence. "Which is why they won't be seeing each other again."

I narrow my eyes at her. "That was between you and me, Imogen," I say through gritted teeth. "Not cool."

She frowns. "You have to know I share everything with Jesse at this point, Audra."

"Even confidential girl talk?"

She shrugs. "Well, I don't tell him *everything*, but the big stuff I share with him, yeah."

Jesse holds up his hands palms out. "What Imogen shares with me *stays* with me, so don't, like, get all upset thinking I'm gonna go relaying everything straight to Franco."

"There's nothing to relay," I say, going for light and carefree. "We hooked up, it was good, there won't be a second time, the end."

Jesse shrugs. "Whatever. None of my business."

"Exactly," I say.

"So." Imogen brings over the pot of spaghetti, now mixed with the sauce; she dumps a monster portion onto a plate for Jesse, and a more rational portion for me, and the same for herself. "Anything interesting happen with your clients today, Audra?"

I shrug. "Not really." I laugh. "Well, there was this one thing. One of my clients is new, not just to me as a trainer, but to working out in general. She just had her first kid and is all gung-ho about not just losing the baby weight but getting into better shape than before. Which is great, right? She's super motivated, great attitude, gives it a hundred percent, never complains when I say one more rep or ten more reps or whatever. So, I've got her doing burpees as a warm-up, and she's rocking it, right? I'm encouraging her, telling her to get one more, blah blah blah, the usual. She's got, like, maybe three more left in the set, she does the jump, the drop down, the push-up, and she's getting ready to jump to her feet. Instead of finishing the jump up, though, she makes a weird squeak noise and drops down to her belly. And I'm like, Kelly, what the fuck? You've got three reps, let's go, let's knock them out." I suppress a laugh. "And she's just like, no. Nope. I'm staying down here."

"What, did she poop herself or something?" Jesse asks.

I laugh. "Not quite that bad, but almost. She peed herself."

Imogen laughs, covering her mouth with one hand, and then groans in sympathy. "I've done a few rotations in the maternity ward," she says. "Apparently that's a thing after you have kids."

"What, you just pee yourself?"

I nod. "I don't mean, like, oops a few drops leaked out. Everyone's had that happen at some point."

"If you're a guy, it happens a lot," Jesse says. "I call it the post-shake dribble. It's annoying as hell."

I bite my lower lip. "No, you don't understand. The poor lady just…whoosh. Peed everywhere. Like, I'm talking her bladder just gave out."

Imogen is sympathy-laughing. "Oh god, the poor thing. That had to have been mortifying."

"She couldn't decide whether to laugh or cry." I shrug. "Fortunately for her, all the sweat towels were gone when I got there today, so I was using one of the full-size shower towels. She wrapped that around her waist and just claimed she'd had a female problem."

"Which is true enough," Imogen says.

"Yeah, exactly."

"Glad I'm not a chick," Jesse says.

I laugh. "Me too! Well, I mean, I'm a chick, but I've never had kids, so I won't be peeing myself anytime soon."

Imogen just quirks an eyebrow at me. "Do I have to remind you of freshman year of college?"

I glare at her. "No. You most certainly do *not* have to bring that up. EVER."

Jesse's interest is piqued, now. "Do tell, do tell."

"If you tell him, I'll divorce you," I say. "Best friend divorce. We'll have to share custody of our Mexican place."

Imogen snickers. "She got hammered at a sorority party, passed out in a flower bed, and woke up having peed herself."

Jesse frowns. "You were in a sorority? I didn't take you for the type."

I blow a raspberry. "Hell no I wasn't in a sorority. I just went their parties because those crazy bitches knew how to put on a bash."

"Ah, that makes more sense." He shrugs, laughing. "Hey, we've all done that. In fact, I can do one better. I went to a party in college, got hammered, and also got food poisoning. So yeah, I woke up in some random dude's spare bedroom and I'd had food poisoning diarrhea everywhere. I barely made it to the bathroom before I blew chunks. It was...god, that was awful. Being drunk and having food poisoning is basically the worst combination on the planet."

I wince. "Oof, that sucks."

He laughs. "Fortunately, the party was at a college I didn't go to, so I didn't know anyone. I managed to get myself cleaned up, stripped the bedding off the bed and shoved it in a trash can outside, and went home."

Imogen shakes her head. "You guys are crazy. I've never done anything like that."

I laugh. "Yeah, because you've always been a goody-goody." I eye her with a mischievous twinkle. "Although..."

Imogen's eyes widen. "No! Don't you dare!"

Jesse eyes us both. "What?"

I shrug. "Oh, nothing. Just...she's not exactly telling the truth when she says she's *never* done anything like that. Her bachelorette party was...um, a little out of hand."

"Audra Donovan, don't you *dare* tell him that story!"

"Tell him the story!" Jesse says, grinning. "It can't be any worse than me shitting the bed."

I grin back. "She was stupid enough to let me be in charge of her bachelorette party."

Jesse's eyes widen. "Oh boy. Big mistake."

I laugh. "Right? You'd think she'd have known better by then. I rented a giant bus with black-out windows and a stripper pole in the middle, and hired a male dancer...we may or may not have gone through a case of vodka that night. And your girl, here, little miss Goody Two-Shoes, she was the drunkest of all."

"It *was* my bachelorette party."

"Yeah, to a raging cockhead you had no business marrying, and I told you as much several times that night, but we won't talk about that. So yeah, she was hammered. I'm talking quintessential white girl wasted. When she was sober, and even just mostly drunk, she wasn't super into the stripper. Who was, let me add, super sexy. But she was all, no I love Nicholas, blah blah fucking blah. Asshole. Anyway, she finally reached super drunk status and finally showed interest in the stripper. Who was, by that point, more of a, um, gentleman of the night, shall we say. Which was part of the reason I hired him, specifically, because I'd heard he was willing to go beyond the mere removal of clothing, if sufficiently financially recompensed."

Jesse rolls his eyes. "So he was a whore, you're saying."

I laugh. "My point *is*, I convinced Imogen to let him give her a lap dance, and she was *really* into it. And I was, honestly, hoping something hinky would happen just so she'd call off the wedding. But alas, instead of getting all up on his jock, she blew chunks all over him *and* peed herself."

Jesse laughs. "The truth comes out!"

Imogen is blushing, covering her face with her hands. "I don't even remember it." She points at me. "You promised you'd keep that a secret, you slut!"

"You said you share everything with Jesse! I figure if he knows the worst, most embarrassing moment of your life, then your relationship is solid. I'm doing you a favor."

"Gee, thanks," Imogen deadpans. "How kind of you."

I pretend to not realize she's being sarcastic. "You're welcome. I just want you and Jesse to succeed as a couple."

Jesse laughs, rubbing Imogen's back. "Like I said, everyone's done it at least once. It's basically a rite of passage to adulthood. Neither of us thinks any less of you for it."

"When she told me the next day what had

happened, I swore I'd never get that drunk again," Imogen says. "And, honestly, I haven't."

Jesse nods. "Do that once or twice, and you're basically cured. It's not really all that fun waking up and having to ask what you did the night before."

The conversation veers, then, and I stay at Imogen's well past when I should, especially considering how little sleep I got last night and that I have a client pretty early tomorrow, but it's better to be here with them talking and reminiscing instead of letting my doubts, fears, insecurities, and desires keep me stuck in a cycle of anger, lust, and self-doubt.

Eventually, I have to go home, and the moment I'm alone, the cycle starts.

I'm going to do something stupid tomorrow, I just know it. I'm already trying to convince myself not to, but it's a losing battle.

THREE

I PULL UP TO THE CURB OUTSIDE THE WAVERLEY PROPERTY, shut off the car, but don't get out. Instead, I sit gripping the steering wheel, trying to talk myself out of being stupid.

"Do *not* get out of this car, Audra Donovan," I tell myself, out loud. "Go home. You don't need the drama, and you don't need him."

I groan and thunk my head against the steering wheel—because I know damn well I'm not going to listen to myself.

"Fuck it," I argue back. "I know why *I* would have snuck out, but I deserve to know why *he* did."

I gather my breath, hold it, and then let it out in an angry exhale. He has me flipping in circles, and talking to myself. I don't need this. But yet, I find myself exiting the vehicle anyway, adjusting my boobs in my bra, tugging my shorts up so the lower edge of my butt shows, and pushing the waistband down to bare more of my abs and a hint of the V-cut leading down to my hoo-ha.

Franco has a thing for my V-cut—I know this for a fact because the first thing he did when he got my clothes off was run his tongue up and down those grooves. I shiver at the memory, and then shake my head to dislodge it; I'm here to yell at him for ghosting on me, not…well, not anything else.

There is, unfortunately for me, a gaggle of guys out in front of the house…which includes the same three bricklayers from the other day. New to the scene are five guys working on the landscaping—laying sod, planting bushes and flowers, carting wheelbarrows of mulch from place to place…

All eyes are on me, and all work stops.

First, yes, it's immensely flattering to know I can still bring a scene to a standstill just by showing up—especially when my forty-first birthday is coming up in a month. But second, it's more than a little mortifying when the three guys doing the brick paving whistle at me.

"Hey, fellas, it's that hot-ass beer lady!" one of them calls, tossing his handful of bricks into the dirt at his feet. "Got any more beer for us?"

"No," I say, giving them a smile. "Sorry, not today. That was a one-time-only special."

"Hey-yo, mama, didn't you wear that yesterday?"

one of them asks, eyeing me blatantly up and down.

"I ain't your mama, or anyone else's," I snark back. "And no, actually, this is a different outfit."

"Looks the same to me, chica."

"Well, it's not. Those were white shorts, these are ivory, that sports bra was cherry red, and this one is navy blue." I lift an eyebrow at him. "Would it be a problem if it *was* the same outfit?"

"Hell nah," he says, backing off. "Just wonderin'."

I stare him down. "I didn't realize this job had a stylist. And I'm wondering if you're being paid to ask me questions, or to lay brick."

He shakes his head and mutters something in Spanish under his breath—which I assume isn't polite, but I'm not about to ask for a translation. I head inside, ignoring the stares as I move past them. I find Ryder in the kitchen at a switch opening, twisting wires together, with green, red, and yellow wire-cap things clamped in his teeth. He sees me, jutting his chin up in my direction as a greeting.

The electrician of Dad Bod Contracting, Ryder is on the shorter side at five-seven or five-eight, but he's seriously jacked—he has the body of someone intensely dedicated to a lot of heavy lifting, and who also watches what he eats pretty carefully, but not obsessively. He has bright red hair—a true redhead, with freckles and pale skin. His hair is short on the sides, longer and messy on top—truly messy, as if he just doesn't give a shit about taking the time to style his hair, but on him, it somehow just works, like he rolled out of someone else's bed. He has a short beard, hazel eyes, and a spray of freckles across his nose, and cheeks that would be almost unbearably adorable if they weren't also insanely sexy. The men of Dad Bod Contracting are…a lot to take in, quite honestly. I've never seen them all in one room before, but Imogen has and she claims it would be bad if I did, because my libido would short-circuit in the presence of so many sexy men. And she may be right, because Ryder's not even my type and I'm attracted to him, same with both Jesse and James. Franco, now…that man is a whole different story. "Attracted" doesn't quite cover the way my libido feels about him.

"Hranco izh downstairzh," he says, around the caps.

"Thanks." I hesitate, and then glance at Ryder. "He say anything?"

Ryder doesn't answer right away, instead finishes twisting the wires together, screws on the cap, and then repeats the process twice more.

When his mouth is empty of caps, he scratches at his short, neat red beard. "To me? Nah. But he wouldn't. Franco keeps that shit to himself."

"Which shit?" I ask.

He sighs. "Um, the kind of shit that has him acting like a cranky dick?"

"Oh."

Ryder takes the switch plate and starts screwing it into place. "Just so you know—"

"Ryder?" I interrupt.

"Yeah?"

"Don't. I'm just going to talk to him real quick."

"Okay, but all I was gonna say is that Franco doesn't like to mix personal shit with business shit, so he may not be super receptive to your visit." He shrugs, and steps away from the finished switch, flipping his screwdriver in the air and catching it again.

"How do you even know it's personal?"

He snorts, his eyes raking over me—not lecherously, not in a way that creeps me out, but making it obvious enough that he appreciates the female body. "Well, you left here together yesterday, and Franco showed up wearing the same clothes as the day before, and he was a cranky asshole all day." He laughs, shrugging. "I'm an electrician, so I have to be pretty good at math, you know? And that's pretty simple addition. Two plus two equals you guys boinked."

I snicker involuntarily at his word choice. "Boinked? What are you, twelve?"

"At heart, yes," Ryder says, laughing.

His phone rings, and I think both of us are glad

for the excuse to exit the conversation without any awkwardness. I have no idea where the stairs to the basement are, so I have to wander the house looking for them. I catch a glimpse of James in a half bathroom, inspecting the grout in the floor tiles and the caulk around the base of the toilet.

I met James once, yesterday. He's the tallest of the four men, at six-five or six-six, and he's built like a refrigerator, if a refrigerator featured broad, heavy shoulders, twenty-inch biceps, thighs the size of my damn waist, and a chest you could use as an anvil. He's...well...he's magnificent, is what he is. He has short, neat brown hair sprinkled with silver at the temples and a matching, neatly groomed brown-and-silver beard. His eyes are a deep, dark, mesmerizing, forest green. Despite being built like a god, he is gentle and kind.

He glances at me as I pass, and stands up to lean out of the bathroom. "Audra, right?"

I reach out to shake his hand. "Yeah—hi, James." I frown. "Wait—if you, Ryder, *and* Franco are all here, why is Jesse off?"

James laughs. "Ryder has some electrical to wrap up, Franco is finishing the wine cellar, and I'm going through and double-checking that everything has been done right and to my personal standards. Jesse doesn't have anything to do here now that the construction is done, so I gave him the weekend off and he's starting demo on a new renovation Monday." He turns the faucet on and off, nudges the mirror to make sure it's stable and centered, and tries the vent fan, then looks at me again. "Franco is in rare form yet again today. Do I have you to thank for that?"

"I can neither confirm nor deny these allegations."

He just laughs again, a hearty, amused boom. "He's in the basement. Stairs are over by the garage."

I wave as I walk away. The basement is bright and airy and open, being a walkout consisting of a large den area, a smaller side room, another half bathroom, a kitchenette, and a workout room with mirrors on all four walls, and a wine cellar; the latter space is where I find Franco. He has a brad nailer and is installing a built-in wine rack—which, from the look of it, has been custom-made by Franco himself. I know he's a carpenter, but this is the first of his work I've actually seen, and I have to say I'm damned impressed. The room is easily twenty-by-twenty with ten-foot ceilings, and the built-in racks stretch from floor to ceiling on three walls, the fourth wall being the glass-fronted entrance. A railing runs around the top of the racks, and I see a ladder with rollers lying on the floor, allowing someone to easily reach a bottle near the ceiling. The racks are works of art, with elaborate scrollwork decorating the face of each diagonal support beam, stained a rich deep mahogany, and polished to a high gleam.

"This is really beautiful," I say, by way of greeting.

Franco glances at me, shock rippling across his gorgeous features before he carefully neutralizes his expression. "Thank you."

"You handmade all of this?" I gesture at the cellar.

He nods. "I did. They're very serious about their wine, so they really wanted this room, especially, to be totally custom."

I frown. "Isn't the entire house a custom job, seeing as the four of you built it?"

He smirks, shaking his head. "Nah, custom means I personally made this built-in rack from scratch. I designed the rack, chose the wood, cut it, shaped it, stained it, polished it, and installed it, as opposed to a prefab rack that I'd have just fixed into place. The cabinets are prefab, for example, because as cool as it is to say you have custom cabinets for your kitchen, they're stupid expensive for a product only nominally better than a readily available version, not to mention if you need to replace or repair a custom cabinet, you're gonna pay out your ass."

"Oh, so I should rethink the custom cabinets I was considering for my kitchen remodel?" I ask, grinning.

"You're remodeling your kitchen?"

I shake my head. "No, I was joking. My kitchen is already amazing and needs no renovation."

"Oh." He reloads his nailer, sets it aside, and then eyes me. "So. Um...you're here."

I lift an eyebrow. "Yeah, unlike you, yesterday morning."

"Audra, can we talk later?"

"You could have at least left a note. Didn't have to be elaborate. Could've been as simple as, 'I had a great time, Audra, maybe we'll catch up again sometime.'"

"I *am* at work, so maybe we could—"

"But no! You just *vanished*. Poof. Gone. I came out of the shower talking to you, but you weren't there. Imagine my surprise."

"Audra—"

"I mean, it was a hookup, goddammit! I knew it, you knew it—we both knew it. I wasn't expecting much—I would have been fine if you were just like, 'yo, I gotta go to work, see ya.'" I say this in my best approximation of a deep, gruff, gravelly voice that is nothing at all like Franco's voice, which is deep but fluid and smooth and quiet.

"I don't sound like that," he says.

"That's not the point." I'm winding up for another salvo, but I'm stopped by Franco's hand across my mouth.

"Audra." His piercing blue eyes are pale and icy.

"I'm working. I can't do this with you right now."

"You're just trying to escape."

He flares his nostrils, which shouldn't be sexy, but somehow is. "I take my work very seriously. The clients are inclined to show up on a whim, without warning. I will *not* be found having a personal discussion on a client's property and on their time. They are paying me to be here, and while I'm here, I'll do my damn job." He pulls a tiny spiral notepad from his pocket, a pencil from behind his ear, and scrawls on it: *Callihan's 7:30*; he rips the paper free from the spiral across the top and hands it to me.

"Callihan's is—" he starts.

"I know where it is," I cut in.

"You have it in writing—I'll meet you there at seven thirty, and you can bitch me out then, okay? Just not here, not now."

I stare at the paper and allow my thoughts to range past feeling pissy at him for leaving, to how attractive he looks with the tool belt and tight T-shirt and tight, ripped jeans and backward ball cap with his Oakleys upside down on the brim, to being irritated with myself for being so attracted to him.

The thought that filters through to my brain past my emotions and libido is that I'd be irritated if someone showed up at my place of work and tried to have a personal discussion with me while I was with a client.

"Fine. Callihan's, seven thirty." I stare hard at him. "You'll be there?"

"I'll be there." He holds up a finger for me to wait, and then crouches to rummage in a toolbox on the floor; he withdraws a huge hammer, old and rusty and pitted, the leather wrapped around the handle tattered and rotting away—he hands it to me. "If you need insurance that I'll be there, take this. It's my grandfather's hammer, and it's one of my most prized possessions. He gave it to me himself when I was eleven."

Something inside me melts a little. "Franco, you don't have to give me your granddad's hammer."

He looks relieved as he takes the hammer back. "Thank god. I've never let that hammer out of my possession in the thirty-four years I've had it." He places it back in the toolbox, and then withdraws something else—an old drill, a huge, heavy, bulky one from about fifty years ago. "This was his, too. Still good insurance that I'll meet you, but not as hard for me to let go of."

"Franco, I don't need a drill. I just need your assurance you're not gonna stand me up to get out of having this conversation."

He places the drill in my hands, and it's even heavier than it looks. "Take it." He grins. "Maybe the insurance is for me, not you."

"Because if you know I have your granddad's drill, you have to show up?"

"Exactly."

I wind the long cord around the handle and body. "In that case, I will take the drill."

He chuckles. "Good idea." He picks up the nailer again. "I have to finish this. I'll see you in an hour and a half."

"See you."

I head upstairs and toward the front door, but I don't get out of the house without passing James again. His eyes land on the drill in my hands, and a deep frown wrinkles his brow.

"Is that…? It is! That's Franco's grandpa's drill." His eyes flick up to mine. "Why do *you* have it? He never lets *anyone* touch that stuff—not even me, and I've known him thirty years."

I don't know how to answer that without giving him an explanation he doesn't need, so I just shrug. "Ask Franco. It's complicated."

I exit the house and scurry to my car before he has a chance to say anything else, and before any of the guys outside can say anything. I set the drill on my back seat, next to my workout bag—the clunky, rusty old drill looks incongruous on the creamy tan leather of my Mercedes-Benz, and it leaves a funny feeling in my gut.

When I get home from work, I take a long, hot, much-needed shower, depilate my legs and hoo-ha, and then wrap up in my favorite robe—a tiny little terrycloth thing that I've had since high school. I do my hair while it's still damp and workable and then sit on my balcony, sipping a glass of cab sav, and flip through my email and various social media notifications, enjoying the sun on my skin. My apartment is on the top floor and my neighbors on either side never go out on their balconies, and there's no building across the street from me, just the parking lot and the back of a strip mall, so I often lay out on my balcony with my robe open for optimal sunbathing. It's my secret to being evenly tanned all over, and one of my favorite ways to relax after work.

Since all I have to do to get ready to meet Franco is put on minimal makeup and get dressed, I let myself relax for a while, indulging in a second glass of wine. I catch up on some light reading—by which I mean my favorite romance author's newest book, a guilty pleasure I'd never admit to anyone, not even Imogen.

My phone dings and a text message alert slides

down from the top of my phone's screen, rudely interrupting a…ahem…a *climactic* scene in the book.

Franco: *I'm ready a little early. Pick you up?*

It's six forty-five. I'm not ready. Nor am I ready to let him pick me up—and to know where I live.

Me: *You just want your drill back.*

Franco: *Nope. Just don't see any point in waiting around another 45 minutes if I don't have to.*

Me: *Fine. I can be ready in fifteen. Text me when you're here and I'll come down.* I text him the address to my building, but omit my unit number.

Franco, after a pause: *That condo complex is less than five minutes from me. I've done renovation work in that building. You leaving out your unit number bc you're worried I'll show up early?*

Me, after a longer pause. *See you outside in fifteen minutes?*

Franco: …

Franco: *yeah, just go ahead and avoid the question. LOL. ;-)*

Me: …

Franco: *We can exchange vaguely suggestive ellipses until doomsday, if you want. I've got unlimited data.*

Franco: … … …

Me: *k bye see you soon*

Me: … … … … …

Franco: *Fine. I'll let you win this round…For now!*

Is he text-flirting with me? Because it definitely feels like he's text-flirting with me. Why would he text-flirt with me? Did he miss the part where he ghosted on me and then refused to talk about it? Sure he was at work, but still. Plus, I'm mad. Why would he flirt?

Ugh.

I glance at my phone and realize I've been sitting here for five minutes stewing on whether or not he was text-flirting with me, and now I only have ten minutes to get ready. And I'm still naked!

I fly into motion, not pausing to think about what I'm doing, just operating on pure blind instinct. Lingerie, a lacy, racy bright crimson set purchased at Fredrick's of Hollywood the last time I was in LA for a trainer's conference. I rarely wear it, but I look damned incredible in it, a fact I verify by taking a quick gander at myself in the mirror before putting on the rest of my outfit. My tits are high and huge and firm—all natural, baby, and still pretty much perfect despite my descent into middle age. My ass pops, a nice taut bubble of athletic roundness. My abs are toned and hard, my thighs are muscular and yet still smooth and feminine.

I pat myself on the butt, checking it for excess jiggle—nope, firm as a Swiss medicine ball.

Yeah—I look pretty damned amazing.

I keep my outfit simple—skinny jeans, chunky black heels, and a black sleeveless V-neck top that shows off both the girls and my arms. Basic make-up—foundation, eyeliner, lipstick, a little color on my cheekbones. Bam—done, and I've got two minutes to spare.

I transfer my phone, wallet, keys, mace, and emergency makeup kit to my favorite clutch, a little black leather thing with rose gold accents that matches well with my heels and top. I want to beat Franco, so I hustle to the elevator; I make it outside just as Franco's big silver pickup with the matching bedcap pulls up, sliding to a stop at the curb in front of my building. Before I can move from my spot on the steps leading up to the building door, Franco has jumped out, leaving his door open, and moves with unhurried grace around the hood to open the passenger door.

I eye him suspiciously as I move toward the truck. "Trying to butter me up with good manners, Franco?"

He takes my hand in his and helps me up into the truck—unnecessary, considering there's a step and I'm not helpless, but it's a gesture that leaves me off-balance with its sweetness. "Nope. Just have good manners."

I snort as I settle into the pebbled black leather of the seat. "Because ghosting on your partner is good manners."

He sighs, an almost inaudible huff of long-suffering as he shuts my door and circles back around to his side. Hopping in and closing his door, he buckles up, turns down the music, and prepares to reverse out of the spot. I take the moment while he's distracted to check him out: clean, dressy blue jeans, perfectly fit to his lean physique, spotless dark brown leather Red Wing boots with red laces, a gray short sleeve polo French tucked—just the front around his belt buckle tucked in. His hair is brushed back and bound into a neat low ponytail, not a strand out of place. Freshly shaven, smelling of clean male and faint cologne, plus a pungent layer of sawdust that I think is just part of his personal scent.

God, he's beautiful. Masculine, vital and vigorous and primal, but just...*beautiful.* Perfect chiseled jawline, sharp high cheekbones, deep-set icy pale blue eyes. He's channeling Brad Pitt in *Legends of the Fall*, especially with that long hair. I'm not usually a fan of men with ponytails, but on this guy it just works, and a little too well at that. And the body I know he's hiding under those clothes?

Gah.

My mouth waters, my thighs clench, and my hoo-ha tightens just thinking about that impeccable crossfitter's body. Every line, every curve, every angle is carved from marble to such perfection that he could be a sculpture by Michelangelo or da Vinci. Being an athlete and trainer myself, I know exactly the kind of dedication it takes to achieve a body like his—not just the hours in the gym, but the devotion to clean, optimal nutrition. For an intensely physical person like me, Franco's body is a drug, and one I could very easily become addicted to.

I notice, too, that the interior of his truck is as spotless and perfect as the day he bought it, but I can see the odometer, and it reads over a hundred thousand miles, so it's definitely not new. A quick twisting glance through the back window into the bed, and I can see his tools and toolboxes, all neatly arranged and tied down and organized.

His eye catches mine. "What?" he asks.

I shrug. "Nothing. Just noticing you seem to have a perfectionist streak."

"Perfectionist streak?" He snorts a laugh as we pull out onto the main road, heading for Callihan's. "Try a friggin' perfectionist *highway*. Borderline OCD, according to the therapist I saw a few years ago."

I eye him, trying to decipher the various bombs he just dropped—he's seen a therapist? Borderline OCD? Where do I start? Why would he admit this to me, someone he barely knows?

"Borderline OCD?"

He nods, checking his mirror as he changes

lanes to get around a slower-moving car. "Yep. Meaning I don't have the compulsion to, like, wash my hands eight times every hour, or turn my locks in a specific order, but I am borderline obsessive about things like being neat and orderly and perfect. It makes me a great carpenter because I can't consider a project finished until it's as absolutely perfect as it can get, but I tend to work slower than someone with less of a compulsion for perfection." He glances at me. "Is that an issue for you, me being a perfectionist?"

I shrug and shake my head. "No, of course not. Just noticing. I'm guessing you've owned this truck from new, and it has a hundred thousand miles on it, but the interior is literally like new. Plus your tools in the back are so organized its mind-boggling."

He laughs at this. "You should see my workshop at home if you think that's organized."

Am I supposed to care why he saw a therapist? I shouldn't. It's none of my business. This isn't a date—it's a meeting to discuss why he ghosted on me.

So why does my mouth betray my curiosity? "Why did you see a therapist?" I glance at him. "If you don't mind me asking."

He rubs his jaw. "Eh…just life. You know?" He pulls to a stop at a left turn light. "Why?"

"Just curious. Most men I've ever met would never see a therapist, let alone admit it to someone they're hooking up with."

"Yeah, well, life is messy. None of us get through life without some kind of damage. Personally, I think every single person should go through a few months of regular talk therapy with a licensed psychologist just as part of mental and emotional self-care." His phone is in a hands-free holder suctioned to his windshield, and he taps at it, changing the song from a twangy country ballad to a newer, pop-bro country tune. "You ever see a therapist?"

I laugh. "I probably should, but no."

"Why not?" he asks.

I shrug. "I dunno. I just never did. God knows I haven't gotten to this point in my life without some damage, like you said, but...I guess I feel like I'm coping well enough on my own."

"Yeah, that's what I thought too," Franco says. "Until I talked to someone."

I laugh trying to make this less weird. "So you're saying I need to see a therapist?"

"No—well, yes. I'm saying everyone does." A pause. "This is a weird conversation for a first date." He makes a face, glancing at me. "But then, it's not a first date, is it?"

"Is it even a date?"

"You're wearing heels and makeup, and I picked you up at your place." He shrugs. "Kinda feels like one."

I sigh. "I know. But it wasn't supposed to be."

"You just wanted to yell at me for leaving like I did, is that it?"

"Pretty much," I admit.

"Coulda done that over the phone. Shit, you could've sent me a text about it." His smirk is galling. "Doesn't explain why you're here, why you agreed to let me pick you up, and why you went to the trouble to make yourself look so good."

I huff. "It took me literally ten minutes to get dressed. I didn't put in that much effort, honestly. I just don't like looking like a scrub when I go out."

"I'm calling bullshit," Franco says, still smirking.

"Excuse me?"

He pulls into the parking lot of Callihan's—a place that feels like a traditional Irish pub crossed with a fancy steakhouse. "Well, just that you showed up at the Waverley site with Imogen the other day clearly having just come from work, or a workout. You'd obviously been sweaty at some point in the day, your hair was all over the place, you weren't wearing any makeup I could see, and you were wearing work-out gear. Not exactly the ensemble of someone who cares what people think of her."

"And?" I dare him to make a bigger deal of that.

"And nothing. I happen to personally find that look sexy as fuck. I'm just calling bullshit on your claim that you don't like looking like a scrub when you go out."

"That was different. I wasn't going out—I was tagging along with my friend as moral support." I gesture at my top and jeans. "This is going-out attire—meaning, I'm knowingly going out in public where I'll be seen by more than just a few incidental strangers. There's a difference."

"You can't just admit you made even a tiny effort into looking good for me?"

I glare. "I made an effort, yes—just not specifically for *you*. I'd have made the same effort if I was going out with Imogen or anyone else." I hesitate. "Why does it matter?"

He shrugs and laughs. "It doesn't. I'm just messing with you."

"Well...don't."

"Why not?" He gets out and has my door open before I realize his intent and, once again, his hand wraps around mine, providing a firm hold as I step down from the truck.

"Because we're not there yet, Franco," I snap, walking with him to the entrance of the restaurant.

"Where?"

"The place where we mess with each other." I snatch my hand from his as we reach the entrance, only belatedly realizing I'd held it the entire way across the parking lot—and Franco parked near the back, in an empty corner. "And this *isn't* a date."

"No?"

I shake my head. "Nope." At least, I *sound* resolute.

"Fine. Call it what you want." He holds the restaurant door for me, letting me precede him into the dark, low-ceilinged interior of Callihan's, and then stands a little too close to me as he waits for the hostess to get off the phone and greet us.

"Hi, can I help you?" She's young, pretty, and wearing a dress that doesn't quite fit in all the right places—and her eyes are all over Franco despite the obvious age gap and the fact that he's here with me.

"Yeah, hi—I have a reservation for two. Morrissey."

She taps at a tablet, and then smiles a little too brightly. "Ah, yes, hi, Mr. Morrissey. Your table is ready. Right this way, please." She leads us to the back of the restaurant, threading a path between tables and booths—I notice, too, that she's putting a little too much sway in her step, for Franco's benefit I imagine.

Bitch.

I mentally rear back at my own unexpected

vitriol—this isn't a date, I said so myself. I have no reason to react like that. For god's sake, let her steal him from me, see if I care. He probably bangs twenty-one-year-old hostesses all the time. Good for him.

She seats us in a booth in the back corner, promises us that our server will be right with us, and then sway/prances away, with only one wistful backward glance.

"That hostess couldn't take her eyes off you," I hear myself remarking.

Gahh—stupid. Obvious.

Franco's eyebrow arches. "Hadn't noticed. And so what, anyway? She's barely twenty if she's a day, and I'm not here for her."

I shrug. "She was putting a hell of a lot of bounce in her step for your sake. Wouldn't be surprised if she slipped you her number while I'm in the bathroom."

"Again, hadn't noticed." He stares me down. "I did notice the way your ass looks in those jeans, though."

I can't help a grin, which I quickly stomp down. "Oh?"

"Yeah. I definitely noticed that."

"What was it you noticed?"

"Fishing for compliments, Audra?" he asks with another of those annoyingly sexy, knowing smirks.

"Yep." I match his smirk with my own, determined

to reset the equilibrium between us.

He laughs. "I noticed that your ass is the most perfect ass I've ever seen." He pauses for effect. "Or felt."

"Thank you." I'm glad it's dark in here so he won't notice my pleased, flattered, aroused blush. "I appreciate that. I do work really hard to keep my ass looking the way it does."

"Your hard work has definitely paid off."

At that moment, an older gentleman in a suit appears at our table, greeting Franco by name and with an effusive handshake. "Mr. Morrissey—how wonderful to see you again!" He reaches behind him to take a bottle of wine proffered by a server. "May I offer you and your lovely companion a bottle of our finest wine, on the house?"

"That's not necessary, Harry, but I'll take it if you're offering."

The man, clearly either the owner or manager, or both, laughs. "I'm not just offering, Franco, I'm insisting. I can't tell you how many compliments we've received on our woodwork after the restoration. Consider it a token of eternal gratitude for a job impeccably well-executed."

After Harry goes through the bottle opening and tasting ceremony and pours us each a glass of a deep, rich, expensive red wine, he leaves us with the server, who takes our order—two ribeye steaks, medium, extra veggies, no potatoes, and side salads to start.

When we're alone, I take a sip of the wine. "Wow. This is amazing. He wasn't kidding when he said it was a bottle of his finest." I eye Franco. "So what was that about?"

Franco takes a sip and nods appreciatively. "That wine *is* really good." He runs a hand down the side of the half-wall separating one booth from the other. "I did all of the woodwork in this place. An employee accidentally set a fire a few years ago, and the place basically burned down. They took the opportunity to totally remodel, and that included having me custom make all the booths, tables, chairs, wine racks, doorframes, everything."

I take a long look around, whistling. "Wow. *Everything*?"

"Every last scrap of wood in here was handcrafted exclusively by me." He says this with no small amount of pride.

As with the wine rack, everything is not just functional, but a work of art. The more I look around, the more impressed I am. "This had to have been an absolutely enormous job."

He nods. "Sure was. Over a year of working nights and weekends."

I boggle. "Wait, nights and weekends?"

He nods. "I do jobs like this on the side—my main job, obviously, is working for James. This was a really massive order, obviously, and well beyond what I usually do."

"You did all this in your spare time?"

He nods. "Yep. It's all reclaimed wood, too. There was an old hospital just outside downtown Chicago being torn down a few years ago and I claimed all the wood. I've got a big backyard, and I dumped it back there to use on future projects. The booths all came from old doors, the tables from old desks...the doorframes are from old floorboards, and the wine racks I pieced together from all over the place. Harry, the owner and manager, takes a lot of pride in being able to say each booth and table is totally unique." He shrugs. "It was a hell of a fun project, and it paid off my mortgage ten years early."

"That's really amazing, Franco. You're an amazing craftsman and artist."

"Thanks," he says, with a warm, proud grin. "Of course, I could've finished in half the time had I used modern tools, but Harry wasn't in a rush so I had all the time I needed."

"What do you mean, used modern tools?"

Our salads arrive then, and we spend a few minutes in silence eating before he answers. "Professionally, I use all the newest, highest-tech power equipment, because on a construction site, time is money. But when I'm crafting furniture, I exclusively use old, low-tech tools. I'm talking antique stuff that my grandfather's grandfather would have used."

I'm even more amazed. "Really?"

He nods, and his expression is bright and open as he discusses this. "Yep. All my woodworking tools I use at home are antiques, some of which I found through antique dealers, or online and fixed up myself, and others which I inherited from my grandfather."

"Why do you use old-fashioned tools? Like you said, wouldn't it be twice as fast to use modern tools?"

He shrugs. "Oh, more than twice as fast. If I use power tools I can make a really beautiful, functional table or whatever in a few hours, whereas the old way takes me half a day of work."

"So why do it the old way? Are you, like, a secret hipster or something?"

He laughs. "God no." A thoughtful sigh. "Um…? It's hard to explain."

"Hard to explain, or you think I won't get it?"

He swirls the wine in the glass. "A little of both, I guess." Another thoughtful pause. "So, my grandfather taught me carpentry. I didn't have the most peaceful home growing up, so going to Grandpa's was a way of escaping, and Grandpa had all these old tools, right? But he had them because that's just what he could afford. He had a drill—that same one you currently have, as a matter of fact—and a table saw and some other things, but mostly, he worked old-fashioned, so that's how I learned. I went to a tech school in high school and got an apprenticeship in my junior year, so I was working full-time as a carpenter by the time I graduated. I learned all the modern techniques, and how to use the modern tools and such professionally, but I've always just found it...therapeutic, I guess, to work the wood with my hands, the way Grandpa taught me. It's calming. I've been making furniture and stuff in my spare time since Gramps first showed me how to make a rocking chair when I was...ten? Twelve? And I've just always used the old stuff. It feels...authentic. It connects me to Grandpa, and to his grandfather, and to all the thousands of years of human history where men have been crafting things from wood, using largely the same tools the entire time. Even modern power tools work in the same basic way as the oldest tools, they're just...faster."

"That's really cool, actually." Yet again, my mouth betrays my better sense. "I'd like to see your workshop sometime."

His eyes narrow, and an eyebrow quirks up. "I thought you were mad at me."

I have to summon the irritation this time. "I am."

He mostly hides a smirk. "I thought we were

here so you could yell at me."

"We are," I say, and now the irritation isn't forced.

The entrees come, then, and the conversation is put on hold as we dig in.

He gestures with his steak knife. "Well? Here I am."

I sigh. "Honestly, I said everything I had to say at the Waverley site. But I'd like to at least know why you left the way you did."

He takes a while to answer. "You're trying to tell me you weren't planning the same thing?"

I narrow my eyes. "Not the point."

"So you're not denying it?"

"What's your point?"

"My point is, I'm guessing you understand just fine why I left like I did, you're just acting pissy about it because I did it to you before you could do it to me."

Damn the man.

"It's rude," I say. "And I wouldn't have just left."

He calls my bullshit with that damned eyebrow of his. "Oh no?"

"No! I'd have at least made an excuse."

"You'd have seen through any excuse I offered."

"True. But in recognizing it, I would have re-spected it for what it was—part of the game."

He leans forward, his blue eyes virulently intense. "And what exactly *is* the game, for you, Audra?" His voice is low, thrumming with veiled, salacious heat.

"You know the game as well as I do, Franco."

"Yeah, maybe, but I want to know what it is for you. I know what it is for me, but I don't think it's the same for everyone."

"The game for me is keeping hooking up simple." I shrug, swirling the wine in my glass. "No strings, no expectations, no weirdness. Just...fun. A little bit of connection with someone, and then an easy, awkwardness-free escape."

Somehow, despite our constant conversation, Franco's plate is empty, and mine is almost cleaned, too, though I barely remember even eating. All I'm aware of is him—his eyes, those pale intense icy blue orbs, and his scent from across the table, and the tightly restrained energy of his presence.

When we're finished eating and the server has removed our plates, Franco pours the last of the wine into our glasses. "Dessert?" he asks.

I frown at him. "Do I look like someone who would eat dessert?"

He doesn't miss a beat. "You look like you *are* dessert."

Dammit, I shouldn't respond to that. I should not—

"You've already sampled all the dessert I have to offer, haven't you?" I hear myself say.

"Hell no," he murmurs. "I think you have a lot more dessert I have yet to taste."

"Dammit, Franco." I huff an irritated, aroused sigh. "I need to use the bathroom."

He just kicks back in his chair, tossing back the rest of his wine as he digs his wallet out of his left hip pocket. "I'll be waiting."

I use the bathroom and then, after washing my hands, I stand in front of the mirror, giving myself a mental pep talk.

Don't do anything stupid. You're a player, he's a player; you both understand damn well how this works. You have all the explanation you need.

Yeah, but I knew all that before agreeing to meet him.

Exactly.

Wait—this pep talk is turning into an argument.

If I'd known beforehand why he left the way he did, then why did I agree to meet him in the first place, much less let him pick me up? And if the whole premise of this *meeting* is to talk about why he left, then why has that been only a small part of our conversation? And why are we flirting like this?

I know that answer all too well.

Deep down, under my consciousness, I knew how this would go, and it's going exactly that way. But it can't go there. I can't let anything else happen. I should call a Lyft and go home.

ALONE.

Don't let him take me home.

Bad idea.

Stupid idea.

Dangerous idea.

I fix my hair, adjusting this strand and that one, tug my top down and plump my tits up, hike my jeans a little higher, wiggle my feet in my heels, and then, with a sigh of irritation at myself, I exit the bathroom.

I find Franco by the hostess stand, discreetly picking his teeth with a toothpick, blatantly ignoring the hostess—who is leaning way over the hostess stand in an obvious ploy to attract his attention with her exposed cleavage.

Sorry, honey—he's got all the cleavage he can handle right here, and mine are real, unlike yours.

Gah, that was catty, even in my own head. Why am I being such a bitch? I mean, it's not like I've actually said any of the catty shit I've thought, but still. And it's not like I even care whether he does anything with the hostess. Or whether her tits are real.

I don't care about any of it. It was just a date.

No, wait—it *wasn't* a date. It was just two people…who have fucked…having dinner together.

And talking about surprisingly personal things.

UGH.

It was a date.

He smiles at me, and his smile is warm and kind and friendly—making me feel even shittier about my catty, jealous thoughts and ridiculous, manufactured irritation. I'm really not even mad that he left like he did, only that he got the drop on me. But I *am* irritated that he knew as much.

"Ready?" Franco asks, holding the door open for me.

"Yep." I sound short and brusque even to myself, and try again, more kindly. "Thank you."

He opens the truck door for me, handing me up, closing it, and then climbing in behind the wheel. He starts the engine, but doesn't pull out of the parking spot. "Something wrong?"

I laugh, shaking my head. "I was calling myself on my own bullshit." I sigh. "And also, the hostess annoys the hell out of me."

Franco digs a slip of paper out of his hip pocket and shows it to me. It's a scrap of receipt paper ripped from a printer, covered with looping, feminine handwriting: *Michelle 630-434-1234 Call me ANYTIME for ANYTHING!* The two words were triple underlined and highlighted in pink, with several hearts doodled around the "anything", just in case her intent wasn't clear.

I blink as I read it. "Wow. Not subtle." I hand it

back to him. "You going to call her?"

Franco snorts as he pulls out of the parking lot. "Not a chance in hell." He stuffs the paper into the bin on the side of his door. His eyes flick to me. "I have other plans, and they don't involve a desperate twenty-year-old."

I gulp; hating the effect his words have on me even if I did love it. "Plans, huh? What plans would those be?"

"Well…I never had dessert," he murmurs, his eyes openly roaming my cleavage. "And I have a hell of a sweet tooth."

A long, long silence.

"Franco…" I whisper.

He turns into my condo complex. "Yes, Audra?"

"This isn't how this is supposed to go."

"No? What were you expecting?" He turns into the lot behind my building and parks in one of the guest spaces. "Like you said, we both know what this game is."

"This wasn't supposed to be a continuation of the game." I unbuckle and open the door, but don't exit yet.

He huffs a laugh, grinning at me. "Oh no? Then I'm not sure what you were thinking, agreeing to go out with me…and letting me pick you up. And pay for dinner. And take you home. And flirting with me."

"I obviously *wasn't* thinking."

He shuts off his truck and unbuckles. "No, obviously not."

I watch him, panicking a little. "What—what are you doing? Where are you going?"

"Walking you up." He smirks. "It's the gentlemanly thing to do… on a *date*."

"Oh." I don't question this until we're at the elevator and he's riding up to my floor with me. "Wait. I wasn't planning on telling you which unit I live in."

He just laughs. "I'm really throwing you off your game, aren't I?"

"Yes, damn you. This whole thing is fucking weird."

I precede him off the elevator and pause outside my door. "Just so you know, I'm normally very, *very* protective of my home. I almost never bring anyone up here."

"Actually, I totally get that. I'm the same way about my house." He laughs, somewhat ruefully. "I guess I don't like mixing pleasure with too many details about my personal life."

I'm standing with my back to my door, and I'm staring up at him, and I understand what he's saying all too well. "Me either. When you mix personal with pleasure, things get messy."

"And I'm a neat freak and a perfectionist, so

having a messy personal life gives me an anxiety attack." He braces a palm against the door over my shoulder, his hard body overwhelming all of my senses, his eyes piercing mine. "I like to keep things neat, simple, and compartmentalized."

"One and done, huh?" I breathe, and watch, annoyed, as my fingers dance across his chest and wander the breadth of his shoulders.

He shakes his head. "No, as a matter of fact. I have a system, and a theory to go with it."

"And what is your system?" I ask.

He gazes down at me, one fingertip trailing up the outside of my bicep, sending shivers down my spine and through my core. "I have a four-fuck-maximum rule."

I laugh, a little too breathily for my own comfort. "I'm pretty sure we broke that last night, Franco."

He shakes his head. "No, you're misunderstanding. Not four individual acts of coitus, but four separate sexual encounters. Meaning, last night was one." He runs his finger up my arm, across my shoulder, over my clavicle and breastbone, and down the valley of my cleavage. "Tonight will be two." He tugs the edge of my top aside to bare the crimson of my bra. "I'll take you to my place tomorrow and fuck you up against my workbench, and that will be three. I'll drive us out to my favorite fishing spot and fuck you in the bed of my truck under the stars, and that will be four. And then…that's it. We go our separate ways."

I keep my breathing steady as he pushes the other side of my top away, baring more of my bra. "I see. And what's the theory that goes with this four-fuck-maximum rule of yours?"

A door down the hall opens, and we both look up, startled; I think we'd both forgotten we weren't alone in this hallway, that it's a public space. I twist away from him, dig my keys out of my purse, and unlock my door. I didn't necessarily mean for him to come in with me, but he did, and I didn't stop him, and then, somehow, my door is closed and my purse is on the floor at my feet and my back is to the door again, and he's everywhere, that cologne and sawdust scent permeating all of my senses.

"Why do you still smell like sawdust?" I ask. "You clearly took a shower."

He chuckles, a smooth, amused rumble. "I was nervous and got ready way too early, so I ended up in my workshop, planing a piece of oak I'm making into a side table."

"Oh." I can't help sniffing him. "I like it."

"I think I also just smell like sawdust, as a person. The scent is ingrained in my pores, I'm pretty sure."

My nose buries against his chest, and I inhale deeply—I'm dizzied by the intensity of my reaction to his scent, the way my heart slams in my chest, the way my core clenches and my thighs shake and my hands clutch at him involuntarily. "It's kind of intoxicating, the way you smell."

He dips, nuzzling his face in my cleavage, inhaling as deeply as I did. "I know the feeling." He lowers himself to his knees, and his hands push my shirt up, baring my midriff and the lower curve of my bra cups; his nose skates across my skin, and his hands cup my waist. "You smell incredible."

"What's your theory, Franco?" I ask, trying hard to sound in control and to cover the shakiness of my voice. Hard to do while his fingers dance around my waist, teasing and tickling my skin above the denim, and then toy with the button and zipper. "About only ever fucking the same person four times, that is."

He touches his lips to my skin, a damp hot kiss just south and west of my navel—I gasp. He transfers this slow touch of his lips eastward, following the horizon of the waistline of my jeans. One kiss, two, three. And then his fingers busy themselves, nudging the brass button through the buttonhole and tugging my zipper down, and then hooking into the lacy crimson elastic of my panties where they're now visible. Tugging them down an inch and then two, he kisses me again, lower, and lower.

Finally, pulling his lips from my skin, he stares

up at me while he hooks two fingers of each hand in the belt loops on either side of my waist, slowly and inexorably peeling my jeans downward, leaving my panties in place. "I came to the theory through a lot of experimentation," he says, his eyes on mine while his hands continue peeling my jeans down my thighs. "Once isn't enough to really enjoy all a person has to offer. It's too impersonal. Enough for a quick release, but that's about it. Once has its place but, in general, it's not enough for me. Two and three times are pretty much the same—still not enough. You get to know the other person, what they like and what you like, but you're still just strangers meeting in the dark. Five and beyond is too much. You risk letting it get personal. After five encounters, you start to sort of instinctively share things, personal things. You start to…connect. You ignore your better sense of things. Four, in my experience, is just right. Enough that you've gotten a sense about the other person, but you can still keep your emotional and personal distance. You can break it off easily with no hard feelings or awkwardness. You've had enough to pretty much know you've enjoyed what the other person has to offer, but you're not tempted to think it could be anything else. You can go your way satisfied, yet not invested."

"Oh," I whisper. "I guess that makes sense."

My jeans are in a pile on the floor off to one side,

and I'm in my black sleeveless top, bra, and panties. He fits my feet back into my heels, levering me a few inches higher once again. Now, his eyes rake down, taking in my cleavage and the red triangle of my thong, and then my thighs. Standing like this, the insides of my thighs just barely kiss, leaving a tiny keyhole between them. In the heels, my butt pops out even more, but facing him like this, he can't really see that.

I start talking, just to cover the unsteadiness I feel at his gaze, at his touch—a nervousness I have no reason to feel, seeing as we've already been naked together.

"Personally, I've always gone with the three strikes rule," I say. "Similar reasoning, though."

"So you're not a one-and-done kind of person either?"

I shake my head. "No, not typically. Sometimes, you meet someone and you just know they're a once and that's it person, you know? But mostly, I like two or three times. Like you said, enough to learn about each other, but not enough to start feeling like it's a *thing*."

"Exactly." His eyes, as pale and icy as they are, blister and spark with heat. "Don't want to risk it becoming a thing."

His fingers dance up the backs of my legs,

tickling behind my knees and skating up my hamstrings. Then, slowly, deliberately, his eyes on mine, he drags all ten fingers down over my buttocks, a teasing, ticklish touch. I catch my breath, a hitch in my lungs. His eyes narrow, jaw tensing.

"Time for dessert," he murmurs.

FOUR

"Dessert?" I question, my voice low, confused; all thoughts have been scattered by the raw hunger in his eyes.

He hooks his index fingers in the straps of my thong at either hip and he slowly drags the undergarment down, down, and off. I don't even have to take off my shoes—he cups my calf and lifts, one foot and then the other, and the red thong flies across the room to land somewhere near my couch. Naked from waist down, still wearing my heels, top, and bra. My core is drenched, weeping, slick and hot and clenching hard at the look in his eyes.

He presses against the insides of my ankles, and I instinctually widen my stance; my hands have a mind of their own, trailing over his head to the ponytail, tugging his hair free to spill loose over his shoulders. I bury my hands in his hair, keeping my eyes on his.

"Dessert," he answers, and drags his tongue over

my seam.

"Oh god."

"We were in too much of a rush last time and I didn't get to taste you." He laps again, slowly, his tongue not penetrating yet, just tasting, teasing.

I have no verbal response for that beyond a gasp as his lips close over my seam and he suckles my clitoris between his teeth, a sudden and wilding assault. Then, instead of pursuing the high he'd started me on, he traces my seam once more but with a fingertip. I watch, mesmerized, as his index finger makes a slow journey over my entrance, back and forth, teasing. His eyes watch me watching him, and I know he sees when I feel the slight pressure he applies to my clit. He sees my reaction when his finger slips between my nether lips, and he sees the way I grit my teeth and suck in an inhalation at the slow, inexorable penetration of his finger inside me. Oh—oh god. He's in no rush, and he knows exactly what he's doing. I expected no less from Franco, but it's still an overwhelming rush of sensation that leaves me dizzy and gasping and trembling, to be played like a violin with such expert mastery. As his finger explores inside me, he brings his lips to me once more, and now his tongue slathers against my clit, working it to hypersensitive hardness. I have a knotted, tangled grip on his hair, bunching the silky mass in my hands. I feel his other hand cup around my buttock, holding me against his mouth.

"God—Franco…holy shit."

He smirks up at me, and I see the slick evidence of my desire smeared on his mouth. "I remember you screaming a hell of a lot louder than that last night," he remarks.

I close my eyes briefly as he trades his words for licks, a series of slow circles against me. "You—you'll have to earn the screams, Franco."

"Do you doubt that I can—and that I will?"

I thunk my head back against the door several times, barely holding back a whimper. "Hell no. But I plan on making you work for them."

Oh god, oh god, oh god—do I ever make him work for them. I keep my moans and whimpers and screams bottled up tight as he laves and licks and fingers and fondles. I bite my lip and nearly sever my tongue, but I keep quiet.

Until he adds a second and third finger, curling them just so, and flicks my clit with his tongue—all this at once is too much, and the ramping climax that sears through me drags a gasping, whimpering, drawn-out cry from me, and then my legs shake and tremble and give out. Franco is there to catch me, standing up and scooping me in his arms.

Dammit, dammit, *dammit*! I didn't want to show

weakness, didn't want to let the orgasm get the better of me, and didn't want to need his arms around me like this. Stupid. Shouldn't have let him in. Shouldn't have gone on the date.

It was a date.

And a damn good one at that, too.

His arms under my thighs and around my shoulders feel much too comforting and comfortable. His eyes on mine are blazing and yet somehow distant—as I know mine are. I know exactly why he chose to do what he did—why he chose to kneel in front of me and go down on me. It's what I'd do, in the reverse situation. Anything to keep from feeling the connection.

Damn him.

Because I do *feel* it. That orgasm was the tip of the iceberg and we both know it. That was one rep in our warm-up set.

I feel him moving, walking—and I only realize then that my eyes are closed and I'm focusing with gritted intensity on just breathing, on not lovingneeding*craving* his mouth and his kiss and his hands and his body.

Jesus, what is he doing to me? How can he make me need this so fucking badly?

He sets me on my bed. When I open my eyes I see him standing in front of my balcony, his back to the glass, facing me. Backlit by the summer sunset, orange and red and gold, bathing him in sun-limned glory. Hair loose, framing his angular jaw and piercing, scintillating blue eyes. He's gazing at me, his expression hard and closed off and inscrutable—and I begrudge him none of that.

I sit up and scoot to the edge of the bed, planting my heels on the Persian rug under my bed that covers my pale blond hardwood floors. I didn't intend for him to come here—my bathrobe is on the floor near the door to my en suite bathroom, my workout clothes are rolled inside out and discarded nearby. A bra hangs from the bathroom doorknob, and my underwear drawer is open, thongs and briefs and boy shorts draped over the edge after my hurried rifling to find the set I'm wearing. My bathroom is a mess, makeup everywhere, a hair dryer plugged in and balanced on the edge of the counter, my box of tampons still sitting open on the floor beside the toilet. The bedside table drawer is open, revealing a Hitachi wand, a Womanizer, and a few other vibrators, strings of condoms of assorted sizes, brands, and styles, lubricant, silk handcuffs, and a sleep mask (read: blindfold).

He sees all this in a sweeping glance, and I remember that he's a neat freak.

"I wasn't expecting or prepared for company," I say, by way of explanation for the mess.

"I'm a neat freak, but I don't expect everyone else

to be." His eyes go to the drawer, pursuing the contents. "I have a lot of questions, Audra."

I'm sitting on my bed, half-naked, trembling from my orgasm, and he's fully dressed, standing across the room with a bulge behind his zipper.

"You can ask, but I make no guarantees to answer, at all or truthfully.

"I'd rather you not answer than lie."

"I figured," I say. "But that's the truth, ironically."

"The blindfold and handcuffs—for you, or for your partner?"

"Either."

"When was the last time you were blindfolded and handcuffed?"

"Three months ago."

"Last time someone else was?"

"A little less than four weeks ago."

"Which do you prefer?"

"Not answering."

"Why?"

"Ruins the fun of discovery."

"So you'd let me use them on you?" he asks, shoving his hands in his pocket—and not so surreptitiously adjusting himself.

"Maybe. Not tonight. And only if I could use them on you."

He sighs. "You know, being a neat freak and a

perfectionist means I also have a bit of a thing for control."

"I figured as much."

He adjusts himself again. "Which toy is your favorite?"

"Can't answer that. They each have their own specific purpose."

"Explain."

"For making myself feel as good as possible as fast as possible, I like the Womanizer. If I'm horny and want to mimic sex without going through the effort of finding a guy, I'll use one of the vibrators." I lift out a large, knobbed, curved, silicone thing with a second smaller stimulator. "Usually this one. If I'm having trouble coming, or I just want to get off hard and fast, I'll use the wand."

He eyes them all, and then his gaze rakes over me. He licks his lips, and adjusts himself in his jeans yet again.

"Do you ever use toys during sex?"

"Not typically, but I have." I cross my legs, blocking his view of my center. "My turn."

"Your turn?"

I crook my finger at him, and he crosses the room to stand a foot or so away from me. "Do you watch porn?"

He shrugs. "Sure, sometimes. Not a lot, though.

I prefer…the real thing, you might say."

"Have you fucked that hostess?"

"God no." He frowns. "You sound almost jealous."

I hate the burn in my chest. "Just wondering."

"I have slept with women younger than me, but ten years' difference is my limit. The thought of sleeping with a twenty or twenty-one-year-old girl makes me feel like a predator." He grins. "You don't have to admit it, but you were jealous."

I hook my fingers in his belt loops—it's a tight fit with his belt, but I have enough purchase to draw him closer. "You want the truth?"

"Yes."

"The whole truth and nothing but the truth?"

"Yes."

I unbutton his jeans, and then pause. "I was jealous. And that pissed me off, because I had no reason and no right to be jealous, and I'm doing my damnedest to squash it. I just didn't like how she was openly hitting on you despite the fact that you were there with me."

He leaves his hands dangling at his sides, affecting an easy, casual stance—his eyes and his slow, deep breathing tell me otherwise. "Even if she'd been within a reasonable age difference, and even if I'd been alone or with a buddy, I wouldn't have pursued anything. Behavior like that is a turn-off to me."

"Good to know. It is for me too." I lower his zipper, and his package springs free through the opening. "Kinkiest thing you've ever done?"

"Not answering."

"Fair enough. Something you've thought about, fantasized about, or otherwise want to do but never have?"

He blinks in silence for a moment. "Damn. That's pretty personal."

"And asking me about my vibrator isn't?"

"There's a difference between how you masturbate and what you fantasize about, Audra."

I nod, eying the bulge, and then meeting his gaze. "True." I reach down and bring his foot up, resting the sole of his boot on the bed between my thighs, slowly untying it. "My answer to my own question, then…" I take a deep breath, and focus on removing his boot and then untying the other one. "This is kind of weird, I guess. I've always had this fantasy of waking up to someone fucking me. I live alone and I've always lived alone, and I've never let anyone spend the night here, and I'd certainly never give a guy I was sleeping with access to my apartment. So it's kind of a forbidden sort of thing, I guess. I don't know. It's not a rape fantasy—that's messed up, and no thank you. The fantasy is always someone I know and trust, and it's always consensual, just…unexpected. I don't know how else to put it."

He nods. "I get that, actually. More than you might imagine." He thinks for a while. "So, let me go back and answer the question I asked you. I obviously don't use a vibrator. I actually don't jack off all that often, because like with porn, I prefer the real thing. I'd rather wait and let it build up until I can find someone to hook up with."

"Bet you've never had to look very hard."

He grins. "No, not really."

"So when you jack off…how do you do it?" I have his boots off, and his socks, and now I tug his jeans off, tossing them aside. He grabs his shirt by the back of the collar and hauls it off, and now he's standing between my knees in a pair of tight black briefs. "I mean, if you don't watch porn, how do you get yourself there?"

He scrapes his hair away from his eyes with both hands, a slow, sexy swipe of his fingers over his scalp. "I have a few photos and videos I use—not taken by me, just…saved for that use. Or sometimes I just think about something recent. A visual memory, know what I mean?"

I grin, nodding. "I do know what you mean. For example, this will probably be a visual memory I'll use a lot down the road."

"What is?"

I pull the elastic waistband away from his erection and slide the black undergarment down to his ankles, baring his huge, glorious cock. I wrap my fist around him, keeping my eyes on his. "This."

He swallows. "Oh." His jaw clenches. "Yeah… me too."

There's a hesitation in his statement, though, and I catch it. "What?" I ask.

He frowns. "What, what?"

"You hesitated just then."

He steps closer, reaches down to grab the hem of my top and drags it off me, tossing it behind him. A deft movement of his hands, and I feel my bra come loose; he breaks my grip on him so he can remove the bra from my arms and toss it aside, and now we're both naked.

"There," he says. "*Now* it's a memory I'll never fucking forget."

"What—the taste of my pussy isn't enough?" I say, teasing.

He answers with all seriousness, however. "Not by a long shot." Franco's hands cup my breasts, thumbs running over my nipples. "These perfect tits of yours are the coup de grace."

I can't help a flattered smile. "I see. I'm glad I could deliver the coup de grace for your spank bank memories." I wrap my fingers around him again. "But I wasn't done creating my own."

"Let me guess…you're finally gonna show me what you can do with your mouth?"

His words bring back a stark, vivid memory of yesterday morning. I shrug—and again, the movement draws his gaze. "Could be. You'll have to stand very, very still in order to find out."

He just blinks at me, and then his eyes rake lasciviously down from my eyes to my breasts, to my core, and then to my hands as I wrap both of them around him, stroking him slowly. He huffs a quiet sigh, a sound of pleasure as I start touching him. His jaw flexes, clenches, and I see his fingers twitch with the need to touch me, to take control.

He cedes it to me, however. At least for the moment.

I have no illusions about how this will go—he'll let me take him to a certain point, but then he'll take over. I know his type, and I know he won't want to "waste" it by letting me take him all the way. Not in a situation like this, at least. I file that thought away—if this goes any further beyond tonight, I'll think about trying to get him to let me take him all the way.

For now, I'm willing to let him do things mostly his way—I just want to get through this without getting myself into worse trouble, feelings-wise.

This is already an unwise decision, to sleep with Franco again. I'm not even sure how we got here—it was just... I just find myself unable to resist him, which frustrates me to no end.

But he's listening, so far—he's absolutely still. Breathing evenly, watching my hands slide up and down, slowly, squeezing now and then, cupping over the head and twisting back down. Thumbing the tip, just exploring the length of him in a way I didn't get to last night—that was a hot and heavy and a wild rampage of sex with little thought to technique or exploration, just abandonment to raw need.

This is different.

I've given up pretending I didn't know this was going to happen—why else would I have shaved my hoo-ha, or put on my most expensive lingerie? I wouldn't have agreed to this whole evening had I not known, at least on some level, that it would go exactly where it's going. More to the point—I *wanted* it to go here.

I told Franco I have a three strikes rule, which is true. But the truth is, that's my maximum limit, and most guys don't get that far. I get tired of them after one. I rarely find a guy interesting enough, attractive enough, or good enough at making me feel good to want more than once with him. Fewer yet are the men who are all of the above. Some men have a special magic which makes me want to seek *his* pleasure. When it comes to sex, I'm selfish. I can afford to be, because men aren't hard to please as a rule. Let them fuck me, and they'll come, guaranteed, and usually it's a case of whether he can last long enough to make it worth my while, much less want more.

Franco, damn him, has all of this by the truckload. And then some. Which is the root of the problem: I just plain old flat out *want* the man in a way I'm not sure I've ever experienced.

It's whetted my appetite for him, if anything.

He's watching—the entire time I've been ruminating and mooning over this whole stupid situation, I've been slowly and gently caressing him. Not in an outright attempt to get him to come—I could do that in a minute flat if I really wanted to—but more just to touch him, to enjoy the feel of him in my hands.

He's getting impatient, I can tell.

I just stare up at him, blinking slowly, stroking and caressing, one hand, two hands, up and down and hand over hand, without rhythm or pattern, until I see his jaw clenching and his eyes narrowing and his hands twitching.

Without warning, I bend forward and take him into my mouth, and it's so sudden and unexpected that he flinches, gasps, and then curses out loud.

"Fucking hell, Audra. Jesus."

I smirk at him, pleased at the reaction I got. "Awww, Franco—I'm just getting started, sweetheart."

He groans. "I wasn't expecting that, is all."

"Sure, sure." I flick my tongue against the tip. "You can go ahead and admit you've never felt anything so good. Flattery goes a long way with me, I don't mind admitting."

He breathes out shakily. "If I admitted that it would be the absolute truth."

I laugh. "I was teasing, Franco—I've hardly touched you. I'm not even really trying, yet."

"Well, it felt like the best thing ever."

"Isn't it the best thing ever, anytime you get your dick sucked?" I ask, stroking his saliva-coated length with one hand.

"Yeah, to an extent. But there's also a definitive, actual best thing ever."

"And my one suck outranks all the other full blowjobs you've ever gotten?" I ask this skeptically, one eyebrow lifted, my hand stilled.

"Would you believe I haven't really received all that many? I'm usually too impatient to let it go that far." He hesitates, sighs, and then continues. "Plus, the truth is, letting someone do that is also an act of giving over control, and I'm not great at that."

"You're doing fine with me, so far," I say, truthfully.

"Yeah, well...you're reaching the end of my patience." Franco isn't a growly sort of guy, on the whole, but he growls now.

"I've barely done anything," I protest.

He laughs. "Yeah, exactly. It feels great, but I'm getting impatient to be inside you." His eyes meet mine. "Which is why I so rarely let anyone give me a blowjob that lasts more than a few seconds before I stop it in favor of other things."

In that case, I want to get another taste of him before he runs out of patience. I angle him away from his body and take him into my mouth. I start slow—just my lips around the tip in a slow, sensual kiss. But then, just as if I was kissing his mouth and getting carried away, I gradually take more and more of him into my mouth, and then once I have a mouthful of him I stroke him with my fists and flutter my tongue against him. More, and more, until I feel him at the back of my throat, and now I turn my eyes up to his, change my angle, open my throat, and take more. He grunts in surprise as I deep-throat him until my lips nudge against his balls.

"*Jesus*, Audra," he hisses.

I smile—mostly with my eyes as my mouth is, um, otherwise occupied. And then back away, only to push forward again. Swallowing, tonguing, cupping his ass with both hands, I watch his reaction.

"Fuck, fuck." He pulls away, removing himself from my mouth with a *pop*. "Fucking hell, Audra."

I wipe at my lips with the back of my wrist, staring at him with all the sensuality I possess. "Told you I'm good with my mouth."

"I believed you, but holy *shit*, woman." He's breathing hard, and his stomach is tensed, and I realize he's backing himself away from the edge. "You weren't kidding."

"Nope."

"You must not have much of a gag reflex. *Damn*."

I grin. "I discovered, totally by accident, that I don't really have one."

His laugh is skeptical. "And how do you discover *that* by accident?"

"That's a story for another time."

He's just staring at me, his expression hard to read.

I laugh, uncomfortable with the intensity in his expression. "What?" I laugh. "Why are you looking at me like that?"

"Because I just don't know what the fuck to do with you, Audra."

I frown. "Um…have really amazing sex with me, and then go home?"

"Not what I mean."

"I know," I breathe. "I'm being flippant."

"I know," he murmurs. "Don't be."

Franco blinks at me. Our eyes meet, and something wild and deep and thrumming and intense sears between us, white-hot and unspoken, unspeakable, unmistakable.

FIVE

I TACKLE HIM, AND NOT AT ALL GENTLY. OUR BODIES connect with a smack and a thud of bone and flesh and muscle colliding, and then I pin him to the bed and straddle him.

There are no thoughts in my head except to *take*.

No thoughts in me at all, beyond Franco.

Need.

Rapacious, ravaging need.

He's stunned by my sudden ferocity. I claw my fingers into his chest, raking them downward as I writhe on top of him, seeking him, desperate for anything physical to take my mind off my emotions. He reaches for me, but I capture his hands, tangle our fingers. He tries to wrestle my hands away, trying to stop me or restrain me or I don't know what, but he underestimates my raw strength, especially that borne of desperation. I battle his grip, keep his hands away from me; our eyes meet, briefly, and I see that if anything, I'm only turning him on all the more, but even that knowledge is a faint, distant understanding. All there is within me is need.

I move, sliding my slick core against him. I feel him. I feel that hot thick hard ridge, and I need it. God, I need it. I shift angles, still wrestling with his attempts to get his hands on me. Then—god yes—I find the perfect angle. The head of him catches against my opening and it's only a matter of sinking my hips forward, thrusting, and he's inside me, and I feel him spearing into me, a sudden hard impalement, my entire being spasming with ecstasy—not from an orgasm but from sheer relief at the feel of Franco, of *him*, this man who has some strange power over me.

"Audra—holy—holy shit, *Audra*..." His voice is ragged, gasping, the breath and sense stunned right out of him.

So thick inside me, so hot, so hard. So *much*. So perfect.

"Franco—" I gasp.

"Wait—wait. Audra, hold on—"

I pin his hands to the mattress, and he lets me, writhing with me. Against me. Thrashing and thrusting under me, giving over to the violent ecstasy of this, a passion so intense neither of us can deny it or control it or stop it.

"AUDRA!" he shouts.

"Franco—Jesus, Franco!" I'm screaming, the climax of our union slamming into me harder and more intensely than ever, than even the climax from the wand and vibrator—this is beyond that. More than that.

I bury my face into his chest and feel his heartbeat, taste it through his skin, my sweat commingles with his and we're moving in perfect unison, his breath mine, and mine his, lips touching, matching breathless gaps and guttural groans—who's making which sound? I can't tell our sounds apart and that too is beautiful.

This is *beautiful*.

I come, squeezing, pulsing around his slick wet thrusts, and that's more beautiful yet.

"Audra!" This time, there's an urgency to his cry. "Wait—you have to stop."

"Can't—I can't!"

"Fuck! You *have* to!" He's desperate, his voice tense and strained.

With a sudden burst of strength, Franco levers me off of him and twists so I'm on my back and he's above me. He's no longer inside me and I'm desperate to get him back, to get more of him. He's gasping, groaning through clenched teeth, hovering over me, pinning me to the bed, every muscle in his body tensed and straining with primal, animal power.

My eyes rake greedily over every inch of him, over every plane and bulge of sculpted perfection, finally landing on his erection, swaying and gleaming above my belly, huge and rock hard and wet.

And bare.

No condom.

"Fuck," I whisper, realizing.

"Yeah…" he snarls.

"You—you—did you—?"

His eyes meet mine. "I didn't come, no."

"Holy shit."

Never, ever, ever in my life, since the first time I had sex, have I *ever* forgotten to make sure my sexual partner was wrapped up. Drunk as a skunk and I still remember.

He's still growling under his breath, every muscle tensed, and I realize he's still holding back.

Oh no, no. That just won't do.

"Franco, let me go." I twist my wrists, trying to break his grip—he's far too strong, even with the gentle grip as he has on me.

He doesn't hear me, too focused on the effort to back away from his edge.

"Franco, let *go*." I put some snap into my voice, and this time he hears me, responding immediately by releasing my wrists.

The second I'm free of his grip, I wriggle

downward, scooting underneath him until his erection is at face level. He's still breathing hard, eyes closed, on his hands and knees. Not paying any attention to anything except his struggle to hold back.

I take him into my mouth, and he grunts in shock. I taste…*us.* Him, me, our mingled essence.

I give him no chance to fight back, to tell me to stop, to be chivalrous or some bullshit. I clasp him in my hands and pump his length with both fists, and wrap my lips around him and suck, tonguing him. There's no teasing or technique or buildup, just a sudden and all-out assault on him with hands and mouth.

"Fuck, fuck, ohhhhh god, Audra, what are you—" he cuts off with a grunt, his hips helplessly thrusting. "Just give me a second to—"

"Mm-mm." I go faster, harder, hungrier—there was something unbearably erotic about what Franco just did, and I'm giving over totally to my instinctual urges. All I care about is him, his pleasure—taking it from him. Feeling him let go, tasting his need.

I hear my mouth on him, my fists—wet slurps and suckling and squishing sounds, and I feel his body clenching, feel him holding back thrusts, hear him grunting, gasping. Instead of faster, now, I use more mouth, one fist around his base pumping rhythmically as I pulse my mouth down around him in deep, fast, wet slides of lips and tongue and throat.

"Audra—" His voice, drowning in desperation. "I can't—I can't hold it—"

"Mmmmhhhmmmm," I moan, urging him to let go. I cup his heavy sac and press a finger just behind it, to his taint, and stroke his thick, throbbing erection all the harder.

"Ohhhh god, Audra, Audra…"

Stop saying my name like that, dammit, with such desperate, vulnerable need.

I just moan, humming around him as I work him with mouth and hands. His next sound is a ragged cry, his hips flexing as he finally gives in to a full thrust—I wasn't expecting it, but I take it and hum in surprise, a sound that morphs into erotic need as he finally *finally* lets go, lets himself move. I feel him throbbing against my lips, feel his balls tensing and clenching, and he thrusts into my throat, moving raggedly.

Lost to it.

I am—he is—we both are.

This wasn't supposed to work like this—I could have just put a condom on him and let him finish any other way. This was supposed to be less personal, less intimate. But somehow it's the complete opposite.

I'm not supposed to feel every pulse of his heartbeat, not supposed to crave his pleasure, not supposed to need his climax, his taste, his desperation, his fury.

"Ohhh—*ohhhh* fuck, Audra—*Audra*—"

God, his voice is raw with tormented need. He gives a final growling gasp, his fists knotting in the blankets, his back arching, his whole being taut as a piano wire—and then, he thrusts, once, pushing into my mouth. I swallowed around him and then backed away so my lips were suctioned around the groove beneath the head; pressing my middle finger just behind his taint, I stroke him furiously with my other hand.

I taste him, heat and musk and salt. Swallowing madly, I take all of him as he comes and comes, spurting thick streams into my mouth and down my throat. Swallowing, swallowing, I still can't keep up and I feel a trickle down the corner of my mouth and over my lower lip.

One last warm flood of his seed, and then, still growling and moaning, his arms shaking, he pulls free and flops limp to his back beside me, breathing as hard as if he'd just done a hundred burpees.

His eyes are open, following me as I roll to sit up.

He reaches up, brushes the pad of his thumb over my lip, wiping away the droplets of his essence; instead of letting him wipe it somewhere or wash it away, I suck it off of his thumb. Just to prove a point, perhaps. I don't even know, honestly.

His eyes on mine are inscrutable. Mine, I suppose, are equally so.

Neither of us says a word.

Franco gets up off the bed and goes into my bathroom; I hear the water running as he washes up, and then I hear him pee, wash his hands again, and then he exits the bathroom. Still naked, and without a word to me, he heads for the kitchen. Curious, I wait. I hear him moving around, and while I'm waiting I use the bathroom and wash, then rinse my mouth. I get back in bed then, and just in time. He enters with two wineglasses full of red wine.

No jokes about needing to wash anything down—the energy between us is solemn and heavy.

Something very serious just happened.

I accept the glass from him as he sits on the bed; we both cover our laps with the flat sheet, but otherwise make no pretense of covering up—no need, and, honestly, no desire to.

I take a long drink, and we sit in silence for a while.

"Audra, what almost just happened—"

"I'm sorry," I blurt, ducking my head to stare at the sheet. "I just—I lost it, I guess. I went a little haywire."

"Are you—if I hadn't stopped, are you on birth control or anything?"

"Yeah, of course. I've been getting a shot since they invented it. But still."

"Exactly—but still."

I sigh. "Nothing like that has ever happened before. I've never forgotten, not ever." I swirl the ruby
liquid in my glass, watching it instead of him. "I don't
know how to explain it, Franco. You just...you made
me *crazy*."

A long pause.

"I'm not blaming you, Franco. It was me. I just—I
don't know." I finally meet his gaze, and what I see
in his eyes and on his face is a mirror for what I'm
feeling—overwhelmed, confused...too much to even
process or comprehend.

"Audra..." He sighs, swirls his wine. "That was
a hell of a lot more than us not using a condom, and
you know it."

No, no, no. I can't do this. Yes, dammit, I feel it.
There's a lot more to it than that. That was supposed
to be a quick fuck; it wasn't supposed to get...*intimate*. It was raw and carnal and not at all romantic,
but it still felt way too personal. Too real. And I don't
want to feel that.

I have no answer for him. I just drink my wine
and try not to think about anything at all.

His eyes are on mine, probing, piercing. "Not
gonna say anything?"

"We both know how this goes, Franco." I toss
back the last of my wine. "Three for me, four for

you—that's our rules, right? We both play the game, Franco. Keep it neat, clean, mess-free, and simple. And...this thing, whatever it is between us, it's starting to get messy and complicated. And, like you said, it's a lot more than you almost coming inside me without a condom on, and we both know it. So...why risk letting it get any messier or more complicated? Neither of us want that, do we?"

He's quiet for a long moment. "No..." he murmurs, "I guess not."

There's a hell of a lot to dissect in that response—the quietness of his voice, the hesitation, the word "guess", the way he didn't look at me as he said it.

I don't dissect it. I don't allow myself.

Franco finishes his wine, then glances at me, a long, slow, burning stare. His blond hair is loose, tangled, falling around his broad shoulders. His eyes flicker inscrutable blue flames, like ice made into fire. I see a quick barrage of things cross his features, and then he shuts down again, closed off, unreadable. I feel myself retreating behind my own walls.

Yet, despite those walls, I feel him.

I feel *us*.

Chemistry.

I've never really grasped the import of that phrase—to have chemistry with someone.

Until now.

Now, I get it.

Certain people just react to each other explosively.

A little bit here or there, and you get some sparks, some smoke, some bubbling. Add too much, and you get a fireball. Franco and I mix to create a fireball—that's our chemistry. Even now, with all this boiling between us, I feel that combustion sizzling.

As hot as what just happened between us was, it hadn't really satisfied a certain deep down craving. That need for *him* won't go away. I still want him. Need him. I want his hands, his mouth. Dammit, I want him above me, beneath me, behind me. All over me.

I feel my nipples harden—a glance to the side reveals an unsuccessfully hidden tent in the sheet; he feels it too.

His eyes meet mine, then go to my breasts, the pink tips hardening into points. My empty glass, spinning idly between my fingers. He sets his glass aside, takes mine, and puts it next to his.

Silence.

I can't take my eyes off that tent in the sheet.

Dammit, dammit, dammit, I want him.

I shift; tug the sheet away to reveal his erection.

"Audra."

I look at him, bold, daring him to deny he wants it too. "I know."

He heaves a breath, holding utterly still other than the sound of his sigh. "We just agreed we don't need to complicate this any further."

Yet he's moving to face me, and then he's above me, and my hands are roaming his shoulders and spine and butt, and then I'm gripping his hardness and he's burying his face between my breasts and I'm biting his shoulder as I caress everywhere I can reach.

"I can't...fucking...*help* it," I groan, and then bite his shoulder again out of raw frustrated need. "I don't want to need you like this, but I do."

He has a condom wrapper between his teeth, and rips it open, withdraws the ring and spits the wrapper aside, rolling the condom on in a smooth motion.

"I know. Me either."

"We shouldn't," I gasp, grasping him, lining him up at my entrance.

"No, we shouldn't," he agrees, surging into me.

I lose the thread of my thoughts, then, as he fills me. I can only cry out, clinging to his broad hard shoulders, fingernails digging into his flesh and raking down as he thrusts into me. His face is buried between my breasts, his lips catching at my nipples, his teeth occasionally nipping the tender flesh. His hands curl under my thighs and lift them. I wrap my legs around his waist, hook tight, and I move in unison with him.

I claw at him, helpless, as he fills me and over-whelms me—I can't breathe except to breathe him, cannot move except to move with him, cannot speak except to cry his name.

I reach climax as he finds his own ragged, gasping, madly thrusting release.

We move together, cry out together. My name, his name, nothing else. Just gusting whimpers, ragged groans, guttural roars, hoarse cries.

When it's over, he goes limp on top of me. I welcome his weight, the crushing warmth of him, his lean bulk on me, his scent and his skin and his everything all over and inside me. I know my fingers are stroking his back, his spine, his shoulders, and I try to stop them, but I can't.

There's a long moment of silence, except for our breathing.

I feel a pressure inside—a hot, ballooning, suffocating *thing* in my chest and gut and throat, an upwelling of…god, I don't know what.

But it's sharp and huge and focused utterly on the man on me and in me and all around me.

And it makes my eyes sting.

I push at him. "I need—I can't breathe. I need to get up."

He rolls off immediately. "God, I'm sorry, I didn't mean to crush you."

I'm off the bed in an instant. "No, that was fine. More than fine." I find my robe, shrug into it, and tie it. "And that's why I can't breathe."

I head to my balcony, rip the door open so hard it slams open and halfway closes again, and lean against the railing, gasping, blinking.

I feel him behind me; I don't have to look to know he's still naked.

"Audra…"

I shake my head. "Franco, don't."

"That was—"

"I said *don't*, Franco!" I snap. "Just fucking don't."

"I don't want to acknowledge it any more than you do, goddammit, and probably a whole hell of a lot less."

"What? Are we gonna trade life stories, now, Franco? Are you gonna tell me why you're a player? Why you have your four-fuck rule? Why you're a forty-five-year-old bachelor?" I feel the defensive spikes shooting out and into my words, but I can't stop them; he's penetrated too far past all my walls and boundaries, and I have to stop him from getting any closer. "You really want to hear why I have my three strikes rule? Why I keep things kinky and casual? You really want to know why I never kiss?" Shit, I didn't mean for that last one to come out.

He doesn't answer any of that.

"No," I say. "I didn't think so."

"Audra—"

"Thanks for dinner," I say. "And the orgasms. They were, honestly...unforgettable. So, thank you."

"We're ending it here, huh?" He sounds carefully neutral, but I don't turn to gauge his expression. I don't dare.

"It's best, don't you think?"

I can imagine him rubbing the back of his neck, or scraping his hands through his long loose hair, but again, I don't dare look.

"Yeah," he agrees, eventually. "It probably is."

"Then I think you should go." I sigh. "That sounded rude, and I'm sorry. I'm not trying to be rude. I just—"

"No, you're right. You're absolutely right. This whole thing is going way past what either of us are comfortable with, and we should just...call it."

"Yeah. We should."

He turns away—I hear his steps on the balcony, and then hear him rustling around, putting on his clothes. I still don't look.

I hear him again, at the open doorway to the balcony. I feel him, more than hear him, if you want to be accurate.

"You don't kiss because you saw *Pretty Woman*," he says.

I laugh, a genuine bark of amused surprise. "Yeah, actually, you happen to be one hundred percent correct. But Vivian was onto something."

Silence.

"So…bye, I guess?"

I turn, finally. He's dressed, put together, and as breathtakingly beautiful as ever. More so, maybe. "Bye."

"You know we're gonna see each other at some point, right?" He scuffs his boot against the track of the sliding glass door.

I nod. "Yeah. And we'll be friends. Just not… this."

He chuckles ruefully. "You really think that'll work?"

I sigh. "No, probably not. But it has to, so it will."

"You gonna ignore me?"

I nod again. "I'll probably be an icy bitch to you, so be warned, and try not to take it too personally."

"Right. Duly noted."

I try to smile, but I can't quite do it. This is the weirdest, most awkward, most uncomfortable parting I've ever experienced. I just want it to be over.

"I'll see you later, Franco." I breathe this, stifling the bizarre flood of icky feelings inside.

"Yeah." He digs his key ring out of his pocket, looks at it, and puts it back. "See ya."

He waves, once, supremely awkwardly, and strides out of my room. Out of my apartment. I hear the door slam. A few minutes later I hear a car door close, an engine start, tires crunch, and then the sounds fade and I'm alone with my thoughts and feelings.

Shit, shit, shit.

I go into my living room to where my purse is still sitting on the floor by the front door. I sit down right there, dig my phone out of the purse, and call Imogen.

"Hello? Audra? What is it?"

I didn't even look at the time. I don't really care. "Imogen? I—remember what I said about really bad or really good?"

"Uh huh." Her voice is tired, but coherent.

"It was both."

"Was?"

"I need so much wine right now."

"Do I need to come over right now?"

"Unless you can get here sooner."

"Sooner than right now?" she says, laughing.

"Can you be here five minutes ago?"

"Oh god." She heard something in my voice, clearly. "That bad?"

"You have no idea," I whisper. "I need to be really, really drunk, and I can't do it alone."

"Audra, you can't drink your way past your feelings."

"Watch me, bitch." I say this with a laugh.

She sighs. "Okay, okay. Ten minutes."

"Bring all the wine!"

She laughs. "How about I bring vodka and we get this done faster?"

"I like the way you think."

"Do we need snacks?" she asks, and I hear her moving around, then Jesse's voice rumbles in the background.

"No. No snacks. Just vodka."

"Jesus."

"Tell Jesse I'm sorry for dragging you away from him."

She giggles. "Oh, don't worry about him. We just finished having some seriously epic sex, so he's fine." I groan, and she inhales sharply. "Oh, I'm sorry, Audra—was that a bad reminder?"

"No, I just—" I laugh. "I just finished having some seriously epic sex, too. Only, that's a good thing for you and not so much for me."

"I'm so confused, Audra."

"Just get here."

"Ten minutes."

It's the longest ten minutes of my life.

SIX

THE SECURITY BUZZER SOUNDS, AND I REACH UP TO STAB the button, allowing Imogen access to my building. An empty bottle of wine and a chunk of 85% dark chocolate sit on the coffee table. I walk over to the door and stick the bottle between the door and the jamb so Imogen will be able to come in and I won't have to get up again.

As I sit on the sofa I hear Imogen approaching, talking on the phone—to Jesse, judging by the low intimate tone of her voice.

"Hi, Jesse!" I yell, as she shoves open my door, bends to pick up the bottle, and then enter my condo.

"Audra, be quiet!" Imogen hisses. "It's nearly midnight."

"Sorry. *Hi, Jesse!*" I whisper-yell.

Imogen eyes the empty bottle and my empty wineglass. "Holy shit, Audra. Did you drink that whole bottle by yourself in fifteen minutes?"

I shake my head. "No. Only half of it. Franco and I had the other half. After round one, but before round two."

I hear Jesse tell Imogen to hand me the phone; I take the handset from her and put it to my ear. "Hi, Jesse."

"Don't get my girl too drunk, okay? Somehow, I doubt she has your liver."

"No, I won't. I'll be getting wasted, but she'll be fine. She'll just have to babysit my stupid ass."

There is a pause on the other side. "Hope you understand if I don't get involved in this."

"Yep. He's your best friend; I'm your girlfriend's best friend. I get it."

"Good. Now both of you *stay there*. I'll come back and get her when she's ready to go."

"You're the best." I sigh deeply. "She's a lucky girl."

"Got that backwards, babe. *She's* the best, *I'm* the lucky one."

"Both ways, then."

"He didn't do anything stupid, did he?"

I laugh. "Yeah, he did." I pause for effect. "He slept with me."

Jesse sighs. "Don't get too crazy. It doesn't actually fix anything, you know."

"I know," I say, cheerfully. "I just don't want to

deal with it right now."

"He's gonna be a miserable bastard to work with for a while, isn't he?"

"Yeah, probably. You can blame me."

Imogen takes the phone back. "Okay, give my boyfriend back." She moves away a few feet and whispers into the phone. I'm not positive, but I think I hear her tell him she loves him.

I wait until she hangs up and puts her phone away and then stare up at her hopefully. "Vodka?"

She laughs, withdrawing a brand new bottle of Grey Goose from her bag. She eyes me. "You're not gonna drink it straight, are you?"

I blow a raspberry. "Things are bad, but it's not *that* bad. I have some strawberry Bubly in the fridge. We can mix it with that."

In a few minutes we both have a stiff drink, and we're sitting on the couch. Imogen knows better than to push me, so we turn on an older Iliza Shlesinger special and I suck down two more drinks before lowering the volume and pivoting on the couch to face Imogen.

"I went to talk to him."

She snorts and rolls her eyes. "Yes, I know. I heard about it from James."

"How?"

"James and Ryder came over for a while earlier

this evening, under the guise of talking about the next project now that the Waverley build is almost done. But really, it was so they could gossip about you and Franco." She laughed, shaking her head. "Men. They act like *we're* the gossips, but they can be just as bad."

"What'd they say?"

"Oh, just that you showed up and you guys talked in the basement, but then you left all upset."

"I was *not* upset. He didn't want to talk about personal stuff at work, and we decided to meet for dinner."

Imogen looks surprised. "Dinner? Like…a *date*?"

She's shocked because I rarely ever go on anything resembling a date. I will meet for drinks to ensure we don't end up at my place, but that's about it. Dinner, coffee, breakfast? Nah. Not likely. Dates are the way you get to know someone, and I'm not interested.

Or I wasn't.

Until I met Franco.

I sigh. "Yeah. Dinner, at Callihan's. A date."

"With Franco?"

I snort again. "No, Imogen, with Jimmy Buffet. *Yes*, with Franco."

"Well, no need for sarcasm," she says, getting up to make another drink for us—we alternate, and I made the last round, so it's her turn. "I was just surprised, is all. Considering the last time we talked about him you were all like, 'eeew, *feelings*, ICKY!'" She says this last part in a faux childish whine.

"I wish I could be mad at you for that, but I can't." I take the drink and sip at it—I'm now starting to feel the effects of the alcohol pretty nicely. "It wasn't supposed to be a date. It was supposed to be meeting to let him explain why he ghosted on me. And then…it just turned into a date."

She frowns. "Um, so…you guys had already slept together, and you were meeting for dinner…"

"And he picked me up here." I say this with a wince, knowing what's coming. "And I let him pay for dinner."

She just blinks at me. "But yet you didn't expect it to be a date."

"I got confused!" I wail. "He's so sexy and easy to talk to, and we flirt without even trying, and…he makes me…god, I don't know. I don't know which way is up when I'm around him. Or, I do, but it's not until afterward that I even realize what's happened. It was just…we were driving home, and then we were up here, and then he was going down on me, and then suddenly it wasn't just fucking anymore."

"I just want to be perfectly clear. He brought you home and you slept with him… *here*, after a date?"

"Yes, Imogen."

Imogen looks confused. "You're breaking all your rules for Franco."

"I know!"

"Did you kiss him?" she asks, knowing about my *Pretty Woman* rule.

"No, thank god." I sigh. "But the last time we had sex, right before I called you…it was…we didn't kiss, but somehow, we didn't need to. The whole thing was like a kiss, but it was our whole bodies kissing. And before that, we'd been talking about how we weren't going to continue the *thing*."

"Continue the thing?"

"Keep fucking," I clarify. "We agreed we'd stop seeing each other, in your old lady parlance."

"And then you slept together again."

"And it was…" I struggle for words. "We… he…I…"

Her expression as she watches me is soft and knowing. "When you came, you felt it in your soul?"

"Yeah, except I felt the whole damn *thing* in my soul, not just when I came." I whisper the next part. "And I couldn't tell the difference between him coming and me coming…where he began and I…and I ended."

Her eyes go wide. "Audra…" she breathes. "You know what that means, don't you?"

"Don't tell me. Please."

"It means you *made love*."

"YOU SHUT YOUR FILTHY WHORE MOUTH!" I shout.

She just laughs. "You did! That's what that is, babe. Hate to break it to you."

"I need a drink," I say.

Imogen laughs. "You've had four, and you have one in your hand."

"I need more."

I stand up, drain my glass, and go into the kitchen. I feel Imogen watching me as I pour two…ish… fingers of vodka into my glass, drain it, hiss, and chase it with flavored sparkling water, and then pour another more rationally proportioned mixed drink. And hooooo, I'm feeling it now.

"You're so gonna regret this in the morning." Imogen laughs.

"My first client isn't until noon," I say. "I'll be fine."

Imogen snorts. "Yeah…you won't be going to work tomorrow."

There's a long pause as I sip and feel the alcohol numbing me. Sweet, sweet oblivion.

Yes, this is irresponsible, and stupid, and will only prolong me having to deal with my feelings. But I just don't know how to deal with this. How to handle my emotions at all, much less regarding Franco.

"Audra, honey, listen—"

"If you're about to bring up The Incident, you can just shut up."

"You called me over here for a reason, Audra. And it wasn't just so I could enable your dealing with this situation through alcohol."

"It *wasn't* making love," I insist.

She sighs. "What happened with Jared was twenty years ago, Audra."

"You said his *name*," I hiss.

"Yes, Audra, I did. It's time you got over that. Jared, Jared, Jared." She stands up and paces around me, gesticulating. "Jared Robert Ellis." She glares down at me. "Say his name."

"No."

"Say it."

"He's not even worth speaking about. I haven't said his name in twenty years, and I'm not about to start now."

"You're just giving him power over you, Audra. *That's* what he doesn't deserve." She takes a drink and then whirls on me. "He's not Voldemort, he's just your ex-fiancé. He was a piece of shit, and he messed you up. I get that. But you have to at least *try* to get over it. To move past it. To stop letting him, and what he did, shape the way you handle everything in your life pertaining to men, love, sex, and relationships."

"Franco said everyone should see a therapist at some point in their lives." I sigh. "Maybe I should."

Imogen stares at me with an incredulous expression. "You talked about therapy?"

I nod. "He said he's seen someone before, and that everyone should do that as a routine part of self-care."

"You never have talked to anyone about Jared, have you?"

I shook my head. "You're the only one who knows about him. I couldn't talk about it. It hurt too bad. The only way I could cope was to bury it and move on."

"Which isn't healthy. Surely you realize that." She eyes me sadly. "You wouldn't even talk to *me* about it."

"I *couldn't*. I don't know how else to say that, Imogen. *I could...not...talk...about...Jared.*" My eyes widen as I realize I just said his name.

"No, and instead you turned to speed dating and casual sex."

I snort. "Speed dating is the last goddamn thing I'd ever do."

"Well, yeah, but you know what I mean."

"Speed dating is matchmaking. I'm interested in the exact opposite."

"I know what you want—casual sex. Jumping from guy to guy as fast as possible."

"Not as fast as possible. I've never slept with more than one guy in the same day."

She eyes me. "Really?"

I stare at Imogen. "You really think I have?"

She shrugs. "I guess I just assume there's not much you haven't done, to be honest." She hesitates. "You tell me about a guy here and there, or complain about bad sex, or a smelly penis, or bad foreplay. Sometimes, if a guy was really good at something, or if you liked him enough, you'd have sex with him a second time. But you never really go much beyond that. You keep the really personal details to yourself."

I frown. "Well...yeah. I mean, you don't want to really know that I slept with a different guy every single day for the first month after my ninety-day post-Jared celibacy period, do you? Or that for the entire five years I lived in that apartment downtown I was fuck buddies with my landlord? Or that I don't do anal because the one time I tried it the guy got carried away and hurt me? That I get checked for STDs once a month? Or that Price, the guy you saw me with that day you walked in, was the only guy to get past one fuck in over six months, and that if you hadn't walked in, he'd have probably made it to three? Or even four?"

"Audra—"

"No, you don't *really* want to know any of that. And to be honest, I'm glad you walked in when you did, because I was letting Price's youthful energy blind me to realizing how silly it was of me to be sleeping with him." I paused. "What else do you *not want to know?*"

"Did you have feelings for Price?"

I shake my head—I realize I'm feeling wobbly. "Nah. It was just really good sex. Now that I've had Franco, of course, everything pales in comparison. But still. Price was good, objectively speaking."

"And you definitely have feelings for Franco."

"I don't know what I have for Franco."

She blinks. "A different guy every day for a month?"

I nod, following her jump back to my previous statement. "It was revenge, I guess. Not like he ever knew, but it was—I don't know—emotional revenge, for myself. Escaping him, or getting as far as possible from what I thought we had."

"I thought you had a three strikes rule?" she asks. "How did that work if you were fuck buddies with your landlord for five years?"

I shrug. "He lived on the first floor, right by the front door. Sometimes, after coming home late from work, he'd leave his door cracked with the bolt out to prop it open. That was the signal. If his door was cracked open, and I was in the mood, I'd go in, lock the door, we'd screw on his couch, usually with

NASCAR on in the background, and a cigarette burning in the ashtray. And then when we were done, I'd go home. I think in the five years I lived there, when we were fuck buddies, we exchanged a total of maybe a hundred words."

She looks perplexed. "I don't understand that at *all*."

I laugh. "It was fun. He was a few years older than me—like, seven or eight. Good-looking guy, great cock. I know literally nothing else about him, and we fucked several times a week for five years. I don't know his middle name, where he grew up, how he came to be the landlord, why he was alone, what happened to his leg, who the woman in the pictures on his mantel was, not a damn thing. It was just sex. Sometimes I'd sit on the couch afterward with him and watch NASCAR for a while, but we didn't talk. Sometimes he'd give me a beer or two."

She shakes her head. "I just don't *get* it. Why? Wasn't it weird or…impersonal?"

"It wasn't impersonal at all. We were both lonely, I think, but neither of us wanted to make it anything more than it was. I don't know what his reasons were."

"What was his name?"

"Tómas." I take a long drink. "He was from Europe somewhere. I know he had an accent. And he was just…European. Uncircumcised, which was different for me, then, and kind of neat." I pause again, thinking. "He had a limp in his left leg, a big scar on the knee. No clue what from, though."

"Was he revenge on Jared, too?"

I shake my head. "No. After that first month, I honestly got just plain tired. That much sex is exhausting. I learned a lot about myself in that month, though. For example, I learned that I love sex and a lot of it, I love men, and I love variety. I don't have any one type. Tómas, for example, was older, tall, kind of thin and not a really physical sort of guy, with dark hair and a permanent five-o-clock shadow. Jared, obviously, was the all-American golden boy. You've met some of the guys I've been with. There's no one type. I just—"

"There is a type, though," Audra cuts in. "Or, rather, one theme tying them together."

"What's that?" I ask, genuinely curious.

"None of them, *not* one that I've ever met, or you've ever told me about, has ever been tall, blond, and muscular, with pretty blue eyes and a perfect jawline." She halts there, for emphasis.

Because that's all she has to say.

That's what Jared looked like.

And…it's what Franco looks like.

Jared had short hair, always neatly groomed,

parted to one side and gelled perfectly in place. He shaved religiously, sometimes twice a day. Worked out obsessively, watched game tapes obsessively, practiced obsessively—football was his entire life, to the point that despite being head over heels in love with him, I sometimes wondered if he didn't love football more than me.

Franco...god. Franco does fit the Jared archetype, now that she points it out. There are certain strong resemblances—compulsive neatness, blond hair and blue eyes, incredible physique.

And that, perhaps, is part of my hang-up.

"Dammit." I stand up abruptly, intending to take another shot or seven, but I wobble, and Imogen catches me and helps me to sit back down.

"Maybe you should hold off for a bit," Imogen says. "Finish what you have and drink some water."

"Are you sure none of my other hookups have had blond hair and blue eyes?" I ask.

Imogen shrugs. "I can't say for sure, obviously, as I know I haven't met even half of them."

I sigh. "No, definitely not even half. Most of them never got even close to my place. Usually I'd go to his place, or we got a hotel room." I hold my head in my hands, I feel really dizzy now. "None of them were blond with blue eyes. Blond, yes. Blue eyes, yes. Both? No. I can say that with certainty."

"So you're attracted to Franco because of that, but also…not repelled, but…mixed up?"

"Yeah." I keep my eyes closed, feet planted on the ground. "You know who else fits that description? Blond hair, pretty blue eyes, chiseled jawline, broad shoulders?"

"No. Who?"

"My dad," I whisper.

"Ohhhhh." She pauses. "That makes *so* much sense."

"Yeah. Dad was…he was such a piece of shit that he makes even Jared look like Prince Charming." I sigh. "Honestly, I thought I was getting Prince Charming when I started dating Jared. I thought he was the antithesis of Dad. The proof that good men do exist."

"Oh, honey."

"Only, it turns out I was wrong. I was getting a prince all right—Prince Humperdink, in Wesley disguise. …And good men don't exist."

"Jesse does. James does. Ryder does." She pauses. "Franco does."

I groan. "Imogen, come on."

She sighs. "What do you expect me to say, Audra? To say that I think you're totally right and justified in refusing to entertain the slightest hint of love? I mean, babe, you act like you're allergic to the word relationship. I know you were burned, and hard, but...you have to move on eventually."

"Nope. I don't."

She hands me a can of sparkling water. "So you're going to cut Franco out of your life and go back to the endless parade of empty, meaningless, casual sexual encounters with complete strangers? Even though you know damn well you have a real and possibly serious connection with Franco?"

"We have *chemistry*," I say as I slug back a double pull of my Grey Goose. "Not just a connection. It's weird and scary and I don't like it. So yeah, Imogen, I'm going to cut him out of my life and go back to the endless parade of empty, meaningless, casual sexual encounters with complete strangers, even though I know damn well I have a real and possibly serious connection with Franco. Because, in the end, I don't think Franco is any different than Dad or Jared or any other scumbag man on this planet." I peer at her, blinking hard to clear my double vision. "I do hope, for your sake, that Jesse, at least, is different. But I will keep my skepticism on that subject entirely to myself."

She smiles, but she looks sad. "Oh, Audra. So cynical."

"That's me. Audra the cynic." I shake my glass, peer at it, realizing it's empty, and that Imogen has been sneaking water into it this whole time, letting me think I was drinking vodka. "Sneaky, sneaky."

She smiles. "That's what friends are for, Audra."

"Love you, bitchface." Very, very carefully, I set down both glass and can, and lay down on the couch. "Nighty night."

She hauls me upright. "Hey now, if you're gonna pass out, you're gonna do it in your bed, not out here."

She helps me into my bed, and I cover up with the blankets, still in my robe. Imogen is in the bed behind me, spooning me.

"Imogen?" I ask, my voice muzzy with impending sleep.

"Yeah."

"Is Jesse really that different?"

"From guys like your dad, Jared, and my ex?" She sighs. "Yes, Audra, he really is. He's as different from guys like them as...god, I can't even come up with a metaphor."

"I'm too drunk and tired for metaphors anyway."

"He's the sun, and everyone else is a candle flame right before it dies from lack of oxygen."

"That's a metaphor."

"He's really that different. There's no comparison." She hesitates. "And his friends are all cut from the same cloth. Meaning, Franco is that different too."

"I wish I could believe that."

"You're not trying to."

I'm fading, then, and can't summon a response. But before I fall asleep, I realize she's right.

The question is…am I likely to change?

Probably not. I've been Audra the cynic for far too long to suddenly become Audra the hopeless romantic.

SEVEN

THE NEXT SEVERAL WEEKS ARE CRAZY BUSY FOR ME—I pack my schedule with clients from six in the morning until seven at night. As well, I've got meetings and seminars all over the state. The results my clients are getting from my workout regimens are making me a little bit famous, on a local level, in certain circles.

It's a mercy I'm so busy because, honestly, I manage to stay so busy I barely have time to sleep or breathe, much less think about Franco. My nights out with Imogen continue as they always have, but she knows me well enough that she doesn't bring it up.

The one time she trie, about two months in, I get up and walk out, leaving her with the bill. A bitch move, I know, but I just can't handle any of it. I can't handle thinking about him, talking about him, nothing. He's cut out of my life.

That move costs me with Imogen, though—she

won't talk to me for over a week, and we skip our weekly burritos and margaritas outing for the first time in years. Finally, I show up at her house unannounced on a Monday night after work, and I'm pretty sure I interrupted a make-out session that likely would have resulted in kitchen sex had I not shown up.

She pulls away from Jesse, leaving her hands on his shoulders, peering at me past him. "Hi." Her voice is flat, wary.

I shuffle a foot against the tile, standing in the entryway to her kitchen. "Hi." I hesitate; apologies aren't really my thing. "Um, so...I'm sorry I walked out and stuck you with the bill. It was a bitchy move, and I shouldn't have done it."

"I literally could not care less about the bill." Imogen plucks a loose thread on the collar of Jesse's T-shirt. "It just hurt that you'd walk out on me like that without a word. I know it's a touchy subject for you, but...it was *me,* for Pete's sake."

"Well, I'm sorry. But I'm just not ready to talk about it."

Regardless if Jesse is listening or not, she sighs and continues, "Meaning you're burying and repressing the whole thing like you did after Jared."

"Dammit, Imogen—"

She holds up her hands, stopping me. "I know, I

know. I won't say anything else—I've known you for two-thirds of your life, Audra, I know better than to think anything I could say will change your mind."

That stings a little—both the resigned hurt and sadness in her voice, and the fact that I know she's right. "Imogen, I'm sorry, I just—"

She shakes her head, sighing, and waves a hand to cut me off. "It's fine. You know how I feel, and I know how you feel, and there's just no point in talking about it. I'm sorry I brought it up. I won't do that anymore." She shrugs. "You're gonna do what you're gonna do—and if you're happy with your flavor of the day, month, week, year, or whatever, that's your business. I'm your best friend and I'll love you no matter what, regardless. Even if I think you're being stupid."

"There's no flavor of anything, I'll have you know," I snap, a little too testily.

"What about going back to your endless parade of empty, meaningless, casual sex?" she asks.

I eye Jesse, knowing whatever I say will most likely get back to Franco.

He holds up both hands, scooting away from Imogen's arms and heading for the backyard. "There's...um...I left a tool in the backyard."

When he's gone, I look back at Imogen. "There's no parade," I tell her.

She seems surprised, and I can tell she's still annoyed. "No? Why not?"

I shrug. "I just...I don't know. I've been too busy."

She frowns. "And I call bullshit."

"I've been working thirteen hours a day, and I've had meetings all over the state the past few weeks. I've been busy."

She just snorts. "Don't forget, I knew you in college. You worked a full-time job, took sixteen credit hours, and still managed to find time to party, study, *and* hook up. So...sorry, honey, but I don't buy it."

I sigh. "Sometimes I wish you didn't know me so well."

She gives me a long look. "You can't do it, can you?"

I lift an eyebrow. "Can't do what?"

"Make yourself sleep with anyone else, now that you've been with Franco." She points at me. "You're hung up on the man. You just can't admit it."

"No, that's not it!" Instead of looking at her, I fiddle with my phone, and then the strap of my purse. "I'm just busy."

She just laughs. "You can lie to me all you want, Audra. I'm still calling bullshit, but I'm not going to push it because, in the end, you can't lie to yourself."

"*So* supportive," I drawl, wryly.

She just shrugs again. "Yeah, well, supporting

you doesn't mean I have to like or agree with what you're doing."

"I have to go."

She hugs me. "I love you, always, forever, and no matter what."

"I love you too, even when you're wrong."

She laughs. "I'm not the one who's wrong, you are!"

I make my escape before either of us can say anything else.

I have a fitness/Crossfit/personal trainer seminar in Chicago the following weekend. I'm staying in a really nice hotel with an amazing view of Lake Michigan. The seminar is an all-day thing and, fortunately, that translates into staying mentally occupied the whole time, so that I can't and don't even try to think about anything but work all weekend. I finally get a little downtime after the seminar has ended on Sunday, and I end up at the bar in the event hotel, sipping red wine, watching the crowd, and trying not to let myself think about anything in particular. I nurse my wine, since haven't been interested in heavy drinking since my bender a couple of months ago.

When my glass is nearly empty, a big male body comes to sit in the seat next to mine. I look up, and see that it's one of the speakers from the seminar, a self-proclaimed Crossfit expert. Having watched several of his videos online, and participated in his workshop workouts at the seminar, I can't really say he's not an expert. His name is...Matt? Matty? Matthias? Something like that. He's sexy, all right: six-something, dark hair, dark eyes, clean shaven, tattooed all over his chest, arms, hands, and legs, pierced ears—a real bad boy rock star look. Plus, he's absolutely shredded, a fact he's obviously not shy about sharing with the world, since his videos are all of him in low-slung shorts without a shirt. Even now, he's dressed like he either just came from the gym, or is about to go, despite the fact that I know neither is true—black shorts cling to his butt and show off his thighs, a tight, sleeveless muscle shirt with his brand logo on it, which is cut to show off his arms, chest, and abs. Overall, the package he presents is visually appealing, but more than a little vain, if not downright egotistical.

He smiles, showing off perfect, blindingly white teeth. "Hey, I'm Matty."

I shake his hand. "Audra."

"Nice to meet you, Audra." His smile widens, and he leans toward me. "You're at the seminar here, right?"

I nod. "Yeah. You're one of the presenters."

He all but preens at being recognized. "Yeah. Matty Corcoran. I run the Shred-Ninety program."

I nod again. "Nice. I did a few of the workshops this weekend. Good stuff. Really smart programming."

I half expect him to launch into another lecture, or a life story about how he started Shred-90 and all that, but he doesn't. "Thanks. Yeah, I noticed you in those workshops. You have a really impeccable form."

I feel a little thrill that he noticed me and my form. "Thanks."

"So, you're a trainer? Out of where?"

"Oh, the metropolitan Chicago area. I'm a local." The seminar is a pretty big one, so there are trainers from all over the country in attendance.

"Nice." He was hoping for a bigger opening, I think, and I've left him off-balance.

Why am I so uninterested? I mean, sure, he's a little vain, but he *does* run a Crossfit program that's gotten attention from celebrities and fitness industry experts alike, which is a pretty big deal. Plus, he's gorgeous, objectively speaking. I should be into him. I should give him more of a chance.

I lean toward him, nudging my glass onto the bar in a subtle signal. "What about you? I've heard of you, but I'm not sure where you run your program out of."

"I'm from LA." He laughs. "I'm a pretty tiny fish in a pretty big pond out there."

"You got a write-up in *Muscle and Fitness* recently, didn't you?"

He preens again. "Yeah, I did. You saw that?"

I almost laugh at how pleased he is. "Yeah, it was a good write-up."

He nods. "Got me quite a few new clients, including a couple low-level Hollywood people."

"Is that your target demographic? Hollywood?"

He laughs. "I mean, yeah. Trainer to the stars has a nice ring to it, don't you think?" He eyes my glass and signals for the bartender. When we both have new rounds—him a sugar-free gimlet and me more red wine—he really turns on the charm. "So, enough about work. Have you lived in Chicago long?"

I shrug. "Yeah—my whole life. I lived downtown for a few years, but the hectic pace and the noise ended up driving me batty, so I moved back out to the suburbs." I sip, and smile at him. "What about you? LA born and raised?"

He shakes his head, carefully setting his martini glass on the bar. "Nah. I was actually born on a military base in Germany. My dad was a fighter pilot and my mom was a nurse at the base hospital. I lived there until I was…fifteen? Then my dad got transferred to Edwards for a training position, and my mom managed to pull some strings to get transferred there, too. I still speak German fluently, as a matter of fact."

"Nice," I say.

Way too much information, bub—that's what

I'm thinking. Why do I care about your life story? If you're trying to pick me up, then quit dicking around and ask me if I want to go somewhere. This talk-talk-talk shit is for the birds.

He seems to expect me to reply with some kind of equally personal information, so I decide to take matters into my own hands. Prove to myself—and Imogen—that she's wrong. I'm not hung up on anybody.

"So, I'm not really one for small talk," I say, watching him steadily.

He takes a sip, eying me with great interest. "No?"

"No. Not really."

His smirk turns eager. "Want to get out of here, in that case?"

"Sure."

He lifts a hand. "Check please."

Within a few minutes, we're stumbling into his penthouse suite. He's all hands and lips, pulling at my clothes, biting at my skin—

And I'm panicking.

Because god*dammit*, Imogen is fucking right. I can't do this.

It's not Franco's mouth. It's not Franco's hands. The way Matty is pulling at my clothing isn't right, and the way he bites my shoulder is wrong. He kisses up from my breastbone to my throat, to my chin, and I put two fingers to his mouth, stopping him before he can kiss me on the lips.

He frowns. "No?"

I shake my head. "No. It's...a thing, for me."

He shrugs. "No big deal." He grins, wiggling his eyebrows suggestively. "I can kiss you in other places, right?"

I swallow hard—because I'm trying to envision him on his knees in front of me, lapping at my core, and all I see is wild, loose, long blond hair and wicked blue eyes. The thought of Matty...doesn't work.

He senses something. "Are you okay?

I sigh. "I'm sorry, Matty. I just...I think I made a mistake coming up here."

He frowns. "Did I do something?"

I shake my head. "No."

"Then what is it?"

I shrug. "I'm just not feeling it. It's not you, I promise."

He lets go of me and backs away, nodding. "Okay, I understand. No hard feelings."

"You're sure? I didn't mean to lead you on, or be a cocktease or anything. It's not like me to back out like this."

He shrugs. "We all have off days. It's cool. I'll walk you back to the elevator."

I adjust my clothes and we walk back down the hallway. It's a bit of a wait before the car arrives at the penthouse, and Matty's gaze is more thoughtful than I'd have anticipated.

"You know, I know I come across as a douchey fitness bro, sometimes. But I'm not, not really."

I eye him warily. "Okay."

"I just couldn't help thinking you seemed a little…sad. That's why I came over to talk to you. A sexy woman like you shouldn't be sad."

I snort. "Even good-looking people get sad sometimes, Matty. And I wasn't sad, anyway."

He frowns. "No? I mean, I could be wrong, but that's the impression I got." He shrugs. "Point is I got the sense you were…lonely. Like you were waiting for someone you knew wasn't going to show up."

The elevator dings, and the doors open. I step on, pushing the button for the lobby. "I'm not lonely, and I wasn't waiting for anyone."

He sticks his foot across the track so the doors don't close. "Since we'll probably never see each other again, I'll just say it." He meets my eyes. "You know what's not sexy? Self-deception."

And with that, he lets the door close and strides with a loose swagger back to his penthouse. The last I see of him is his back, emblazoned with his Shred-90 logo, and his impossibly wedge-shaped physique.

When the doors close and the car begins its downward journey, I thunk my head back against the wall.

"Goddamn you, Franco Morrissey."

I make it another month without seeing Franco. And, let me tell you, it's the longest month of my life—preceded by the longest two months of my life. It's been over ninety days since I've had sex—Franco being the last. I tried again with a guy at a bar near my house, but the same thing happened—I saw Franco in my mind's eye, felt him, smelled him, heard him, and couldn't follow through. That guy wasn't as gracious as Matty Corcoran had been, but whatever…he was a businessman on a work trip from Minnesota, so it's not like I'd see him again either.

I'm going through the motions at this point, just trying to maintain the status quo.

I meet with Imogen every Friday, and we talk about everything, but we don't talk about Franco.

One evening I went to dinner with Jesse, Imogen, James, and Ryder, and it was fun. Franco was out of town, delivering a dining room set he made for an online customer an hour west of Skokie, and without Franco, the group wasn't quite the same, and no one seemed to know what to say to me for fear of making things even more awkward, which only made it all the worse. I ended up faking period cramps and went home. Imogen knew better, of course—we've been synched to the same cycle since high school, so she knew I wasn't on my period but, bless her heart, she didn't say anything.

It's been ninety-four days since the last time I saw Franco, and I'm alone in my favorite drink-alone dive bar. It's a tiny, dirty, dingy hole in the wall walking distance from my condo, and by now the closing bartender knows me by name, and he also knows my beverage of choice.

I'm scrubbing it this evening—my comfiest capri sweatpants, a sports bra, and a thin zip-up hoodie, with a Rogue Fitness ball cap. I'm two glasses in—going slow, because I refuse to let myself devolve into binge drinking to avoid my problems. Regular drinking, sure. But not to the point of drunkenness. Just enough to let me think about *anything* besides Franco.

And how resolutely I refuse to miss him.

Or want him.

Or need him.

Gah—it's not working. But I'm far too stubborn to quit.

I'm scrolling through the news app on my phone when I feel a body sit down on the seat beside me.

Expecting it to be either a regular intent on chatting me up, or a newcomer intent on picking me up, I ignore the person.

"Audra? Is that you?" It's a female voice.

I look up, and see Laurel Madison.

She's a former client of mine, and probably one of my greatest success stories—which is due entirely to her, and not me. When we met, Laurel was a thirty-four-year-old single mother to a hellion of a six-year-old boy. Overweight by at least fifty pounds, unhappy, lonely, stressed, prediabetic, she had a muffin top even the most aggressive compression Spanx couldn't hide. Her breasts were big but flat, her belly wobbled and bulged, her thighs jiggled, and her butt waggled. She came to me in tears, refusing to weigh in, admitting to eating mostly garbage at work—which was waitressing at a chain restaurant—drinking too much when she got home, and bingeing on ice cream.

But, under all that, she was a beautiful woman, with gloriously long hair as glossy and black as a raven's wing, perfectly natural tan skin with an amazing complexion despite a garbage diet, and a warm, kind, funny, loving personality. At first, she was subdued in our sessions, unwilling to push herself, and painfully reserved. It wasn't until I got her out of the gym setting that she started to open up a little bit: I took her grocery shopping, showed her how to pick healthy foods, and made suggestions for things even her picky son would eat. I showed her stevia-sweetened soda at the local health food store. When we were at her house unloading the groceries, her son asked if I was going to "train Mommy to be happy again," which made Laurel cry.

After that, she started pushing herself a little harder in the gym, and started buying healthier foods. The first big roadblock came six weeks in—she'd dropped four sizes in her clothing, but her weight hadn't really gone down, and she was getting discouraged. That was when I showed her the before photos—she'd refused to weigh in, so I'd let her off by taking front and side-view photos, knowing how vital it can be for clients to see progress when they're struggling.

By the end of a year, she was down to a healthy weight and fat percentage, was making consistently positive, healthy nutritional choices, and had been forced to buy an entirely new wardrobe—which she had been able to afford thanks to leaving her waitressing job for a position managing a local nonprofit animal rescue and shelter.

Now, almost two years later, she looked better than ever. Trim, fit, glowing…with slightly larger, firmer, perkier breasts than the last time I'd seen her. She also had mascara running down her cheeks in twin tear-tracks.

"Laurel? Wow! You look amazing." I laughed, taking a bar napkin and wiping at her cheeks. "Running mascara notwithstanding."

She laughed, sniffling. "Yeah, I—had a bad breakup." She tried a tremulous smile. "How are you?"

I sighed, and realized I didn't have the energy to pretend to be hunky-dory—Laurel had always been sharp and insightful, and would see through it anyway. "Eh, I'm here." I snorted, gesturing at the bar. "And considering where *here* is, I'd say not great."

The bartender, Eric, a burly, bearded, tattooed, potbellied older guy, poured a pair of shots of whiskey and slid them toward us both. "Hey, I resemble that remark."

"Ha ha," I drawled, taking the shots and passing one to Laurel. "Thanks, Eric."

"Just don't weep into the whiskey, that's all I ask."

"Wouldn't think of it, pal. I'm straight ice, through and through, you know that."

"You'd like to think so, wouldn't you?" He smirks at me, and then turns to pour a fresh beer for an old regular.

I turn to Laurel. "So. Bad breakup, huh?"

She sighs. "Really bad."

I look her over. She's put together, wearing a navy skirt and a pale coral top, with a string of pearls and an elegant updo. Her black hair is glossy and healthy, not a hair out of place, and her skin is so tanned and perfect even I'm jealous of it. Her eyes are a pale grass green, her nose petite and pointed, slightly upturned.

I shake my head. "You really do look amazing, Laurel. It's hard to believe it's you."

She smiles. "Thank you. I feel great—I'm eating clean, working out regularly."

"Looks like you're moving up in the world, too." I indicate the pearls and the ensemble—the skirt and top look pretty pricey.

She shrugs. "Our nonprofit got absorbed by a larger five-oh-one group, expanded, and turned into a chain of nonprofit rescues around the area. And I just got promoted to regional manager today, so yeah, that's a pretty big step up."

"Regional manager, huh? That's awesome!"

She sighs. "Yeah. I was all excited, ready to bring my big news home to my boyfriend…who promptly blindsided me with a breakup announcement the second I walked in. And I'd been thinking of asking him to move in with us, too."

I wince. "Ouch. Why did he dump you?"

She shrugs. "I have no clue. I thought we were doing good. A year and a half together, and then, bam. He just dumps me for no reason. 'Sorry, babe, it's not working. I'm out. See ya.'" She affects a gruff voice for this. "Whatever. Asshole."

I hold up my shot. "To the assholes in the world—most of which have dicks."

She snorts a laugh. "I'll drink to that." We do our shots, and she eyes me. "So. What's new with you?"

I shrug. "You know—the same. Clients, seminars, working out."

"No man in your life?"

I laugh. "I think we talked about this when we went out to celebrate you letting me go as your personal trainer."

"Yeah, you said you don't do relationships, you just do men."

"Right. Like I said, same ol', same ol'."

She stares me down, hard. "Bullshit."

I thunk my forehead against the sticky bar top. "GODDAMMIT! Why does everyone have to keep calling me on my bullshit?"

Laurel laughs. "I just stepped in something smelly, didn't I?"

"Where's Nate?" I ask, referencing her son in an attempt to change the subject.

"With my mom." She seems like she's taking the bait. "When Derek left, I sort of lost it, and Mom came to my rescue, told me to go out and get my shit together. Nate is nine, almost ten, loves football, hates Brussels sprouts no matter how much bacon I put in them, watches *Star Wars: The Clone Wars* on repeat, despite having seen the entire series at least five times through. And let's see, what else…? Oh yeah—nice try, Audra, but you can't bait me into avoiding the subject."

I groan, and wipe at my forehead with a bar napkin. "You need to wipe this bar down better, Eric," I call. "It's sticky."

"It's a dive bar. S'posed to be sticky."

I laugh. "Can't argue with that logic." I sigh, taking a long drink of ice water before going back to my wine. "So. Looks like you're moving up in the world in the breasticular region, too."

She cackles, glancing down at her breasts and lifting them. "These puppies? Yeah, it was my thirty-sixth birthday gift to myself. After losing all the weight, my poor boobies had dwindled down to these horrible, ugly, flat, stupid little sacks of flab. So, I saved up and got some implants. Nothing crazy—this is about what they were before I had Nate and then gained all the weight after Paul and I split."

"Well, they look damn good."

She smiles. "Thanks." Her eyebrow lifts. "So. What's your deal?"

I let out a long, frustrated sigh. "Just a guy. We hooked up, there were feelings, I don't do feelings and neither does he, so we went our separate ways, but I can't get him out of my head and it's messing with me hardcore. No big deal, I'm fine."

"Why don't you do feelings?" Laurel asks.

"Long, long, long story," I say.

She nods, and sips at her drink. "Fair enough." She nudges me with her shoulder. "You should try feelings sometime, though. I've heard they're pretty great. Everyone's doing it."

I laugh, showing her the mascara-smeared napkin. "Yeah? What about this?"

She waves a hand. "Nothing's free. You want happiness, you gotta go through some shit to get it. I was happy with Paul until that fell apart, and I was happy with Derek until he dumped me. Eventually I'll find someone that sticks. Until then"—she shrugs—"there'll be breakups, assholes, and more than a few nights alone with some Halo Top and my vibrator. It's all part of the process."

"How can you be so *laissez-faire* about it?" I ask.

She shrugs. "Because I've experienced enough of the entire cycle to know the good times are worth going through the breakups. Sex is awesome, and sex without feelings is pretty great too. Believe me—I've had my share of hookups both before and after Paul, Nate's father. But sex with feelings? There's nothing like it. The emotions, the connection, the belonging?" She shakes her head, sighing. "There's nothing like it."

"Even when it gets taken away?"

Laurel nods, holding my gaze. "Yep. After Paul, I went through a phase where I thought love was a sham and all men were scumbags, but that didn't last long for me. Most people are, on the whole, decent. If you're looking for it, you'll find that most men are decent guys. Not perfect, and to find a really amazing one seems to require quite a search, in my experience, seeing as I haven't found one myself yet. But are they all cheaters and liars and assholes? Nope. That's too broad of a brush, I think. It's also too easy to find what you're looking for, if all you're expecting to find are fuckboys and assholes."

"Were you always this wise?" I asked.

She nods. "Yep."

I laugh. "Oh, well, okay then."

She laughs too. "It's just that when you were my personal trainer, all of our conversations were focused on me and my health. We rarely talked about you."

I stare into my wine—which is cheap and gives me a headache, another reason I don't drink much. "Yeah, well, I rarely talk about me with anyone, even Imogen, my best friend of almost thirty years."

"Daddy issues, intimacy issues, trust issues, or all of the above?"

I stare at her balefully. "Are you a nonprofit manager, or a shrink?"

She pats my arm. "Here, right now? Neither. Just your friend."

"Oh." I take a moment to think. "Probably all three."

My phone rings at that moment, and I glance at it before answering—*James Bod: Dad Bod Contracting.*

"Sorry, I should take this," I say to Laurel, who nods and checks her own phone. "Hello?"

"Hey, Audra. This is James."

"So caller ID tells me," I quip.

He snorts. "Don't be a smart-ass. Reason I'm calling is to invite you to a little get-together I'm having this weekend. An impromptu, informal Dad Bod barbecue at my place." He hesitates. "All the guys will be there, plus Imogen, obviously, and I think she's bringing a friend of hers from work. If you want to bring a friend or two, the more the merrier. I'll be making steaks and burgers and dogs, and I think everyone is planning on bringing a side or some drinks. It'll be low-key and fun. Just wanted to give you the invite."

I sigh. "*Everyone* will be there, huh?"

James's growl is one indicating he has no patience with nonsense. "I know you and Franco had your issue, but you're both adults. You can handle a party with mutual friends, can't you?"

I feel chastised. "Yes, James. I can handle a party with mutual friends."

"So you'll be there? It's this Saturday. I plan on firing up the grill around four, but everyone is welcome whenever till whenever. I'll text you my address."

"I'll be there." I eye Laurel. "The more the merrier, you say?"

"Yes ma'am. Bring something, or just bring yourself. There'll be plenty of food and drink, and some to spare."

"I may bring a friend. We'll see. Either way, I'll be there. Thank you for inviting me."

"Course. See you Saturday."

I stuff my phone back in my purse—it dings a few seconds later with James's address, but I ignore that. I glance at Laurel. "You busy Saturday?"

She brightens. "Actually, I'm free. My mom is taking Nate for the weekend to celebrate his birthday. I take him out the weekend of his actual birthday, and then Mom takes him that whole following weekend. It's fun for him, and gives me a weekend free. What's going on?"

"A barbecue at a friend's place."

She narrows her eyes at me. "Just a barbecue, huh?"

I shrug, endeavoring to look innocent. "Yep. And, sure, there *may* be at least two single, good-looking, successful men there, and you *may* just be coming off a breakup, but that's purely ancillary. I just want to invite you to the party. We lost touch after you *fired* me, and I feel like we should stay in contact this time."

She huffs. "I didn't *fire* you, I just didn't need a personal trainer anymore."

I laugh, elbowing her. "I know, I know—I'm teasing. I do want you at the party, though. The guy I had the weird thing with, Franco—he'll be there, and I'll need all the moral support I can get."

"Single, good-looking, *and* successful?" she asks, rightfully skeptical.

"They're contractors—builders. Decent, nice, salt-of-the-earth, sort of guys. And yes, seriously good-looking."

"Names and descriptions?"

I smirk. "You'll have to come to find out."

She sighs. "Fine."

"Send me your address and I'll pick you up on the way."

"Sounds good," she says.

After that, we hang out at the bar and talk until much later, much later than I should stay out, considering my first client is at seven thirty in the morning. But Laurel is fun to talk to—it's past midnight by the time we say our goodbyes. I walk home since it's only a block down and around the corner from my condo, and Laurel takes a Lyft home.

Laurel's words ring in my head as I trudge into

my condo and flop face first onto my bed. Despite the hours of conversation in between, all I hear is her saying: *Sex with feelings? There's nothing like it. The emotions, the connection, the belonging? There's nothing like it.*

Dammit.

That's it exactly—she pinpointed the emotion I couldn't name, the thing that's stuck with me the most strongly in the months since Franco and I slept together.

Belonging.

In those moments in his arms, I belonged. It was fleeting, and foreign, but amazing. I just…fit.

I groan, and push off the bed. I strip, brush my teeth, use the bathroom, and flop into bed again, hearing Laurel's voice on a loop. *Belonging.*

It was a fluke, though, wasn't it? It had to have been a fluke.

It *was* a fluke. A one-time-only performance, unrepeatable—with him or anyone else. I just have to accept that.

Don't I?

EIGHT

I T's Saturday, a little past four in the afternoon, and I'm lounging with my feet in the cool water of the beautiful in-ground pool in James Bod's backyard. Sipping a sugar-free mojito made by Ryder, I'm listening to an absolute darling nine-or ten-year-old-girl with beautiful nut-brown hair in frizzy, braided pigtails. She is telling me everything there is to know about a series of books called Ever After High. We've been sitting together for fifteen minutes, and I thought I'd be bored when she sat down and started talking, but I'm not. I haven't gotten a word in edgewise, and we haven't even exchanged names.

I'm amused and bemused.

"...And then—and *then* Raven wouldn't *sign the book*! I just knew it!" She pauses to take a breath.

A deep, bear-like voice booms from far overhead. "Nina."

I look up, and so does the girl beside me. James,

his massive frame blocking out the sun, Oakleys, as usual, perched on his nose, a can of some local IPA looking tiny in his gargantuan paw is speaking.

"Yes, Papa?"

Papa? I frown up at him.

He waggles a finger at the girl—Nina, it seems her name is—and then at me. "Are you talking *at* her, or *with* her?"

Nina wiggles uncomfortably. "At her."

"A conversation is…"

"A mutual discourse between two people."

"And a monologue is…"

"Something nobody outside of a theater ever wants to hear," Nina replies in a way that indicates this is a commonly repeated lesson.

Nina kicks her feet in the water, watching as James—her father—ambles away across the yard again. "I tend to go off into monologues a lot and not let anyone else get a word in edgewise. Papa says I need to learn to listen more and talk less."

"Listening skills *are* important," I say. "As are introductions. I'm Audra Donovan."

She shakes my hand and smiles at me. "I'm Nina Bod." She points across the yard at another girl with similar brown hair in similar messy, uneven pigtails, who seems to have Imogen and Jesse cornered by the adult drinks cooler. "That's my little sister, Ella."

"Nina and Ella Bod, hmmm?"

She nods. "Yep. We're named after Papa and Mama's favorite singers, Nina Simone and Ella Fitzgerald." She pauses, takes a breath, and then launches into another monologue. "Mom died when I was five, and Ella was only one. Mom was gonna have a baby, but Papa says things just went sideways, whatever that means. Mama went to be with Jesus, and so did the baby. I don't really remember her very much, 'specially 'cause Papa misses her so much he won't talk about her ever, and Ella doesn't remember her at all, so it's just me remembering her. Which is super hard, sometimes, but I have an old photo album under my bed with pictures of her. Plus, Papa has this old camera and he used to take a lot of pictures of her, but then she died so he stopped and I stole the camera and now I keep it under my bed and look at the pictures sometimes. But that's a secret. I don't think Papa would stop me, but he'd get sad and he's just starting to be less sad, even though you can't really tell most of the time unless you know him really well like I do, since he's such a grumpy old bear all the time, but he really is a lot less sad now than he used to be."

"Wow, I—"

Nina claps her hand over her mouth. "Ooops. I shouldn't have told you any of that. Papa says I need to learn to keep private business private and not go spewing our collective family tragedy out to any old person who'll listen to my ever-running mouth."

I laugh. "I won't tell him you told me, how about that?"

She glances at James who's popping the top on a beer and eyeing us. "Oh, I think he already knows. He's a really good guesser at things like this."

I laugh. "I imagine he is."

She glances at me. "Are you Imogen's stubborn girlfriend who Papa says is making Franco act like somebody pooped in his oatmeal?"

I snort, choking on my drink.

She sighs, shaking her head. "Me and my mouth. I wasn't supposed to repeat that either. But I'm curious."

"He said that to you?" I ask.

She shakes her head solemnly. "Oh, no. Papa never talks like that in front of us. But sometimes the uncles come over and they drink that nasty brown stuff and talk loud, and I hear them because Papa thinks I'm sleeping but I'm not. Uncle Ryder and Uncle Jesse came over the other day and *they* were talking about Uncle Franco, and *they* said it was because Imogen's girlfriend was being stubborn, and *they* were the ones who said that oatmeal thing about Franco. Even though I know for a fact Franco doesn't eat oatmeal, because he stayed the night one time and Papa made oatmeal for us the next morning and Uncle Franco wouldn't eat it because it had something called carbs in it."

"So you have Uncle Franco, Uncle Ryder, and Uncle Jesse."

She nods. "Yep. But they're not our real, actual uncles, you know. Papa was an only child, which is why he's so bossy with us. It doesn't make sense to me, but Papa says a lot of weird stuff. The guys are Papa's best friends, and Papa says they're like brothers, so that's why they're our uncles."

"You're lucky to have so many awesome uncles, huh?"

"Yeah." She looks at me. "But if you could do something to make Uncle Franco go back to normal, I'd really appreciate it. He's been kind of lame lately, and I'm *so* not here for it."

I laugh hard, because Nina is really something else. "Yeah, I'll see what I can do. No promises, though."

"What did you do, anyway?"

I sigh. "Well, that's hard to explain, kiddo."

"Hard to explain, or hard to explain to a ten-year-old?"

I laugh again. "Can't put much past you can I, Nina?"

"Nope. Papa says I'm too smart for my own good, and just smart enough to know it."

"Sounds about right, I'd say."

She eyes me again, and I can tell that she's not finished with me yet. "So, did your husband die or something?"

Again, I choke on my drink. "What? God, you're something else." I wipe my chin, and then wipe my hand on my skirt. "No, I've never been married."

"What? You've never been married? Do you have a boyfriend?"

"No."

"So why are you alone? You've got to be as old as Papa, and he says he's two days older than dirt. Plus you're pretty, so it can't be because you can't get a man."

I shake my head. "He's not that old, actually. Forty is the new thirty, you know."

She frowns. "That doesn't make any sense."

"No, I guess not. I'm alone because I like being alone."

"I think Papa would say that's donkey splat."

I rest my drink against my forehead. "Even ten-year-olds are calling me on my bullshit," I mutter to myself.

She grins. "You shouldn't say curse words in front of me. I'm like a parrot, but smarter."

"Then you're smart enough to know not to repeat it."

"I've heard Papa say that one, too, so it's not like I've learned it from you."

"Well, thank god for that." I glance down at her. "Would you mind if I went and talked to some of the other adults now, Nina?"

She shrugs, smiling at me. "Nope. I'm gonna go ask Uncle Ryder if I can play Candy Crush on his phone."

I glance at Ryder. There's a huge spreading oak in the backyard, and at some point James made a huge swing out of thick ropes, half a tractor tire, and a wooden plank—the swing is easily big enough for two adults sitting side by side, and Ryder is on it with Laurel beside him, the pair chatting easily. They're laughing, leaning close, thighs touching—I picked Laurel up and we drove here together, and spent the first few minutes making introductions all around, but it was obvious within minutes that she and Ryder were interested in each other, so I made sure to leave her an opening to go talk to him without me.

I pull my phone out of my purse, which is sitting on the ground a few feet behind me, out of range of the pool, and extend it to Nina. "Here, play on mine. It looks like your Uncle Ryder is having a conversation."

Nina clearly misses nothing. "Ohhhh." She grins.

"Well, that *is* the kissing swing."

I frown at her. "The what?"

"Papa calls it the kissing swing." Her face falls. "He used to, at least. He never goes on it anymore. Him and Mama used to sit on it and swing and kiss while I played out here."

I feel like there's a hell of a story in between Nina's throwaway comments, especially since I didn't realize James even had children.

Nina hops up. "I just remembered my best score is Fruit Ninja on Uncle *Franco's* phone, so I'm going to ask if I can borrow it."

And off she scurries, prancing and dancing, spinning and tripping and twirling and stumbling in the way of little girls. She goes right up to Franco and tugs on his shirt, putting her hands together in a pretty-please gesture. Franco grins down at her, and that smile of his is heartbreaking and heart-warming and panty-melting all at once, because he very clearly absolutely adores that little girl with every fiber of his being. I watch him play tough guy before relinquishing his phone. Then he gently, playfully shoves her away; her response is to full-on bodycheck him, all without pausing in her frantic two-fingered assault on his phone.

Franco's gaze travels the backyard, hopping from Jesse and Imogen, who are still dutifully listening to

Ella's diatribe, to Imogen's friend Nova—whom I've only briefly met for a minute when I first arrived—who is busily mixing drinks in the kitchen, and then to Ryder and Laurel. As he sees Ryder and Laurel on the swing, he nudges James and points them out. James's face goes through a quick series of expressions: joy at his friend clearly crushing on the new girl—yay for me and my matchmaker skillzzzz!—and then to pain and wistfulness. He must be remembering the times he's spent on that swing. His reply to Franco is something muttered under his breath, which I can't make out.

Franco's gaze slides, inexorably, to the pool. To me. My heart patters in my chest, as his eyes meet mine. We've managed to avoid each other so far, but it's only been twenty minutes. And those twenty minutes have been tension-filled. Nina provided me with a lot of distraction, but I've been hyperaware of Franco and every move he makes.

I look away, return my phone to its pocket in my purse, and head inside to talk to Nova. A newer friend of Imogen's, Nova Benson is one of the tallest women I've ever met, probably standing right at six feet, and she's built like an Amazon. Strong, fit, clearly no stranger to the gym; she's just flat-out statuesque—the Greeks and Romans couldn't have carved a more perfect representation of a powerful warrior woman.

Nova has bright, flaming red hair, bright vivid blue eyes, and a mischievous hint to her smile, something I noticed the moment I met her and notice again now as I join her in James's kitchen. She must've just come from work, as she's wearing maroon scrub pants and the same kind of sneakers Imogen wears to the hospital. Instead of the matching scrub top, Nova wears a white, ribbed tank top, and an electric blue bra underneath, both of which show off her breasts. Somehow, though, Nova makes the look seem casual and sexy and effortlessly cool all at once, especially with a pair of mirrored aviators holding her hair back, and a stunning number of bracelets on both wrists: braided-thread friendship bracelets, silver bangles, an Alex and Ani bracelet with a dozen charms, a worn black leather cuff on each arm, a plastic hospital bracelet on her left wrist—that one is old, and very clearly has a story behind it—there are too many bracelets to count, extending halfway up her forearms. My first thought, which comes out of my mouth the moment I'm in the kitchen with her, is:

"Do you take all those bracelets off every night, or what?"

Nova laughs, shaking both wrists, making the various bangles jingle. "Yep! I have a whole dresser drawer dedicated to bracelets. I couldn't possibly wear the same ones all the time—that's...that'd be anathema to the entire point of wearing them."

"Does it take forever to put them on every day?"

She shrugs, and goes back to muddling the mint. "Not really. A minute or two, depending on how many I'm wearing. I was working today, obviously"— she gestures at her scrub pants—"so this is a minimal amount."

"Are there any you don't ever take off?" I ask, blatantly fishing for the story of the hospital bracelet.

Which is where her eyes go. "That one," she says, tapping it. "But that's an old, painful, shitty story and this is a party."

I feel bad, now, asking about that. She smiles at me, and the hint of mischievousness is there, and also a knowing expression that tells me she knows I was fishing and doesn't mind, and also forgives me for bringing up the past.

I'm impressed by the amount of expression she can put into a single look.

She slides a pink cutting board toward me, on which are a handful of limes and a knife. "If you're going to pester me, at least make yourself useful."

"We're making more sugar-free mojitos?" I ask, slicing limes in halves and then quarters.

She nods, squeezing limes into a bowl and adding more mint. "Franco got a taste of yours before Ryder brought it to you, and he wanted one, and then everyone wanted one, and Ryder tapped out after making yours, and I used to be a bartender in college, so...here I am, making eight mojitos." She shrugs. "Well, sort of mojitos. I'm using extra lime juice and a touch more pure LaCroix instead of adding simple syrup, so it's not really a mojito, but it has the rum and the lime and the mint, so we're just calling it a mojito."

She slides a glass toward me.

"Try that one. I made it for myself to test the recipe."

I sip at her drink, and I blink in surprise. "Wow. I thought Ryder's was good. *That's* amazing."

"Yeah, well, that's what six years of professional bartending will get you."

"Six years, huh?"

She shrugs and goes back to muddling mint in the lime juice and doling it out into the glasses. "I have my MS in nursing."

"A masters in nursing? What do you do? Which department?"

"Neurology. I'm an assistant to one of the top neurologists in the area." She gestures outside. "I have the names right, right? Franco is the one with the long hair, with whom you have some sort of complicated history, Ryder is the other ginger at the party, and James, our gracious host, is the one who looks like The Mountain from *Game of Thrones*, except a little older and a hell of a lot sexier."

I nod. "That's the gang. And obviously you know Jesse."

She adds the rum next. "A little. Imogen invited me over for a glass of wine one night, and he came over for a while, as well." Her eyes shoot to mine, questioning. "I'm not sure if he lives with her, or she lives with him, or both, or neither."

I laugh. "I don't know either, honestly. I think it's complicated. I know she's at his place a lot these days, but he also basically remodeled her entire house himself, and is still working on it, so he's there a lot, too...I don't know. It works for them, so whatever." I feel like I've deftly avoided the question of Franco.

"And Franco? What's your deal with him?"

I sigh. I guess I was wrong about the "deftly" bit. "Um. We had a thing. Now we don't have a thing. The end."

Nova dips her middle finger in the lime juice and flicks it at me. "Nice try, but I'm an expert at topic avoidance technique. You can't bullshit a bullshitter."

"That wasn't an avoidance technique," I say, upping the ante by chucking an entire half of a lime at her head. "It was a shutdown technique. A little-known tactic called *I don't want to talk about it*."

Nova must have taken kung fu with David

Carradine or something, because she snags the flying lime out of the air with a lazy swipe of her hand. "You asked about my bracelet, so I asked about your obviously still-a-thing thing with Franco."

"Ahh," I say, laughing. "I see how it is."

"Tit for tat."

"Hopefully it's not tit for tit," I say, "because you'll win that game, I'm afraid," I say gesturing with the knife at her absurdly massive mammaries.

She snickers, shaking her breasts at me. "Be afraid—I've knocked people straight the fuck out with these monsters."

James and Franco enter at that moment, stopping short at the open sliding glass doorway between the back porch and the kitchen, their eyes wide, watching the scene between Nova and me unfold.

Nova lets out a short breath, waves the muddler at the men, grinning easily. "Shoo, now, boys. Nothing to see here."

James tugs on his beard, his eyes hidden, perpetually, behind his Oakleys. "Not sure if I believe that. I might need another demonstration of whatever was going on just now."

"Not likely, bud," Nova says. "Sorry. That was a girls' club conversation, and you don't have the right equipment to be a member."

I don't have any quippy comebacks—Franco is in

the room with me, and I'd almost forgotten how he tends to suck all the oxygen out of my lungs, along with all of the sense out of my head. I hear voices, James and Nova, mainly, but it's all just buzzing, like the adults in Charlie Brown movies. Franco is staring at me, his expression as unreadable as ever, and I'm staring back, and probably drooling.

He's as casually dressed as I've ever seen him, in a pair of cutoff khaki shorts and an old, faded, black Garth Brooks concert T-shirt with the sleeves cut off. He's barefoot, which, for some reason, makes me horny.

Or maybe it's just him; it's probably just him. But there's also something about his bare feet that makes me shivery and quivery.

Franco isn't grinning, or even smirking. His gaze is hooded and heavy-lidded, his granite jawline pulsing as he grinds his molars together. His hands are shoved deep in his pockets, and his chest is rising and falling a little too deeply to be normal. I notice a surreptitious movement in one of his pockets, and I realize he's adjusting himself; his zipper is tight, and seems to even swell further the longer his gaze remains locked on me.

I still have the knife in my hand, and I'm squeezing the handle so tightly my knuckles hurt. I'm breathing hard, my chest rising and falling raggedly, rapidly, just like Franco's.

"Audra." I hear a voice, saying my name, as if not for the first time. "Hello?"

I blink and shake my head to clear the hypnosis. "What?"

Nova puts the straw in her mojito to my lips. "Have a drink."

I take a long pull, and discover she's added an extra dose of rum because *whoa*. But it's exactly what I need to burn away the effect of stupid, beautiful, mesmerizing Franco. Just for good measure, I take another long pull.

"Why don't you just go ahead and give me this, huh?" Nova says, as she takes the knife from me, slowly and gingerly.

"Yeah, good idea," I murmur without taking my eyes off of Franco's.

Abruptly, Franco spins on his heels and stalks across the backyard like a hungry predator deprived of its meal. At the very farthest corner of James's sprawling, acre-and-a-half backyard, there's a downed tree, an elm that was struck by lightning. It has already been partially cut into huge chunks. Nearby is a shed, which narrowly missed being smashed by the tree when it fell; Franco goes right to this shed, yanks open the door as if it offended him, leans in, and comes out with a massive chainsaw, a heavy, wedge-headed ax, and a pair of safety goggles.

I almost laugh at the fact that even pissed off, or whatever Franco is in the moment, he still remembers to wear safety gear. I'm not laughing, though. He starts the chainsaw with a single furious jerk of the starter cable, and uses it to cut a six-foot-long chunk of the tree into smaller sections, and then tosses the chainsaw aside in favor of the ax. He sets a length of wood on end, hefts the ax up over his head and brings it down with slaughtering, vengeful force. The piece of wood splits apart into two, each half flying two or three feet in opposite directions. He grabs one half, splits it into halves again with just as much angry force, and then repeats it with the other half. All four newly split quarters he tosses into a pile, and then starts the process over again with another chunk.

Watching Franco split wood makes me horny.

I want to go over there right now, rip the ax out of his hands, and beg him to take me right up against the pile of wood.

His muscles shift and ripple as he swings the ax, and he lets out an audible grunt of exertion as he brings the ax down to slam into the wood.

"You finished with those drinks, Nova?" I hear James rumble in his growly, rippling, bass voice.

I blink, tearing my gaze away from Franco, and turn back to the kitchen just in time to see Nova topping the drinks off with slices of lime, her eyes on her work rather than James. But her attention, it's still somehow clear, is entirely on James. The air crackles, sparks, and sizzles with energy.

His eyes are shielded by his Oakleys, but it is perfectly clear that his eyes are locked on Nova as she gathers three glasses in one hand and two in another, leaving James to snag the last two. They exit the kitchen together, not talking, a foot of space between them, leaving the last drink for me, even though I still have Nova's original glass in my hand.

But somehow it's empty.

I watch James bring his two drinks across the yard to where Franco is tirelessly splitting wood, each chop as viciously powerful as the last. James stands aside, waiting for Franco to pause, and then hands him one of the glasses.

Franco takes it, stirs the drink with the straw, and then sucks the entire thing down in a matter of seconds; he hands the empty glass to James and goes back to splitting. James shakes his head and walks away, sipping his own drink more sedately.

I'm lost, watching Franco split wood, and I can't help wondering if he thinks I'm fooled as to why he suddenly feels an urge to hack at a poor innocent tree.

A few minutes later, Nova glides in, leans a hip against the counter beside me, and fans herself with a hand. "Holy moly…that *man!*"

"I know, right?" I say, still helplessly watching Franco.

Nova laughs. "I mean, yeah, but that's not who I meant." She gestures at James, who is currently locked in an arm wrestling match with Jesse; Jesse is a beast, all right, but he doesn't have a snowball's chance in hell against James, whose gargantuan bicep is bulging and rippling with exertion, the veins popping.

"Oh." I sip at the new drink, knowing I'm acting like a lush, but unable to help it. "Yeah. James is… something else."

"And those girls of his? God, they're just darling!"

"I didn't even know he *had* daughters," I admit. "But I don't know him that well."

Jesse, Imogen, and James all troop into the kitchen right as I'm saying this, and James plops onto a stool next to Nova.

"If you're in here, who's watching the meat?" Nova asks. "I only came because Imogen promised me a thick, juicy steak."

James gestures at the grill with his drink. "Ryder. He's a better griller than I am. I got 'em started, and he's finishing 'em. We have a system."

Jesse laughs, a mocking guffaw. "Yeah, a system we had to figure out after you ruined I don't even know how many hundreds of dollars in steaks because you suck at grilling, but you're too damn stubborn to admit it, or ask for help." He glances at Nova and then at me. "We had to agree to let him start the grill and put the meat on, but then when it was time to actually flip it and finish it, either Ryder or me take over, because Franco is almost as shitty at a grill as James."

"Hey, I can make a hell of a grilled cheese, okay?" James says, defensively.

"Yeah, but Nina's are better."

"And who taught her?" James asks.

"Me, dumbass!" Jesse says, stabbing James in the back of a hand with plastic drink sword. "*You* don't even use mayo!"

James rumbles something unintelligible, which I assume isn't polite. And then, louder, "Whatever, fucker. So I'm not a great cook? Who gives a shit?" Still not polite, but I feel for James.

I pat him on the shoulder. "I'm on your side, James. I can't even boil water."

Imogen laughs. "No kidding! You tried to make spaghetti once in college and damn near burned down the entire hall."

"How do you even do that?" Jesse asks. "It's *water.*"

"She forgot about it, let it boil over, and then it totally evaporated, and then the pot started scorching." Imogen is laughing helplessly now. "I came over to borrow her notes and found the pot *on fire*. Audra was in her room, the door closed, with—uhh—" she trails off awkwardly, not wanting to embarrass me quite *that* much, apparently.

"I was exploring the mysteries of the female orgasm," I say, affecting a prim tone. "And I may have gotten a little carried away. It could happen to anyone."

Of *course* Franco chooses that moment to enter the kitchen, dripping sweat and breathing hard. He hears my statement, stiffens, his jaw clenches, and he turns right back around and goes back outside. He crosses over to the grill where Ryder is flipping the steaks, burgers, and hot dogs, a drink in one hand and tongs in the other, gesticulating with the drink as he tells a story to Laurel, who is visibly hanging on every word, her eyes locked on him, watching him, clutching her own drink in both hands as if for dear life.

Franco snatches Ryder's drink from his hand mid-gesture, slams it back, and then returns the empty, and walks away without a word to either of them. Ryder stares mournfully into the empty glass, calling a sarcastic "Yeah, sure, help yourself, dick!" after Franco.

Laurel laughs as Ryder shakes his head in disgust before turning to finish flipping the meat. She takes a tiny sip of her drink from the straw, and then fits the straw up to Ryder's lips. He turns his eyes to hers, quirks an eyebrow, and then takes a long sip. He says something, she nods and shrugs and smiles.

Ooh, things are heating up in here! James and Nova, Ryder and Laurel...? I wonder which will be the first to pair off?

Nova and Imogen are exchanging glances, and then Imogen kicks my shin gently with her bare foot. "I think he heard you."

I snort. "You think?"

She shakes her head. "The sexual tension between you two is so thick you could cut it with a spoon."

Nova laughs. "Cut with a spoon and eat it like ice cream, because that tension is *delicious*. You should've seen the way they stared each other down. I'm pretty sure Audra might be pregnant from how hard Franco was eye-fucking her."

I huff, wishing I could come up with a witty, searing denial. But I can't. Because I'm also fairly certain I could be pregnant from the way he was eye-fucking me. "It's a little sexual tension, so what?" I glance at James. "We're both adults. We can handle a party with mutual friends."

"Yeah, but the question is can the rest of us handle the tension between you?" Imogen says. "Because it's so thick the air is dripping with it."

"So, James." I say, a little too loudly. "How did I not know you had two adorable daughters?"

Imogen laughs. "I didn't know either until I showed up here today, and if you count my original call to Dad Bod, I've technically known James longer than I've known Jesse!"

James rolls his shoulders. "I'm protective of them. I don't bring them around work very often. I work with my three best friends, so it's already hard to keep work and personal separate, but I try not to let my work life bleed into theirs too much."

I gesture at the kitchen and the backyard in a sweep of my hand. "But we're all here?"

He nods. "This is entirely personal. Me, my three best friends, my buddy's girlfriend, and a few of her friends, just so it's not a total sausage fest."

"But I've known you, on at least a little bit of a personal level, for months now, and the fact that you have two daughters has never once come up," Imogen says. "It *is* a little weird."

James sighs. "Like I said, I'm protective of them. I wasn't keeping them a secret from you, I just…" He shrugs. "They've been through a lot. I'm a little weird about it, I guess." He pushes off the stool. "I'm gonna go see how Ryder's doing with the meat."

After he's gone, Jesse raps his knuckles on the island countertop. "He only brings certain people around the girls. Me and the other guys are it, usually, plus the nanny he's had watching them after school since…well, since things changed for him. It's his story to tell, though, not mine, which is why I've never said anything either." He gestures at Nova, Imogen, me, and Laurel as she enters at that moment. "It's actually a really huge step for him to let outsiders into this party. It's usually just the four us and the girls every year."

Laurel is looking flushed, her tan skin pinking at her cheekbones. She's visibly bursting with something to say, fidgeting with things on the counter, glancing at me and the other girls, and then at Jesse.

Imogen notices this, and pushes at Jesse's shoulder. "Hey, Jess? I think Ryder and James and Franco could use a little more help out there."

Jesse eyes the other men, who are standing around the grill talking, occasionally glancing this way. "Oh, they're fine."

Imogen smiles up at him, lifting an eyebrow suggestively. "I think they *could* use your help, actually. I'm pretty certain."

Jesse's eyes widen. "Ohhh. Right. Yeah. Got it." He heads for the doorway, pauses, turns around and flips open a cabinet over the fridge and snags a bottle of Dalmore. "Just gonna take this." And then he's gone, only to return to grab four glasses from a different cabinet. "And these. Sorry. Leaving. Bye."

Imogen laughs at him, covering her love-smitten grin with one hand. When he's actually, truly gone, Imogen shakes her head. "Gosh, I just love that guy."

I shake my head, my stomach flipping at the way she's looking at him, at the obvious and ice-melting love between them. "You look like you're about to pop, Laurel. Spill it!"

Laurel squeals, clapping her hands. "We've got a date!"

My eyes bug out. "A date? Already?"

Laurel nods, barely suppressing giggles of excitement. "Next Friday!"

Nova is just smirking. "That was fast."

"No kidding," Imogen adds.

Laurel shrugs, batting her eyelashes with a cutesy grin. "What can I say? The man clearly can't help himself. He just knows a good thing when he sees her."

I laugh. "Where are you going, do you know?"

She shakes her head, her jet-black hair waving loose around her shoulders. "Nope! He asked me if I wanted to go out with him sometime soon, and I said yes, and he suggested Tuesday or Wednesday, but I have late meetings both days and he has a union softball game Thursday, so we're going out Friday!" She's positively vibrating with excitement. "I asked him if he had anywhere specific in mind, and he said yeah but it'll be a surprise. Which I'm fine with." Laurel squeals, claps her hands again, and then settles, turning to Nova. "Soooo, Nova...I saw you and James getting a little cozy over by the beer cooler earlier."

Nova keeps her expression blank. "We...were... just talking."

Imogen rolls her eyes. "Why are you playing coy, Nova? It's just us girls."

Nova shrugs. "I'm not playing coy, I'm just...a little reserved about some things."

Laurel snorts. "What is there to be reserved about? You like the guy, he likes you. You were cozied up on the cooler, talking. So what?"

Nova busies herself mixing drinks—something complicated with a lot of rum and a lot of vodka and not a lot of mixers—probably more for something to do than because anyone really needs another drink. "My life is complicated and there's no room for anyone in it, especially not a guy with two daughters. So yeah, I like him, he likes me. But that's as far as it goes." She shrugs, not looking at any of us. "Just how it is, whether I like it, or want it that way, or not." Her gaze sweeps us. "There. You wanted to know, now you know. I think it's time to eat."

Nova abandons her effort at making drinks, taking one and leaving three finished and several half-begun, and exits the kitchen. Her long, loose, shimmery, fiery copper hair sways down her back as she moves out into the sunlight, which catches on her hair and on the many bangles and bracelets on her wrists, lighting her up with sparkles and glints and shimmers.

Imogen takes one of the drinks and sips it. "No sense leaving these to go warm." She sighs, watching Nova. "I was hoping she'd loosen up a bit once she got here, but I guess I was wrong."

"She seems super cool, though," I say. "I like her."

Imogen nods. "She's awesome. We met in the cafeteria, as we tend to work similar shifts a lot and usually take lunch at the same, and have ended up eating lunch together pretty much every day. She doesn't talk about herself very often, and I just get the sense she keeps her personal life very buttoned up, you know? But on any other topic, she's, like—she's this firecracker, just exploding with energy and opinions and personality. I just love her to pieces, but I wish she'd let me in a little."

"Well, you do tend to want people to spill their every secret to you the moment you meet them," I tease, exaggerating just a little.

Imogen rolls her eyes at me. "I'm *personable*. It's what makes me such a good bedside nurse. Any time there's a really cranky, difficult patient, I get sent in because I can handle them and get them to calm down and open up. It's just one of my gifts. But Nova?

She's a tough nut to crack." She pokes at me with a finger. "Nova is a lot like you, actually, Audra dearest. You have this inner wall around yourselves where you keep all your painful little secrets, and you never let anyone in, or even anywhere close. The only reason I know as much about you as I do is because I've known you since before either of us got our first periods, and I've been there for literally every major and minor life event since." She gestures at Nova, who is watching Franco chase Nina and Ella around the yard with what looks like a live snake. "I just can't help wondering if she has her own Imogen. I feel like she doesn't."

I rest my head on Imogen's shoulder. "Everyone should have their own Imogen. But they can't have you—you're mine."

She pats my head. "I think Jesse might disagree with you on that point."

I wrinkle my nose. "I guess I can share you with him." I point at Laurel, faking a glare. "But don't get any ideas, missy. You try to steal my best friend, and you'll be in trouble."

Laurel just laughs. "I wouldn't dream of it."

"Calm down, Audra. No one is stealing anyone. Plus, there's enough of me to go around, I'm pretty sure." She pats her butt. "No matter how many burpees you make me do, Audra, I think I'll just always have a big ass."

Laurel cackles. "Honey, you're preaching to the choir, here. I lost sixty-six pounds in a year and a half, gained about ten pounds back, and literally *all* of it is on my butt! No matter how I eat or work out, those ten pounds are just stuck—right *here*." She grabs and shakes a butt cheek in gesture.

"Like I've been telling Imogen for literally years—" I start, but Imogen cuts me off.

"You shush, woman," Imogen cuts in. "You know as well as I do that build and genetics play a part in all of this. You work your ass off and you're fanatically devoted to how you eat. I get that, Audra, I see it, and I respect it." She leans against Laurel and they bump hips. "But some of us are just doomed to have big butts."

Ryder and Jesse squeeze through the sliding glass door right then, overhearing the tail end of the conversation.

"And speaking for a vast majority of heterosexual males on planet earth, and probably more than a few women of the other persuasion"—Ryder lifts his glass in a toast, his entire posture and voice reverent and serious—"I say, thank you sweet baby Jesus for that."

Jesse clinks his glass against Ryder's. "Amen to that, brother."

We're all laughing now, because the men are just

so serious about it, and it's funny and endearing.

Franco pushes in, then, followed by the girls, who are chattering in overlapping chorus. "Make way, make way," Franco says. "Mr. Snakeypants wants to say hi to everyone."

He assumes center stage in the kitchen, a three-foot-long garter snake in both hands, one hand pinioning just behind the creature's jaws to keep it from biting or escaping.

Laurel dances back, shrieking. "What the hell is wrong with you! Why would you bring a live snake into the kitchen? Get it out!"

Franco just laughs. "Oh calm down, it's just a garter snake. He's totally harmless. His name, according to Miss Ella here, is Mr. Snakeypants. Which, personally, I feel is a wonderfully appropriate, and not at all suggestive name, for a snake."

Ella, the younger of the girls is dancing in circles, chanting, "*Mis*-ter *Snakey*-pants! *Mis*-ter *Snakey*-pants!"

Nina, trying to be more subdued now that there's a larger adult audience, reaches out to touch the top of the snake's head. "He slithered right over the top of my foot and didn't even bite me. I was a little scared—but not *too* much—because then he just sat there on my foot looking up at me, so I called for Uncle Franco, who caught him and he was chasing us with him because snakes are kind of yucky, but he's nice and not too yucky, even though his skin feels weird."

"Snakes are yucky, full stop," Laurel says. "Now put Mister Snakeypants outside before I faint."

Ryder is laughing. "Let me see him." He reaches out, carefully takes the snake by the back of the head from Franco, letting the rest of the long body wrap around his arm. He moves over to Laurel, who dances around the island, screaming, until Ryder traps her in a corner of the kitchen. "Just calm down a second. Jesus! Look at him! He's not even doing anything."

"I don't care! It's a *snake!*" Laurel hisses.

Ryder is keeping his distance, but not letting her escape. "Have you ever touched a snake?"

"No, and I don't plan to."

"Just try it," Ryder says, his voice smooth and low. "He won't hurt you. I've got him, so he can't. But he probably wouldn't anyway."

"No."

"Just touch the top of his head."

Laurel meets Ryder's eyes, hesitating. "You're sure he won't bite me?"

Ryder makes sure the snake's head is pointing away from Laurel. "See? He can't. I've got him."

"It's okay, Laurel," Ella says. "I was scared too, but it's kind of tickly, that's all."

Laurel reaches out, yanks her hand back, and

then steps closer to Ryder, moving up behind him and peering out around his bicep. "You're sure you've got him?"

"Yes!" Ryder laughs. "And if he's gonna bite anyone, it'll be me."

"What if he does?" Laurel asks, still hesitating with her fingertip an inch from the snake's body.

"It'll hurt, I'll get a tetanus shot, have a couple sweet puncture wounds for a few weeks, and that's it. They're no threat to people." He grins at her. "I've been bitten before, actually, several times."

"By a garter snake like this one?"

"Ummm, no. Well, yeah, by a garter once when I was a kid." He pauses for effect. "I got bit by a copperhead while swimming in a lake in Louisiana, and by a rattler while hiking in Colorado. And by a few other harmless ones other times."

Laurel stares at him. "I can't decide if that makes you a badass or a dumbass."

"A little of both?" Ryder says.

While all this is going on, I've somehow ended up standing next to Franco. He washed his hands and is drying them on a handful of paper towel. His eyes are on me, and mine on his, as if neither of us can seem to help it.

"Hi," he murmurs.

"Hey."

He gestures at the reptile in Ryder's hands. "You say hi to Mr. Snakeypants yet?"

"I'm good." I can't help a smirk. "That name was your idea, wasn't it?"

He laughs. "No! I swear. It was all Ella."

Silence descends between us, even with the commotion all around us: Ryder and the girls take the snake outside to let him go, Laurel is squealing again and everyone else is trooping outside to find places at James's extra wide, extra long picnic table.

Which leaves Franco and I alone in the kitchen, just staring each other down, not saying a damn word.

"Why'd you have to go chasing snakes, Franco?" I murmur. "I was doing so well at ignoring you."

"You were not. You were staring at me every chance you got."

"Like you haven't been doing the same?" I counter.

He shrugs. "Sure. But you're wearing a dress that basically screams to be ripped off. So I can't be held responsible for staring at your tits, which are, to be fair, all but out there."

"I didn't realize it would be a problem for you."

"Oh, it's *definitely* not a problem." His smooth voice is deep, feral purr.

Nearly everyone is sitting down, at this point, which provides me with an exit. "Time to eat." I push past him, holding my breath so I don't accidentally inhale his scent, closing my eyes so I'm not tempted to turn them up to his.

I feel him watching me as I make my way outside and take a place at the picnic table—on the very end, with Ella beside me, Ryder beside her, and Jesse and Imogen across from me; the only other open spot at the table is on the other side and at the other end... far, far from me.

The meal is...honestly, one of the most relaxed, convivial, and enjoyable of my life. The food is plentiful and delicious, the drinks flow freely—but not to excess, as everyone seems to be pacing themselves well, at least partially out of respect for our two youngest members. The conversation is easy, with friendly ribbing between the guys, and rolled eyes between the women, and constant chatter from the girls.

When the meal is finally over, James and Franco set to work building a bonfire in the fire pit at the back of the yard, near the downed tree and the pile of split wood, which is now much larger thanks to Franco. Within a few minutes, they have a roaring blaze flickering and dancing in the boulder-lined fire pit, and the rest of us are dragging deck chairs and loungers and kitchen stools across the yard. James plops down on the massive, gnarled, flat-topped stump of the downed tree, which seems to be his personal spot—the fire pit, indeed, appears to have been put in place specifically so he could sit on the stump and poke at the fire. Franco drags over a section of the tree, flips it on end, and sits on it next to James, and Ella crawls up onto his lap. Franco, without missing a beat, hauls her up and settles her in place; a familiar dance for them, it seems.

My heart is not melting. Nope, it sure isn't. NOPE NOPE NOPE.

Nina drags a chair to sit by her dad, resting her head against his arm. Gradually, everyone finds a spot, and the fire grows brighter as the evening grows darker and the stars start to pop and prickle against the blackening velvet sky, and there's a drowsy, contented wash of cross chatter.

Nina, apropos of nothing, hops up, runs back into the house and reappears after a moment, dragging two hardback guitar cases. They're almost too big for her skinny frame to carry, but she manages to haul them across the yard to the fire pit. She plops one case at her dad's feet, and the other at Jesse's.

"I'm bored!" she announces. "Papa and Uncle Jesse should play some tunes!"

James rumbles wordlessly. "I haven't touched that in years, sweetie."

"Yes, you have," Nina argues. "I heard you playing it in your room the other night. You were playing super quiet like you didn't want me to hear, but I heard because I can't sleep sometimes. You were playing that one song you like to play a lot."

James sighs, nudging the case with the toe of his boot. "That's different. Nobody wants to hear that."

Nova, sitting next to him, bumps him with her shoulder. "I don't know if I'd say that's true."

"It's just an old sad song I play when I'm bored," James says, staring at the guitar case.

"You mean when you're sad because you miss Mama." Nina says this quietly, gazing somewhat nervously at him from lowered lashes.

"Nina," James growls, the rumble a clear and dire warning.

"What? It's true! I'm not saying anything private! I just wanna hear you play again. It's been so long and it's a perfect night for it and you don't have to play *that* song. Uncle Jesse can pick and you can play along like you guys used to."

Jesse unclasps the guitar case, flips it open, and pulls out a beautiful acoustic guitar. He settles it on his lap with easy familiarity, plucks the strings one by one, and adjusts the tuning. "I'm game if you are, buddy," he says to James.

James sighs again, a deep, gusting breath of resignation. "Fine. A couple songs. But if you pull this mess again, girly, you're in trouble."

Nina claps happily and plops down in her chair, settles her chin in her hands, and watches, eyes sparkling in the firelight, as James tunes his own guitar. Jesse is already noodling, strumming a chord here and there, plucking out little riffs, humming under his breath—finding the tune, I suppose. I glance at Imogen, curious.

Sitting beside me, Imogen leans close. "I've never actually heard him play before," she whispers, excited.

"I didn't even know he was a musician!" I whisper back.

"He mentioned he plays in a cover band sometimes, but I guess they sort of disbanded and he's been too busy lately with Dad Bod to play."

After some more noodling, Jesse settles in to play a recognizable melody: "Hotel California" by the Eagles. After a little guitar intro, he starts singing the lyrics, and I'm not sure what I was expecting, but it wasn't for Jesse's voice to be so amazing. It's deep, raspy, charged with intensity, beautiful. After a minute, James joins in, strumming around the melody. His voice is deeper, smoother, providing a harmony to Jesse. They go through that song, and then transition to "Jesse's Girl", which makes Imogen blush and snuggle against Jesse's arm. After that, they do "Fade to Black" by Metallica, and then "Stairway to Heaven" by Led Zeppelin.

The songs they do and the way they play the melodies and harmonize tells me Jesse and James have been sitting around bonfires jamming to those tunes for decades.

Nina, leaning sleepily up against James's arm, gazes up at him. "Play the song, Papa."

"No." A gruff, terse, monosyllabic refusal.

"Please?" Her voice is cracking, sad.

"Dammit, child." He sighs. "It's more'n just me and your uncles this time, Nina."

"So?"

"So...it's hard." He scrapes at a guitar string with his thumbnail, making a raspy hum.

"Good thing you're so tough, huh, Papa?" She nuzzles closer. "Please? And then I'll go to bed. Promise."

James sighs again. "Fine."

"*Fuck,*" I hear Jesse mutter, under his breath so low probably only Imogen and I could hear him. The word is hissed, bitten out, a sound raw pain.

James plucks a slow, sad melody, and then sings—"Every Time We Say Goodbye", by Ella Fitzgerald. Jesse doesn't accompany him on this one, and his expression is neutral, almost shut down.

As are Ryder's, and Franco's.

This song is clearly thick with meaning for all four of them, and for Nina.

When the song is done, James lets the strings hum the final note until the sound quavers into silence. The guitars both go back in their cases, and then James lifts a now almost sleeping Nina into his burly arms, while Jesse scoops the long-since slumbering Ella into his. Imogen follows Jesse inside, and Nova follows James. Ryder and Laurel rise, too, and wander off into the darkness beyond the pale orange light of the dying fire, murmuring to each other in low tones—it sounds like Laurel is asking about the song, and Ryder is giving what seems to be the party line for Jesse, Franco, and Ryder when it comes whatever happened with James and the girls' mother: "It's not my story to tell, it's his."

And, just like that, Franco and I are alone at the fire.

I'm not drunk, but I've been slowly drinking all night, leaving me loose and floaty.

"If I asked you about Nina and Ella's mom, would you tell me?" I hear myself asking.

Franco slowly shook his head. "It's not—"

"Your story to tell," I say, in unison with him. "Gotcha. Nina told me she was going to have a baby and went to be with Jesus, and so did the baby."

Franco blows out a tight breath. "Yeah, that's pretty much all there is to tell." He pauses, considering; I finally let myself look at him, and find his piercing blue eyes fraught with sadness and hazed with old memories. "She was Jesse's sister."

"Oh my god. I'm so sorry to hear that. I had no idea. Were he and Jesse friends before they got together?"

"Reneé." This is from Jesse, standing behind me, startling me; I twist and see Imogen hanging on him, gazing up at him lovingly, sadly. "Her name was Renée. James and I have been friends since middle school. We met in seventh grade. We got in a fight during lunch, and my sister broke it up. The three of us were inseparable after that. We met Ryder and Franco a few months later, when all of our parents collectively decided to sign us up to play flag football through the local YMCA. To get us out of their hair, I guess. But yeah, James and I were friends long before he and Renée started dating, which was in high school." He pauses, laughing. "Franco's stupid ass had a crush on her too, actually."

"It wasn't a crush. Your sister was hot as hell, so half the guys in town had a crush on her. And I knew James was gaga for her, anyway." Franco says this with good-natured irritation.

"And you were hot for Lacey Wright at that point, too, weren't you?" Jesse asks, steering the conversation away from Renée.

Franco stabs the fire with a piece of stick. "Who

wasn't? Of course, the problem with Lacey was that she had no problem getting with any guy who'd pay her the least amount of attention."

"Which included you, am I right?"

"Shut up. We went on one date."

"Yeah...*date*." Jesse says this with a snort.

"Are you done?" Franco snaps. "Because I could bring up Amy Collins...or Judy Fredrickson...or Prissy McLane."

"Oh god, *please* don't bring up Prissy McClane," Jesse pleads.

"We all tried to warn you."

"Like we all tried to warn you about—" Jesse starts.

"I will stab you in the eye with a cinder if you say another fucking syllable," Franco snarls.

Jesse laughs, holding up his hands, palms out. "Okay, okay. Jesus, dude." He stops laughing, and eyes Franco. "That's some seriously old history, man, get over it already."

Franco shoots to his feet and stalks away, ripping his hair out of the ponytail, shaking it back and combing his fingers through it, and then retying it as he vanishes into the shadows.

I glance at Jesse, who's still standing behind me. "Let me guess, more old history that's Franco's to tell and not yours?"

"Yep." He smirks down at me. "But if you could get him to tell you about it, it might explain some things."

"She'd have to do some explaining herself, though," Imogen says. "And she's as miserly with her history as the rest of you seem to be." She pauses, and I realize what she's about to say it. "She'd have to tell him about Jared."

"Dammit, Imogen," I snap.

She shrugs. "Like Jesse said, it's old history. We all have it. No sense hoarding it like it's something precious. Just get it out there and move on. Quit letting it have this hold on you."

"Easy for you to say."

She frowns. "You think it was easy for me to get over Nicholas? Just because I have Jesse now, and I'm happy as can be with him, doesn't mean I'm *over* what Nicholas did to me. I've just found something worth having that makes it easier to keep moving on, one day at a time. It's a choice—I made a *choice*. And it wasn't *easy*."

I get to my feet with an aggravated huff. "Whatever." I grab my bag and head for the house, just to get away from Imogen's truth.

"I guess we get the fire to ourselves, huh?" I hear Jesse say, and then the thunk and spark of a log hitting the fire, followed by the renewed crackling of flames devouring the fresh fuel.

I see shadows in the distance—Ryder and Laurel strolling along the fence line of James's property. I angle away from them to give them their space and privacy. Where to go? Where did Franco go? I want to know so I can go anywhere else. The house seems like a safe bet—but, as I head for the kitchen, I see James and Nova standing chest to chest by the fridge, her hands on his shoulders, his on her waist. They're not kissing, though, and their body language is tense, as if they're fighting the obvious attraction between them. I see Nova shake her head and pull back, twisting away from him, then James scrubs a hand through his hair, mussing his usually neat brown locks.

Nope, not going in there.

The eight-foot-high wood-slat privacy fence surrounding James's backyard runs up to the side of the house, dividing Jesse's property from the neighbors'. A large gate that spans the driveway up near the front corner of the house separates the road and the rest of the property. I see moonlight glint on the metal gate as it swings open on silent hinges, only the slight rattle of the latch giving him away.

Headlights approach from the street, then turn and bounce up onto the driveway, and silhouette Franco's form. His head is down, arms swinging loosely.

He's leaving?

As I walk up to the front of the property, I notice that the gate is tall, and looks like it was handmade from metal piping and rods and spindles; it's heavy but well-balanced on oiled hinges, swinging open slowly as I give it a push. Behind me, the fire flickers orange at the far end of the yard, and Imogen and Jesse are small, conjoined shadows. Just as I turn to close the gate behind me, I see Ryder and Laurel slip back to the fire and sit down.

A car door opens and I hear a voice identifying Franco. The vehicle is a late-model Kia sedan with a pink LYFT sign on the front dash, driven by a middle-aged man in a Sikh turban. I'm lit by the headlights as I approach, and the driver turns to see if Franco wants to wait for me.

He leaves the door open, one foot in the car and one on the pavement. I stop beside him, staring down at him.

I don't say a word; neither does he.

After a silent moment, energy crackling between us in a storm of unspoken tension and awareness, Franco slides over and extends a hand to me.

I place my palm in his, and lower myself into the car, and shut the door.

"Ready to go?" the driver asks, his voice quiet and soft and thickly accented.

No, is the thought that runs through my head.

"Yes, thank you," Franco murmurs.

With a few taps of the cell phone in the hands-free holder suctioned to the windshield, the driver begins the journey; I recognize the address as being a street in the subdivision near my condo complex—the street in question is a lovely, sleepy, quiet little avenue, tree-lined, with small, tidy houses on large lots.

We're going to Franco's house.

My eyes meet his, and my heart squeezes, flutters, does flips to match the somersaults in my stomach, and the tremble of my hands.

NINE

It's a slow, silent drive from James's house. The driver has the radio on very low, playing wailing, skirling, toe-tapping Indian music at odds with the tension in the car between Franco and me. The driver's head bobs in funny little sideways shakes in time with the rhythm, and he mutters something under his breath in his language, as if he's singing lyrics to the song that aren't present in the radio version.

There are about six inches of space on the seat between Franco and me; we're both buckled in, my purse on my knees, his hands loose on his thighs. I want to meet his eyes, but I'm scared; if I look at him, I'll say something, and I'm not sure what that would be. So I keep my eyes on his hands, noticing little scars here and there hidden among the lines and fine hairs. They are strong hands, powerful but careful, and skilled and gentle.

I have a split-second image rushing through my

head: his hand stutters down my hips, clutching at my thighs. I blink, shake my head to clear the image, but the damage is done. My stomach clenches, and my thighs press together. I drag my eyes away from his hands, because no part of him is safe to look at right now.

Even his nose is a danger zone: I remember the way it felt, nuzzling against my skin as his tongue lapped at my core.

I feel my nipples harden, and I notice his eyes sliding sideways, flicking down to my breasts, and lingering there.

I glance out the window to distract myself and see that we're passing my condo complex, which means we're less than five minutes from his place. We turn right into a subdivision, and the trees arch overhead, obscuring the waning half-moon and the few twinkling stars visible in the Chicago suburbs. A left turn, and then a right, and the street we're on now is narrow and paved in old, uneven cobblestones. The houses here are older, well-kept ranches and bungalows, and the trees lining the street are thick, venerable old oaks with wide-spreading branches and broad leaves and gnarled roots that threaten to ruck the sidewalks out of true.

The driver pulls into a narrow driveway in front of a low-roofed ranch with gray siding and white trim, a bright crimson door, and neat, simple land-scaping consisting mostly of box shrubs. There's a picture window to the right of the front door with a flower box underneath, planted with a neat line of red geraniums. Even from the outside, I can see Franco's handiwork everywhere, and his penchant for neatness and order. The grass is neatly mowed and edged and fertilized, verdant and green, the landscaping beds cleanly mulched and clearly defined. There's a de-tached garage beside and behind the house a ways, with Franco's truck sitting out in front of it, and I can see a hint of the backyard.

"Here you are," the driver says, putting the Kia into park. "Thank you, and please to enjoy your eve-ning." He draws the last word into three distinct syl-lables: EVE-en-ing.

"Thanks, you too," Franco replies, exiting on his side.

I get out on my side and follow Franco up the driveway; he has his phone out, tapping to rate the driver and apply a tip, and then the device goes back into his rear pocket and he's digging out his keys. He bypasses the front door in favor of the side, unlocking it and pushing it open, letting me in first. The side door leads directly into the kitchen, which is small but feels spacious, with dark floors and light cabinets, concrete countertops and stainless steel appliances.

The light over the stove is on, shedding a low, inviting yellow glow. After Franco closes the door behind him, he relocks it out of habit, tossing his keys onto the nearby counter.

There's an abrupt silence following the initial jangle of his keys on the counter.

It's cool in his house; my skin pebbles, and my nipples harden further into diamond points. Or… maybe it's just because I'm alone with Franco in his home.

I'm standing in the middle of his kitchen, my arms crossed over my chest. Franco doesn't look at me, just withdraws his phone from his pocket, plugs a charger cable into it and tosses it onto the counter near his keys; his wallet joins it. He's wearing flip-flops, which just seems weird, as he typically wears boots of some kind. He kicks them off and uses his feet to line them up neatly next to the door, beside his familiar steel-toed work boots and a pair of battered cross-trainers.

God, the tension.

It crackled between us all afternoon and evening, sparked and caught fire in the car…now, the tension is a raging inferno. All I'm aware of is him. Every particle of my being is attuned to Franco, and only Franco. He's just standing there by the side door, hands at his sides, his eyes on me. That inscrutable blue gaze is fixed, laser-like, on mine.

My thighs are pressed tightly together, and my core is weeping with frustrated, agonized need. The last few days I haven't even been able to bring myself release, unable to reach climax on my own. I tried several times but failed, and failed, and failed, leaving me a worked-up, frustrated disaster. Only several brutally punishing workouts have saved my sanity.

Now I'm here, and he's here, and I have no idea what to say, or if I should make the first move, or if he will. I don't even know what that move should be, or what I want it to be.

The tension has burned away any remaining haze from my buzz, leaving only need and awareness of Franco.

His eyes leave mine, raking slowly down to my protruding nipples, clearly visible through the thin dress. Down again, to my center—his nostrils flare and his brow furrows and his jaw grinds, and his hands flex at his sides.

And his zipper tightens.

Yeah, you bet your ass I notice that.

How long have we been standing here, staring at each other in silence? Seconds? Minutes?

Franco lurches forward unsteadily, dragging in a harsh breath. He's not drunk—at least not on alcohol.

It's me. Us. Need.

"Goddammit," he breathes.

"Franco, I—"

I have no idea what I was going to say. But it doesn't matter.

Before I can get out another syllable, his mouth slams up against mine, his lips scouring, tongue slashing. I whimper in surprise, stiffening all over at the unexpected assault of his mouth on mine, but then need takes over and the taste of his mouth takes over and the heat and wet of his lips and tongue take over, and I melt up against him. My arms are trapped between us, and I slither them out from between our bodies so I can feel the crush of my breasts against his hard chest and the hammer of his heart beating just like mine. I cling to his strong neck and hold him and—I kiss him back.

Abruptly, he rips away, panting. "I had to."

"I know," I whisper.

He turns away from me, breathing hard. And then turns back an instant later, his eyes blazing. His hands assume control then, and I'm powerless to stop him even if I wanted to: he plucks at the knot at my nape and the top of my dress sags forward, and then he tugs the top down to my waist. My nipples can't possibly harden any more, and now they tingle and ache, and my breasts feel heavy and full under his ravenous gaze. He buries his face against my shoulder, and I feel his teeth nip the thin, sensitive skin on my shoulder blade, and then his tongue slides down. I'm gasping under the warmth of his lips, but his hands are busy as well as his mouth. He pulls the rest of my dress away, and hauls down my thong, and I'm naked in front of him. My core tightens and clenches, and desire seeps out of me and I know he smells it.

"Franco," I whisper.

He just grunts, continuing the journey of his mouth toward my breast. I paw at him, rip at his shirt, tear it off and throw it aside. Claw at his flesh, raking my nails down his broad rippling back and then scraping them up the ridges of his stomach and over the hard slabs of his chest, and then I yank at his shorts, too impatient and desperate to feel him and taste him to bother with zippers and buttons. But the stupid shorts actually fit properly, so I have to slow down and take my lips from wherever it is they're kissing in a frantic barrage. I have to stop kissing him so I can pop his fly open and yank down the zipper. Then, finally, I can shove the shorts off him, along with his underwear.

As soon as his erection bobs free, I grasp it, moaning at the feel of him in my hands. I caress him as he sucks my nipple into his mouth, and I stroke him as he kisses my breasts with the same wild passion as he kissed my mouth. He groans at my touch, and I'm whimpering, and we're still just standing in the middle of his kitchen.

His teeth saw at my nipple and then he suckles on it, and my knees go weak, shaking, and then give out. Franco catches me, lifts me up, and scoops me into his arms.

Dammit, dammit, dammit—my heart is palpitating and hammering and flipping, and my stomach is fluttering and every nerve and synapse and sense is singing and attuned to Franco, to his body and his strength. His eyes are on mine... and mine are on his lips. I'm so close.

But I don't kiss him. I don't dare...do I?

I'm still breathless from his kiss and his mouth is right there, and I need to taste him again, need to feel that moan as his mouth slashes across mine. Screw it. My arms tighten around his neck and my lips slant over his, my tongue finding his lips and then his tongue and I'm breathing him, tasting him. The kiss is breathless. Aching.

Exquisite.

Heart-rending.

Perfect.

How long? I don't know, but not long enough.

Finally, his arms shake from the exertion of holding me there. He moves into another room, and I have the brief sense of being in his living room—a couch, a TV, a glass coffee table, an easy chair. And then he's twisting again and I'm weightless—he's thrown me onto the bed. I land with a *whump* onto a firm mattress covered by a thick comforter—there's no time to breathe or to move or to assess his room.

There's just Franco.

He's crawling across the bed to lever over me, filling the space above and around and everywhere with his male scent and heat. We don't touch, for a moment; he stares down at me and I stare back, his eyes flicking with blue fire. His fists press into the comforter beside my face. He's searching me—looking for what? I don't know.

The same thing I'm looking for when I stare back into his glacier-blue eyes: something I know I'll find in him, if I only look hard enough.

But do I *want* this?

I hate this sense of falling, the vulnerability I feel in myself as I gaze up at him, my desperation for his touch, my acquiescence to his kiss...my need for another kiss and another, when I've gone *years* without kissing anyone simply because it's too intimate and too real and too connective—

Deep down I'm terrified of connecting with someone again and having them rip it away from me. I only barely survived that betrayal with my sanity intact—I'm stronger now, but also far more fragile. A strange dichotomy, but true.

Dammit—god*dammit* I feel something hot stinging my eyes, a prickling dampness blurs my sight as Franco stares down at me and there's nowhere to hide.

His big, rough thumb brushes gently across the corner of my eye, and he lowers his face slowly down to mine, and this—this kiss is unlike the previous ones. This one is not desperate or wild.

This one is slow.

If the other kisses were manic with unbridled passion, this one is deeply, intentionally fraught with it, constructed with precision and elegance to prove what passion truly is.

I fall into his kiss effortlessly, tumbling into it without even thinking. My hands are buried in his long silky blond mane, and I feel his stubble under my palms, feel his cheeks moving as he kisses me into utter stupidity.

The prickling in my eyes is only made worse by this, and I hate how my heart twists and unfurls and reaches upward as if to soar past my slashing tongue and into his mouth and into his chest to braid and twine around his heart.

I hate, too, how the kiss doesn't seem to end, but only to morph into a new kiss followed by a pause for breath and another kiss, how our flesh slides like silk on silk and my hands know his body, *know* blindly and perfectly each curve and angle and plane of him. I hate with shaking ferocity the way he can make me moan when he does *that* with his tongue and how he can make me arch my back and shudder when he paws hungrily at my breasts and how my legs saw at his and splay apart for his questing touch—that seeking nudge, that warm press...it's him. *Him.* His beautiful thick hot hard erection sliding against the tender inner flesh of my thigh and then grazing my nether lips and spreading me apart and I whimper at the touch of him, gasp at the intrusion of him as I welcome him, tipping my hips upward without hesitation to take him within me.

God, I try to tell myself I *hate hate hate* the way he looks at me, understands me, feels inside me, like he's always been there, and always will be there. It's as if him being inside me is me finally finding my home.

His forehead brushes mine, his hair falling to either side of our faces, our lips touching but not moving, not meeting not kissing, just both of us moaning in harmonic unison at the perfection of the gliding slide of our union, the wet slippery hot tightness of him moving through me, my legs wrapped around his ass and my hands clawing at his shoulders and raking down his back so deeply he'll have marks in the morning. I feel him pushing deep, as deep as he'll go, and I angle my hips up and draw my knees upward to take more of him. One of his hands is under my neck, his thumb brushing at my earlobe and the corner of my jaw, and the other supports his weight.

We move together.

His groans fill my ear and travel, echoing and rebounding, into my soul, his groans of such sweet abandon that I know he's never known a moment like this any more than I have. Those sounds, those breathless gasps, those quiet feminine sobs—is that me? I'm a screamer, a shrieker, a thrasher...not this writhing, undulating, clinging, half-weeping, half-whimpering woman. But it is me—it's me as I fall apart beneath Franco, it's me as I understand how fully I belong to him.

I tell myself I hate it.

I fight it.

But I might as well try to hold back a tsunami.

It's like trying to contain a supernova.

I can't...and I don't want to.

I can't hate it, and I can't fight it.

Because, at this level of intensity, hate and love are essentially indistinguishable.

Franco is panting, now. His grunts are breathless, his movements frantic. Wild. Feral. His grip on the nape of my neck is fierce and unbreakable, and I must look at him now—I have to turn my eyes up to his, have to open my eyes and stare into his drowning blue gaze and not look away, because my own movements are just as frantic, just as desperate. My body is a wild beast, undulating madly as I slash my hips against his, levering my legs around his waist and clinging to his shoulders and writhing with all my strength against him as raw unfiltered passion crashes into me and explodes through me. I feel him—all of him. I feel with every molecule of my body all that is Franco as we unite.

I feel him driving through my clenching core, and I feel him throb, feel his balls tense and shudder as he cries out, and I feel him pulse and engorge and I'm spasming around him, clamping down on him like a vise, making me feel every shudder and pulse and throb as he orgasms all the more intensely. I seize around him, wailing past sobs, my teeth sinking into his shoulder to muffle myself, and then I feel Franco tighten and stiffen above me and his movements become harsh and ravaging, and his grunts are deep and feral to counterpoint my high breathless cries.

A hot wet rush floods through me and Franco is groaning and his face is buried between my breasts and I'm clutching him against me with my whole body arching up off the bed into him and against him, and I'm unable to even scream for the paralytic power of the climax that crushes me in that moment, snatched out of me at the feel of Franco unleashing himself inside me.

We cling to each other through the smashing waves that follow, gasping and groaning and whimpering.

"Franco..." I whisper his name.

"Audra," he breathes mine, sounding nearly as stunned and broken as I feel.

There is a long, long silence, Franco lying partially on top of me, his weight beautiful and welcome and somehow tender and vulnerable, my fingers toying with his hair, his breath on my skin, his erection softening inside me.

Something wet and hot drips through me, and my breath catches in a sharp gasp as awareness lances into me.

I clutch frantically at his face, tilting it up so I can look into his blue eyes. "Franco, we just—"

"I know." He rolls with me and I find myself sheltered in the circle of his arms, and I've never ever in my life ever felt so small and delicate and safe as I do now.

"Franco, we can't just—" I start.

"Can we *not*? Can we just...for one minute, *please*, can we just not? None of it." His voice is ragged and raw. "Just for a few minutes. I'm just a guy, you're just a girl, and we're just having this moment.

You and me, together."

"Okay," I whisper. Because…he's perfectly right.

I just breathe, resting my cheek against the warm, firm cushion of his chest, feeling his arm around my waist, his hand resting on my hip. I settle a hand on his belly, and I listen to him breathing, listen to his heartbeat. It's a soothing sound, the gentle susurrus of his breath, and the steady thump-thump of his heart.

But there's the seeping of his seed sliding out of me, wet and hot. And I can't just forget that. I can't ignore it.

"I—" I shake my head, pushing away from him. "I need to—I have to clean up."

Franco stops me with a hand on my breastbone. "Stay there. I'll get a washcloth."

I lie back down hesitantly, and Franco goes out into the bathroom, the pale firm roundness of his tight ass mesmerizing, even then. The bathroom isn't en suite, so I only hear him. I hear water running, and I assume he's cleaning himself up and then he returns to the bedroom, and even more mesmerizing than his butt is his cock as it dangles and sways between his heavy thighs. It's not often I stick around long enough to get a look at the guy when he's not erect, so this is kind of interesting for me, to be honest. And, despite the stress and pressure and fracturing intimacy and tense vulnerability of the moment, I find his flaccid member incredibly intimate.

He's standing over me, a washcloth in his hands. His eyes fix on mine, and he hesitates. "I haven't done this, like…ever, actually. So, um. I'll be gentle."

"You—what?" I ask, not sure what he's talking about. "OH!"

This last is a gasp of surprise as he tugs my thighs apart, and then with an exquisitely gentle touch, he uses two fingers to splay apart the tender folds of my center and uses the warm, damp washcloth to wipe me clean, dragging the cloth upward, folding, and swiping again, until I'm clean.

My throat closes and the prickling in my eyes returns, and my chest is somehow tight as a drum and hammering like one.

Because that was, without a doubt, the most tender, most intimate, and most vulnerable moment I've ever experienced in my life and I'm in no fucking way ready for it.

It makes my heart hurt.

It makes my head spin.

It makes everything inside me tense up, freeze, paralyzed in a breathless panic.

When I'm clean, Franco straightens, holding the washcloth in one hand, his eyes on mine. His brow is furrowed in deep, troubled grooves.

The hand holding the washcloth shakes, almost

imperceptibly. I know he was as affected by this as I was.

"We just had sex without a condom," I whisper, blinking up at him—blinking, because I refuse to acknowledge the stinging blurring heat in my eyes as anything other than...something I don't want to think about.

"I know," he mutters back.

"I've never, ever, ever had sex without a condom. Not once, ever, in my whole life, even though I've been on birth control since I was fifteen." I hesitate. "And, um, I get tested regularly, so I'm...you know, clean."

"I haven't either, even when I was married." He meets my eyes briefly. "And so do I, and so am I."

I sit up very, very carefully, not taking my eyes off of his. "You were...*married*?"

He closes his eyes briefly, as if he can't believe he just said that. "Shit." He opens them again. "I...yeah. I was. For almost six years, back in my twenties."

"And you never once had unprotected sex with her?"

He is so visibly tense that I kind of wish I hadn't asked. "No. She...um. She hated birth control. Said it whacked up her hormones, so we...no, we always used a condom." He winces. "It's weird talking about this with you. I've never talked about it at all, with anyone, let alone like this."

"Like this?"

He indicates me, himself, and the bed, all in one gesture. "We're still naked, we just had sex, and it was…"

"Something?" I suggest.

His laugh is disbelieving and amused. "Yeah, it was something all right."

We are both silent. What do I say? I can see him trying to figure out the same thing.

"Audra, I…" Franco starts. Trails off.

"I can't believe we did that," I say just to fill in the quiet.

"I know. Me either."

"I just…I got…I got carried away," I say. I look at him again, after long moments of looking anywhere but at his eyes. "I *never* get carried away."

He nods. "Me too, and me neither."

"How did it happen, Franco?" I ask, tugging the blanket up and clenching it under my arms. "How did we…how did this happen? How did we get here?"

"I don't *know*, Audra." He sits on the edge of the bed, and I'm drawn into his eyes, into his lean frame, his tan skin and hard muscles. "If you'd known this was going to happen when you got into the Lyft with me, would you still have come with me?"

I'm having terrible difficulty breathing. "I…" I

blink hard. "I don't know," I whisper.

"You don't?"

I swallow hard. "No, that's not right. The answer is yes, I would." I'm somewhere between panting and breathless. "Okay? I would."

"What if…" He turns his eyes to mine—don't say it, don't say it, please fuck don't say it, I hear myself chanting in my head. "What if you get pregnant?"

"I'm on the shot, and I have been for years. I've never lapsed." I'm swallowing hard. "I'll swing by a pharmacy and get a Plan B, though, just to be safe."

He clenches his jaw so hard I hear his teeth grinding in the silence. "Plan B." Even his voice is hard.

"Yeah." I'm confused by his reaction to it—the mere mention has him tenser than ever and almost angry. "Is that a problem for you?" I know I sound pissy, but if he's going to turn all controlling about this, we're gonna have problems.

"No…no." He softens his voice. "No, it's not a problem."

"Then what's with your reaction just now?" I ask.

He shakes his head. "Nothing. Just…a personal thing."

I frown. "I'm naked in your bed. I still have your cum leaking out of me, Franco. I think I can handle some of your *personal* stuff at this point."

He takes a deep breath. "I need a minute."

He rockets to his feet, stomps across the room; yanks open a bureau drawer, snags a pair of shorts, steps into them, and exits the room in a skirl of male scent and pissed-off energy.

I'm not sure what just happened. Maybe he's getting a drink, or taking a breath in the kitchen. He said he needed a minute, so I don't want to follow him. God knows this is a crazy situation, and I understand he might need some time to process it all. But I'm confused. I don't know what I'm supposed to do.

He was married?

We just had unprotected sex. It was the first time for both of us, even though we're both over forty. I've never had sex without a condom.

And now…I have.

Despite all that, the memory of it makes my heart palpitate and squeeze because of …our connection. The kisses, and the sheer intimacy of the sex.

But I refuse to think about that other word that's bubbling around in my head. I won't say it, won't think it, won't even entertain the notion of it.

That's *not* what it was.

I hear a door close.

He's gone?

I feel a bolt of panic at the idea he might have left.

I tell myself to calm down. Just relax. Breathe.

This is his house. Where would he go? Talking a walk, getting a breath of air?

Yet still, there's panic inside me.

After all that just happened between us…he just walked out?

Several minutes pass and then the panic and anger and fear spur me out of his bed. I open his closet and grab the first button down I see—a white long sleeve dress shirt that looks nearly new. I slip my arms in the sleeves, button it up, and then roll the sleeves up. Just putting on the shirt, knowing he's worn it, makes me feel calmer.

I take a deep breath and leave his room. Exiting the hallway, I find myself in the open-plan main area; it's clear Franco has done major remodeling here. It's simple, clean, neat, and beautiful. Dark floors, light walls, simple decor, with a few personal touches here and there—photos of Franco with the other guys in various stages of life: as kids, teenagers, young adults, adults, and current. There's a woman in a few of the photos, and I assume it's Renée, James's wife and Jesse's sister. I see no photos of Franco's family, though. No siblings, no parents, obviously nothing of his ex.

I head into the kitchen, peering through the window over the sink, which overlooks the back-yard—I see the garage door is open and a light is on.

His workshop. I'm already out the side door ignoring the fact that I was giving him time. But I'm already across the driveway and standing in the open garage door, watching Franco. Still clad in nothing but his shorts, he's bent over a mammoth slab of wood balanced across two sawhorses. He has a simple tool in his hand—damn if I know the name of it—and he's running it across the piece of wood, moving with the grain in long, slow, smooth, precise strokes. Little curls of wood peel away, and he brushes these away between strokes. Every ounce of his attention is on his work, and each movement is as slow and precise and methodical as the last.

I don't know how long I stand there, leaning against the side of the garage, watching him. But I realize I've calmed down, the anxiety and concern are gone, and I'm totally relaxed.

I could watch him forever, says a little voice inside me.

TEN

AFTER SEVERAL MINUTES, HE LOOKS UP AND SEES ME. "Sorry, I just..." He lets out a breath. "You wanted to see my workshop, sometime. Well, here it is."

I look around—the room is quite large and it is filled with all sorts of tools and equipment. Everything is arranged in the neat, obsessively orderly fashion I would expect of him. The tools are all old, made of wood and handworked metal. There is a stack of wood on the floor in one corner—a castoff pile, it looks like as all the pieces are different sizes and kinds and shapes. There are also several crates and boxes of metal parts—handles, knobs, pulls, hinges, hooks, knockers, locks, and other parts I don't know the names of—as well as stacks of wrought iron spindles and sundry other larger pieces of metal.

"It's amazing," I say, with unfeigned candor. "I love the way it smells in here."

He smiles. "Me too. Reminds me of Grandpa." He crosses the garage and hangs the tool on a peg, making sure it hangs just so before leaving it in place.

I spy a stool tucked under the workbench, which runs along the rear wall beneath the pegboard of tools. I go to it, slide it out, and sit on it, crossing my legs as demurely as I can—this isn't going to be a sexy conversation.

There's a jar of rectangular, thick pencils that look like they've been sharpened by hand, and Franco withdraws one of these pencils and goes over to the wood on the sawhorses, standing back and staring at it for a long silent moment before leaning over it and dragging the pencil carefully and precisely around the perimeter, marking the new shape.

He says nothing to me, and I realize I'm going to have to ask.

"Franco…what just happened? Why did you react like that?"

He ignores me as he continues to draw an oval inside the rectangle of the piece of wood. When he finishes the outline, he stands back, tucks the pencil behind his ear, and turns to face me. He just looks at me for a moment, and then sighs. There's another stool near mine, and he hooks it with a bare foot and pulls it out. There's a small block of partially worked wood on the workbench, just a vague shape—he sits on the stool, takes a small fixed-blade knife from another little cup, and starts whittling at the wood.

He still hasn't said a word.

"Franco?" I ask, wondering if he even heard me.

He just keeps whittling, but finally pauses and looks at me. "I was twenty-one. I met her at this big kegger. James and the others were there, too. It was a U-of-I party, lots of upperclassmen and lots of girls from several sororities. A real rager, out of control, the kind of thing that would get shut down by the cops if it wasn't out in the middle of a damn cornfield. She was by the bonfire with her friends, nursing a cup of beer, just watching and laughing and sticking with her friends. Which I totally understood, because I didn't really stray too far from Jesse, Ryder, James, and Renée either. Ryder knew I was crushing on her and dared me to go talk to her. So I did. Got a fresh cup of pissy-ass beer and went over." He shrugged. "That seemed like it, for me. I liked her, a lot. I called her the next day and asked her out—"

"You didn't wait three days?" I ask, teasing.

He snorts. "That bullshit is for pussies." He whittles a bit more, and I start to see a recognizable shape emerging from the wood. "We went out, and hit it off. Went on another date, hit it off. Two dates led to three, and then we'd been going on dates for two months, and she finally asked if we were exclusive."

"Were you anti-commitment even then?" I ask.

He twirls the knife in his fingers. "Eh...yes and no. Not as much as I am now, because of what happened, but yes, I was to an extent, even then."

"Why do you think that was?"

He goes back to whittling. "Shitty example growing up, I guess."

"Parents had a messy split?" I guess.

He shakes his head. "Nah, they're still together, actually."

"Something else?"

"It's complicated." He works the knife in a circle, digging out a little divot. "I'm from a long line of Irish Catholics on both sides. Real zealots, too. Not just Mass once in a while Catholics, but real-deal, super-committed stuff. You went to mass every Sunday; you confessed, you got confirmed, the whole thing. I have memories of going to Sunday Mass with Grandma and Grandpa and Mom and Dad, Dad's brother and his whole family, Mom's sister and hers... they're all from this area. There was a time when I was a kid when we all went to mass together every Sunday." He shrugs. "It was a big part of my childhood, to be honest."

"So how does this translate into what you just said?"

He carves a little ear, long and rounded on top.

"Catholics are vehemently against divorce, even under the worst circumstances. And my folks grew up in families that took the faith even more seriously than they did when I was growing up. Super stiff, formal, traditional backgrounds. You just did *not* get divorced, no matter what."

"I see…"

He pauses, eyeing his carving with a critical eye. "My parents were…they weren't suited for each other. Mom was super modern and forward-thinking, independent. Wanted a career, wanted to wait before having kids, wanted to travel, refused to wear skirts or dresses to Mass just to piss off her dad and grandfather. Dad was more traditional, wanted kids right away, wanted her to play the housewife and not work. They clashed a lot and, honestly, I've never been sure why they got married at all. I'm not sure if they ever even *liked* each other."

"Were you the reason they got married, maybe?" I ask.

"You mean, was Mom pregnant so they were forced to marry?" He shakes his head. "No, I did the math. I wasn't conceived until they'd been married almost six months. And they never had any other kids—I'm an only child. I've never understood it." Another sigh. "Things in my home, growing up, were…chaotic, at best. Dad was a heavy drinker, so was Mom. They were verbally abusive to each other, always shouting and calling names. Think of the stereotype for an Irish Catholic family from Chicago, and that was us. Dad was a die-hard Cubs fan, grilled in the winter, shoveled snow in shirtsleeves, drank Jameson as religiously as he went to Mass and confession. Never hit me, I should point out. Wasn't like that. But he and Mom would go at it, you know? Like, bad. Mom would throw plates and Dad would smack her sometimes, and Mom would smack back."

I wince. "Yikes. That sounds awful."

He nods. "It was shitty. They loved me, though, and I never doubted that. Dad took me to ball games and taught me to ride bikes and all that shit, and Mom fixed my scraped knees and walked me to school and packed my lunches. But once they started drinking and fighting with each other, I couldn't deal, so I'd ride my bike to Grandma and Grandpa's." He taps the workbench. "I bought their house from them when they moved into the nursing home."

I blink. "Wait…so this is your grandparents' house? This is the same garage where your grandpa taught you carpentry?"

He nods. "Yep. I haven't changed this garage at all, except to replace the siding, roof, and garage door. Inside is the same as when I was a kid. Different tools, maybe a bit cleaner and neater, but mostly the same."

"Wow. That's…that's really cool, Franco. No wonder it feels so…" I shrug. "I don't know. Homey. Nostalgic. I don't know."

He smiles. "Yeah, exactly. I've never had words for it either…at least not hokey ones."

I can't help the soft, tender expression I feel on my face. "So, what are the hokey ones?"

He hesitates. "I just…I feel Grandpa out here. He's here. I feel his spirit, his presence, whatever you want to say. When I'm out here, it's almost like I'm with him again."

"You must have really loved him."

He laughs. "Oh yeah. He was a real hard-ass, though. Don't get me wrong. Expected perfection. Probably where I get it. He'd make me redo a piece if I got one small thing wrong. An entire week's worth of work, he'd just trash it if I got it wrong. But it was out of love, wanting me to do my best and expect the best from myself."

"So, your parents."

He nods. "My parents…like I said, it was chaotic at best." Another long pause. "On top of the fighting, they were unfaithful to each other pretty consistently all my life. I remember cutting class and taking the bus downtown with my buddies as a kid, and seeing Dad on the street with another woman. He saw me, I saw him, and he just shooed me away. I asked him later, and he said I'd forget it if I knew what was good for me. A few weeks later I got sick at school so I came home early…and Mom was in bed with one of the neighbors. She told me to just keep my mouth shut. Same thing would happen regularly on both sides, and I realized eventually that they both knew the other was cheating, and they just…went along with it."

He goes back to carving. "And it's not like they didn't sleep with each other—the house I grew up in had real thin walls, you know? So I heard them going at it a *lot*, drunk and sober. So, between the drinking and the verbal and physical abuse and the infidelity, I just grew up with this distorted view of marriage. I *knew* other families weren't like that, but all my buddies growing up went through divorces with very few exceptions, and it just messed them up. So I was like, is it better or worse for them to get divorced? I wasn't sure, you know? Like, having two parents was cool, but they were fuckin' nuts. Mom fucked half the neighborhood, and most likely the mailman and a few contractors, and Dad had a little black book full of names with little marks next to each one, four lines in a row and then a fifth line across them, you know? Numbering how many times he'd slept with each. My dad was a *busy* man, lemme tell you. I happened to see that little black book once. I couldn't get over it."

"That's sad," I say. "And gross."

He nods. "I know." He sighs. "I guess I come by it honestly. Although I've never kept track, and I don't cheat."

"That doesn't seem like you, Franco," I said hazarding a guess. "So your parents' example soured you on monogamy and marriage to begin with, and then…"

He stops carving, holds the piece up; it's a little rabbit, about three inches tall, sitting on its hind legs, head twisted as it looks to one side. It looks so lifelike I almost expect it to dart away off his hand and hop across the workbench, but he's not quite finished yet.

He glances at me. "Then everything with James and Renée happened. You heard it from Jesse, or at least part of it, and some from Nina, it sounds like. The little scamp can't keep her mouth shut to save her life, God love her."

"Can you tell me what happened?"

"Since you know the shape of it, I can tell you how it affected me. If you want more than that, you'll have to ask James."

"No thanks. He scares me a little."

Franco chuckles. "He should. He is a little scary. You shoulda seen him fifteen, twenty years ago— you think he's a beast now? He was all-state offensive lineman at Illinois, and even went through an NFL combine."

"Like, to go pro?"

Franco nods. "Yep."

"But he didn't?

"Nope. It was a combination of reasons. He got in a car accident and hurt his knee pretty bad the year he did the combine, which he could have rehabbed. But Renée was against him going pro. While he was in the hospital, she asked him if he really loved football enough to want to do it every single day for the rest of his life until he got too old to play, or got hurt again. He thought about it, and thought some more, and realized he didn't love it that much. He just enjoyed it. But he had other passions, other things he enjoyed doing—namely, building. He'd been working for a construction company through most of high school, and he really liked it. He'd gotten some pretty big promotions, even in high school, and he saw a viable path forward in the company, so yeah, he let football go and pursued construction."

I shake my head in awe. "Wow. That's...I don't think many men who could have gone pro would have chosen not to."

He nods. "That's James. And honestly, that's Renée, and the effect she had on him. He'd have gone through physical therapy and rehabilitation to get his knee back in playing condition, and then gone pro. I don't think he ever questioned it until she flat out asked if he was sure that's what he wanted. That's how she was. Smart, thoughtful, practical. Always looking at things from a different angle."

Another long pause, as Franco examines his carving, which seems mostly complete. "James and Renée were just meant for each other. She balanced him out, challenged him, kept him guessing and thinking when he can be kind of a plodder, straight ahead, no stopping for anything kind of guy, and she needed him to keep her grounded. They were together all through high school, got married a year and a half later…and then they just did life. They spent a few years just being married, working, taking vacations, having fun. Then they wanted to start a family, but they had trouble with it." He pauses again. "That's part of James's story, though. Point is, they ended up with Nina and then Ella, and they were just deliriously happy. Quintessential family with a nice house and some land, two sweet kids, enough money to be content…and then Renée got pregnant again and they were even happier. It was all normal and fine, and she went in to have the baby, and…something happened. I'm not really sure what, but something went wrong and she died, and so did the baby."

"Jesus."

"Yeah." He's quiet again for a minute, sanding the figure he'd carved. "It was hell. He fell apart. All three of us quit our jobs and moved back to town to help him. All four of us lived with him and the girls for the first year and a half, until he was in a place where he could function without us. He'd barely been functioning, on any level, when we got there. Not bathing, not eating, not sleeping, not going to work. He was the general manager of the company then, second only to the owner, who had also lost his wife some years earlier, and he understood where James was at. So he gave him all the time he needed to get his shit together. We forced James to get back to normal, and then we hired a sitter and created a tag-team so the sitter and James's parents and in-laws could watch the kids for a few days, while we took him out on a three-day bender. Got him hammered, took him to a hotel, and got him to cry it out."

Franco is silent again.

"Eventually, he was able to deal with being alone with the girls, and we all figured our own shit out. We'd sort of…put our lives on hold, in a way. James needed us, you know? So, we were there. That's when James started Dad Bod. The owner of the company James had worked for, like, half his life at that point, wanted to retire, so he sold the whole thing to James for a steal."

He eyes me. "Yeah, I know—where does this tie into my earlier reaction? What happened to James after Renée died really fucked with my head. Like, I already felt like marriage was bullshit, and love was stupid and fake, and then after Renée died and James just completely fell apart, I was like, why the hell would I want to put myself through that, even if love was real? I mean, *they* had it all, the real deal…and look what happened to James." He shrugs. "I developed the four-fuck rule not long after that."

I frowned at him. "You skipped something kind of important, I think."

He sighs. "Maria."

"Your ex."

He nods. "Yeah. Maria."

"You were hoping I wouldn't notice you'd glossed over that?"

He laughs quietly. "A little, yeah. I don't like talking about it." Another long pause; he seems finished with the rabbit, and he sets it on the counter, twisting it this way and that, examining it again. "So, Maria and I got married six months after we met."

"A little fast."

He growls. "Yeah, no shit. Everyone warned me. James flat out didn't like her, Ryder thought she was hot but didn't trust her, and Jesse told me I was dumbass for taking it beyond a little fun with her."

"Ouch. But you didn't listen?"

"Nope. I was *in loooove*." He turns the word into

a mocking, whining drawl. "Infatuated was more like it. The truth, unpalatable as it may be, was that she was hot as fuck, but it was surface hot, you know? Like, she had no depth. I see that now, after twenty years, but I was clueless then."

"Twenty-one and blinded by the titties, huh?" I ask, laughing.

He frowns. "Yeah, pretty much." A pause. "She was just...glamorous, I guess. A little shy, but a tiger once you got to know her. Loved the fast life, shiny things. She liked me because I was a middle finger in the air to her very traditional Columbian parents, who wanted her to marry a good Columbian boy. I mean, I was Catholic so I had that going for me, but I was white, and they hated that. Plus, she was maybe just as blind and infatuated as I was."

"Cock-blindness is real, Franco."

He laughs. "Oh, I know." He nudges the rabbit toward me, and I pick it up, looking at it; it's a beautiful piece, a true work of art...and he did it just as something to do with his hands while he talked. "It was great for the first six months to a year. We got a nice little place downtown, I had a job at a condo remodeling company specializing in high-end units, and I got paid like a boss. But things started to go downhill fast after the first year. She wanted a new car, and then she wanted a bigger ring barely two years in. And then she wanted us to go out more, even though I was working eighty hours a week to afford the pricey apartment with views of the lake that she had to have. She would stay out after work and not tell me where she was or what she was doing. I wanted to trust her, to be confident in what we had, but it was hard, you know? Because, deep down, I didn't really trust her, or myself, or our marriage. I think deep down, I knew we were playing house, you know? Two dumb kids playing at marriage. It wasn't real for either of us."

"That sucks."

He laughs bitterly. "Yeah, tell me about it." He sighs. "That was just the beginning."

"Oh, no."

"Oh, yes. Three years in, and things were terrible. She was never home, always out with her friends, shopping, spending money. She had a job, but it was fluff, paid shit and nowhere near enough to cover her spending habit. But it was the being gone all the time that got me, though, you know? Like, I'd come home to an empty condo, make my own dinner, eat alone, go to bed alone, and she'd come home at whatever time stinking of alcohol. I'd go out with her after work every once in a while, but I had to get up early for work so it was hard, and I just didn't like her friends or the whole crowd she hung out with. They were all vapid, shallow, and selfish—kinda like her, I guess. Then, one day I was at work and my boss was sick as a dog. It was early, like barely seven—I'd gone in to finish something, and Maria hadn't even come home from the night before. That happened a lot, so whatever, but that morning I had a niggling feeling in my gut, but I ignored it."

"This doesn't sound good."

"Yeah. So my boss sent me to the pharmacy to get some Dayquil and shit. Well, this pharmacy was near the jobsite, but far from our condo. Nowhere near where any of our friends lived, and nowhere near where they partied either. So, I'm in the pharmacy, looking for the medicine for Rob. And I hear a voice up by the pharmacist's counter. A familiar female voice. Asking for Plan B."

"Shit."

He just sucks in a breath, holds it, stares at the counter, and then lets it out slowly. "I froze in place for a minute. Like, no way. What? Why would she need Plan B? We always used a condom and she hadn't even been home the night before." He shakes his head. "Then it sank in. She needed Plan B because she had just had sex—unprotected sex—with some other dude."

"Ouch. That fucking sucks."

"So I got my shit together and went to stand behind her as she was waiting for the pharmacist to complete the order. She had a drink in her hand, an iced coffee, I think. She was done up, made up, looking prim and proper as ever. She even had an overnight bag, which I guess she kept in her car and I just never realized it. So, yeah, she opened the box right there and took the pill in the store, and then turned around and literally bumped into me."

"What did she say?"

He laughs, once again with vicious bitterness. "She was shaken, because she knew she'd been caught red-handed, and that there was no point in even trying to deny it. So she didn't. I didn't know what to say, so I just turned around and left. Went back to work, went home. She was there, and we got in this huge fight. She accused me of working too much, never being home, so she was lonely, what was she supposed to do, blah-blah-fucking-blah."

"So she had the nerve to try to blame you?"

"Oh yeah. But out of fear, because her parents were even more Catholic than mine, if you know what I mean. Divorce wasn't an option for either of us. Like, just no. Her parents would disown her if she got a divorce, and mine would stop talking to me for who knows how long."

"So what'd you do?"

"I stayed with her." He sets his carving knife back in its place and scoops the shavings into his palm and discards them in a nearby trashcan. "For another two, almost three years."

"Three years? Why?"

"Divorce wasn't an option. I don't know how to explain it if you didn't grow up like we did." He shrugs. "It was three years of hell. I hated her. I got myself tested for STDs, and then refused to touch her. I worked, and I went home, slept in a different bed. Avoided her. She tried her damnedest to get me back, made all sorts of promises, tried to seduce me, every trick in the book. But I just...I couldn't do it. I'd grown up seeing my parents hooking up with different people, and I hated that as a kid. My wife, cheating on me? Oh, fuck no. More proof that marriage was bullshit."

"And you did that for three years?"

"Yep."

I blink hard, thinking. "You didn't touch her?"

"Nope."

"At all, for three years?"

"Nope."

"And you never cheated?"

"Fuck no. I'd have been justified, some would say, but that's not me. So no, I didn't touch her and I didn't cheat."

"So you were celibate for three years?"

"I got real acquainted with my own hand, let me

tell you." He sighs. "If you really want all the gory details, there was one time, near the end, that I let her touch me. I was lonely as fuck, and it was a weekend. She was gone, as usual, because after it became clear I wasn't giving in, she went back to her old ways. So, Friday night, I got wasted at home alone. It was awful, and only made me feel shittier. So I went to bed. Woke up to a hell of a dream—my wife loved me again; she'd never been unfaithful. She was in my bed, sucking my cock, and it felt amazing. It was only afterward that I realized I wasn't dreaming, that she really was in my bed. She'd gotten drunk, come home, saw me in bed and got horny or something, decided to try one more time to get me back. That, apparently, was just her way of doing it. I kicked her out, and I wasn't nice about it either. I was…well, I was pretty awful, actually. Said some really nasty shit to her. I was still drunk, but it doesn't excuse it. I just…I felt nasty, slimy, and just…dirty, for having let her do that to me. I just wanted nothing to do with her."

"Oh god, Franco. That is so terrible. I don't even know what to say."

He nods. "I know. I'm over that. I'm just explaining how I felt then." He pauses for a minute. "Actually, that was kind of the tipping point for me, now that I think about it. I was talking to James about it on the phone—he'd never understood why I wouldn't just divorce her cheating skank ass, and I never had a good explanation beyond the Catholic guilt thing, and my parents." He pauses again. "And then James was like, dude, the approval of your parents means nothing to you. You're not a practicing Catholic anymore. You're ten times the man your old man is, and you deserve to be happy. If not happy, then at least free. And who gives a flying rat fuck how it makes Maria feel? She's the one who brought this all on herself."

"Hooray for James!"

He laughs. "Yeah, hooray for James. He still had Renée then, and he was pretty optimistic about life.

"So I went and got papers drawn up that same day. Took them to her, lied to her face and told her I had proof she was cheating, and that if she signed the papers now I'd make sure she got her share of what I had, which was a decent chunk, back then, or she could fight it and get nothing."

"She fought?"

"Oh no, nothing that simple. She bargained. Bartered. Nickel-and-dimed me for every last penny I had. She knew I was desperate to get clear of her, and she used that to fuck me over. And I let her. Gave her the condo overlooking Lake Michigan, the fancy new car I'd bought her right before I found out she was cheating, plus some investments I'd made."

"Damn," I say, whistling. "She fucked you *hard*."

"I wanted out. It was just stuff, just money, what did it matter? I was truly desperate. Once I realized I could be free of her, that I didn't have to stay with her out of some misplaced obligation or religious guilt or something, I was crazy to get free, so I just agreed to everything." He shrugs. "I left that marriage at age twenty-seven, flat broke and angry as hell at the world. I got a one-room basement apartment in one of the most dangerous areas of Chicago, worked my ass off to rebuild my savings. Spent the next ten years or so working my way up at the company, got to the point that I was on the verge of making the leap up into high-level management. And then, the very day I was supposed to sit for an interview for a management position at the company I'd been working for, I got the call from James that Renée had died in childbirth."

"Jesus, Franco."

"Yeah. I'd been coming down here every weekend to hang out with them for years at that point—I'd just seen Renée the weekend before. I'd felt the baby kick." He's quiet, wrought with memory. "Then bam, gone. Dead. No warning, no goodbye—one of my best friends and my best friend's wife, gone. So I quit my job that day with zero notice, broke my lease, packed up, and came down here. Lived with James and the girls until he was on his feet, and then moved in with Grandma and Grandpa until they moved into the home, at which point I bought this place."

"When did your grandparents pass?"

"About a year after they went into the home. Grandma died first, and Grandpa went about a week later, because he couldn't be without her. He told me as much. I was visiting him and he told me he wanted to go be with Beth. He was lucid to the very end. I held his hand and told him to go be with Grandma, that I'd be fine. He asked if I was sure, and I said yeah. I told him I loved him, and he closed his eyes like he was going to sleep. Got this big smile on his face, and just stopped breathing." He's silent a long, long time. "Damnedest thing I ever saw. Just…gone, by his own choice, naturally. He just…let go."

"That really beautiful, actually."

"They were together sixty-four years." He sighs. "If anything could make me believe in love, it was them."

I think of what we just experienced together, and I wonder if that applies to me at all. But the moment that thought enters my head, I mentally and emotionally recoil. No! Don't wonder that. I don't want that responsibility, that burden. I don't believe in love any more than he does, so why would I want to factor into him believing it?

I don't.

Simple.

Franco stands up, crosses to the pile of discarded wood pieces, squats and sorts through the pile until he finds something he finds suitable in some way, and returns with it to the workbench. Curious, I watch while he twists the piece of wood this way and that— it's a block about six inches by four inches by three inches, a pale, soft-looking wood. He selects a different knife than the one he'd been using; this knife is thicker, longer, with a differently shaped blade. Slowly, carefully, he begins shaving off slices of wood at a particular spot, each movement of the knife made at a precise angle and for a specific purpose.

He glances at me as he carves. "So. I showed you mine, now you show me yours."

"I was afraid you'd say that."

ELEVEN

FRANCO QUIRKS AN EYEBROW AT ME. "YOU HAD TO KNOW I would ask. You can't think I'd tell you my deepest, most painful memory and not expect the same in return from you, can you?"

I laugh. "No, I knew you'd ask." I take a moment to watch his slow, sure movements of the knife, gathering the courage to tell my own pain. "Mine is pretty similar to yours, actually. It's all rooted in childhood, you know? I've actually got an Irish background myself, obviously, with a name like Donovan. We weren't Catholic at all, though. I mean, we were by background, but none of my family was practicing in any meaningful way beyond Christmas Mass, Easter Mass, things like that. My dad was—is, to this day—a piece of shit. Human garbage, and I don't say that lightly. There is, legitimately, no human being on the planet I despise more than my father."

Franco's eyebrows shoot up. "Damn. He must

really suck, then."

I blow out a breath. "Yeah, that's the understatement of the millennium." I pause, thinking, and then continue. "I don't feel much better about my mom, but for totally different reasons."

I rarely talk about or even think about this, so it's difficult to get the words out, and I pause frequently in the telling.

"They met at a bar, hooked up a few times, dated on and off for a few months, and then my mom came up pregnant. She wheedled enough money out of him for an abortion, but couldn't seem to keep clear of Dad for whatever stupid fucking reason. Went right back to him. Ended up pregnant again, with me, this time. Why she didn't abort me, too, I'm not sure. Maybe he wouldn't pony up the money again, or couldn't, or she didn't find out in time. I don't know."

Franco frowns at me. "It couldn't have been, oh I don't know…maternal instincts to want to keep you?"

I laugh at that, and not kindly. "Oh no. Nope. Definitely wasn't that. Mom never wanted to be a mom, and she told me as much in so many words when I was…eighteen? Nineteen? She didn't come out and say she didn't want *me*, per se, just that she'd never wanted kids. I'm pretty sure as soon as she was able to afford it, after I was born, she went and got her tubes tied so there'd be no risk of getting saddled with any more damn kids." I shrug. "So there's that element—I was a burden to her, and even more so to my father. They were never married, and still aren't, but they've been circling each other for forty-some years, getting into blow-out fights, breaking up, getting back together—it's happened too many times in my life to even begin to count. I'd stopped keeping track by the time I was in fifth grade. The cycle was this: Dad couldn't keep his dick in his pants, but he's a lazy good-for-nothing son of a bitch who can't keep a job, can't do his own laundry, can't pay his own bills, can't cook his own food, so he needs my mom. And she, in turn, is lonely and sad and hardwired for codependency. She needs to be needed—just not by me; I've never counted in the cycle. So Daddy Dearest would go out drinking, pick up bar tail, get caught cheating because he's the least tactful or circumspect human ever to walk this earth, and my mom would lose her shit, break up with him, kick him out, swearing up one side of the trailer and down the other that it was the last damn time."

Franco has the block into a recognizable shape at this point—a bird, it looks like, something wheeling on a wingtip, a raptor with a sharp beak and extended talons. All this in a matter of minutes, with a few economical strokes of his knife; now that he has the major shape outlined, he switches to a smaller, sharper knife for more detailed work.

"Well, about two weeks later she'd be horny and lonely and maudlin and had herself convinced he'd learned his lesson, and that he'd be sick of McDonald's and Mad Dog and dirty clothes, and he'd come crawling back and turn on the charm. And ohhhh yes, good ol' Pop could be a charming motherfucker when he wanted to be; even I wasn't immune to it as a kid. He'd lie and manipulate and promise and charm and wheedle his way back home and into her bed, and things would sort of stabilize for, like, a week or even a month here and there." I sigh, fiddling with the rabbit he'd carved. "Then the whole thing would start over again. He'd stray, and she'd find a condom wrapper in his laundry or lipstick on him somewhere or she'd get a call from one of her many gossip hound friends telling her he'd been seen stepping out with so-and-so. He never really tried to hide it, I don't think. I mean, Dad's a lot of shit, but he's not stupid. He just didn't care enough to bother hiding it. I don't know. And Mom is just…weak. Needy, and without enough self-esteem to kick his ass to the curb for good."

"That sounds about as chaotic as my own childhood."

"Oh yeah. And the fights they'd get in? Oh man. Cops were at our door regularly. I was on a first-name basis with a few of them by high school because they got called to our trailer so often. I'd have to sit outside with one of them while the other went in to talk to Mom and Dad, and sometimes they'd take me for ice cream or to Seven-Eleven for a Slurpee. I honestly wished more often than I care to admit that one of those officers would just take me to *their* home, or at least just leave me on the street and not make me go back home. I was so sick of Mom and Dad's bullshit that being homeless sounded more appealing most days."

Franco's eyes are sympathetic. "I know the feeling, trust me."

I wave a hand, hating how even now it hurts to talk about this old crap. "I know better, now. I was lucky to have a roof over my head, food in my belly, and that they never hit me, and that Dad never did anything gross to me, or let his friends do anything. I mean, I knew plenty of kids, just in my trailer park, who went through all that and worse, so I knew even then that I was better off than a lot of them. But it still just sucked, you know?"

"It's tempting to compare yourself both ways, isn't it?" Franco says, pausing to look at me. "To people who have it worse, and to people who have it better. But you can't. You can only really understand what you're going through yourself."

"So true, that," I say. "So, yeah. That was my

childhood, and it really messed up my view of love and marriage. Like, if *that's* love, I want zero fucking part of it. And, honestly, I had nothing better to even compare it to. My grandparents weren't in the picture and never have been, for reasons I'm not certain about. Family dysfunction, I guess—the kind of shit all of them never got over, so they just don't see each other. I've seen them for Christmas a few times, and I'd get the occasional birthday card, but that's about it."

"And then?"

I laugh. "You just want to get to the really juicy stuff, huh?"

He shrugs, grinning at me. "Yep, basically."

"And then...I was so eager to escape Mom and Dad's cycle of horse crap that I found ways to stay at school. Which for me ended up being sports. I played volleyball, basketball, tennis, soccer, did track...anything and everything, as long as it meant I could stay at school and practice, or work out. By junior year I was one of our school's top stars in track and field, volleyball, and soccer. I was literally always either at practice or in the gym. I had it so I only had to go home to sleep, and only then for as little amount of time as I could manage and still function, which is a habit I've never been able to break, even to this day. I got almost a full-ride between volleyball and track scholarships, and the summer after I graduated I moved to an apartment on campus and never went back."

"Was that with Imogen?" Franco asks.

I shake my head. "No, actually. We've never lived together. We were best friends all through school, and we ended up going to the same college just by virtue of accident or fate or whatever, but we never lived together."

"Oh. I guess I just assumed you had."

"Nah, we almost did, but we decided against it. I think we both knew we'd kill each other. We're too different in the way we live, so our friendship was better off with a little space built into it."

Franco laughs, flipping his knife between his fingers. "Oh man, I can't even begin to tell you how tough it was, that year and a half Ryder, James, Jesse, and me all lived together in that three-bedroom, two-bathroom bungalow. Jesse and I shared a room for the first two months, until we convinced James to let us update his basement into a workable living space for one of us. So then Jesse moved down there and I stayed in the bedroom, while Ryder stayed in the garage, which left one bedroom for James, one for the girls, and one for me, with Ryder in the garage and Jesse in the basement."

"The garage?" I ask.

"Yeah. One of the first things James did when he bought the place twelve or fifteen years ago was to turn the garage into an extra room, so that's where Ryder stayed from the start. The garage is James's official Dad Bod Contracting office, now." He pauses, examines his carving, twisting it this way and that to look for flaws, spots one, and sets to work fixing it. "Jesse and I almost killed each other on a daily basis while we shared a room, though. We nearly came to blows a few times. James never knew, though, and still doesn't. I know he knows it was tough for us at times, especially early on, but he never knew how hard it was for two grown-ass men, used to independence, to share a single tiny bedroom."

"It's amazing that you guys did that for him."

He shrugs. "Not really. He's our best friend. Our brother. We'd do anything for him, and he'd do anything for us—and we have, in every possible way over the years." He eyes me. "You can't tell me you and Imogen aren't the same way. In fact, I know you are—I've seen it."

I nod. "Well, yeah, but you guys quit jobs, broke leases, moved, and shared a house. Those are not small sacrifices."

He waves a hand at me. "Enough about that. Get to the good stuff." He eyes me with humor. "And by that I mean the really horrible shit that probably scarred you as bad Maria did me."

In a patently ridiculous attempt to leaven my own mood, I make the wooden rabbit hop around the workbench, singing "Little Bunny Foo-Foo", tapping the carving on the bench at every repetition of "bop-pin' 'em on the head." It makes Franco laugh, which makes me laugh, but I can't put off telling Franco the unvarnished truth any longer.

"Okay, so I met Jared my sophomore year at State. He was an all-state quarterback in high school, and ended up all-state in college, too. I met him on the track—we were both doing wind-sprints early one morning. He was the real-deal golden boy, you know? All-American good ol' boy from the Illinois countryside. Drove his grandfather's restored pick-up, lettered in three sports in high school, prom king, valedictorian—the star quarterback who led his team to state championships three years in a row, because he was the starting varsity QB by sophomore year in the most competitive high school football program in the state. Tall, built, perfect blond hair and pretty blue eyes and a dazzling white smile."

Franco rolls his eyes. "Sounds like a douche."

I laugh. "Well, he was, and still is probably, but I didn't know that then."

"Well, of course not. With those kinds of qualifications, who would ever think that of him?"

"And to be fair, he was really good at covering his douchey-ness."

"They always are."

"They?" I ask, eyeing him curiously.

"The biggest douches on campus. I didn't go to college in the traditional sense—I went to trade school via an apprenticeship, so my personal experience was different than most, but I spent a lot of time at Urbana-Champaign with James and Renée, so I got to be pretty familiar with how places like that work."

"Right. Well, he was the king of the campus at State, like he'd been the king of the campus in high school—it was a continuation of high school for him, I think, just on a larger scale. More attention, more fanfare, more glory." I pause, gathering my thoughts and memories. "So, you have to be aware that I was… pretty much the opposite of him. A nobody. I mean, sure I set a few records for volleyball and track, but who really cares about that? I was the tough girl from the trailer park. Back then, I didn't really dress the way I do now; I lived in athletic gear—track pants, hoodies, gym shorts, cross-trainers, nothing tight or revealing. And by the time I met Jared, I had a pretty interesting reputation already."

He lifts an eyebrow. "Meaning what?"

"Meaning I'd been assaulted on campus late one night my freshman year—only, I kicked the shit out of the guy so bad he had to be hospitalized. And then another guy tried to pick me up in the cafeteria one day, and I publicly roasted him, as the kids on the internet like to say. I mean, I was brutal. Shit like that happened a lot to me, and I developed a reputation as a hard-ass ice queen. I had no patience for guys, be-yond…you know. Getting into their dorms and back out when I was done with minimal drama."

"And then you met Jared."

"Exactly. So he's this golden boy, and I'm the girl who beats guys up and roasts them in the cafeteria so bad they all but run away crying. I've mellowed a lot since college, if you'll believe it." I laugh, and Franco laughs with me. "It was an unlikely pairing at best. But I could go to the gym, or the track, and keep up with him—and not just keep up, but challenge him. Obviously I lifted less in terms of weight, but he had a hard time matching me in terms of raw intensity. He liked that. He wasn't…it didn't faze his sense of manhood, I guess—and it does a lot of guys—but I'm never willing to back down or put out less than my full effort."

"Nor should you." He eyes me. "You're a beast, for real. And that's sexy as fuck, to me."

"Thanks for that." I can't help a smile, but I've got more to tell. "Anyway. Jared wasn't threatened by me, and that made me feel like I could be…I don't know—a girl. Stupid, but I don't know how else to put it. I'd had to be tough all the time—my trailer park growing up was a rough place, and my apartment wasn't great either, so I was always this tough, strong, take-no-shit chick. Still am, actually. But Jared let me feel like a girl. Still not exactly what I'm trying to say, but I don't know how to put it."

"He made you feel safe and feminine." He's not looking at me as he says this, but somehow his full attention is still on me, and fiercely intense.

I catch my breath. "Yeah. Exactly." I breathe again, after a moment of pushing all kinds of emotions away. "So...somehow, we ended up together. Girls *hated* me, after that. I mean, real hate. Death threats, evil eyes, nasty notes, real high school shit from these dumbass girls who were supposed to be grown women. All because I dared date *the* Jared Ellis. *Me*—the ice bitch. He didn't seem to care about any of that, and neither did I."

"So far so good, right?"

I laugh. "Yeah, so far so good." I sigh, humor fading quickly. "I started embracing some of my femininity with him—he encouraged me to wear girlier clothes, and I tried it, for him. I hated it, but I did it. And I got attention for it—girls making fun of me and being more jealous than ever, and guys trying to hit on me before they realized I was Jared's girlfriend. I had a love-hate thing with that attention. I liked feeling and looking more feminine, and I liked the attention, but I also hated it at the same time. I dove headfirst into my relationship with Jared. Just blind, headfirst, all-in. I lived at his dorm as much as I did my own apartment, and took the role of girlfriend as seriously as I took studying and working out. I was happy. I loved him. He loved me. He was the antithesis of everything my dad was—Jared was proof that decent men existed because, until him, I'd been sure a good-looking and decent man was as much a myth as unicorns and one hundred percent effective birth control."

"Funny that you put those two things together," Franco remarks, finally finishing carving the eagle and beginning to sand it.

"Yeah, well, the little girl in me always wanted to believe in unicorns, and the woman of loose morals in me always wanted to believe that birth control would totally protect me from disease and pregnancy."

"Your Catholic is showing."

I laugh hard at that. "No kidding. It pops out now and then." I continue my story—and now I'm getting to the hard part. "We dated sophomore year, junior year, and senior year. We were like, six months from graduation and I was sure he was going to propose any day. I had my acceptance speech ready, and had even practiced it in the mirror, as embarrassing as that sounds. And I feel it's important to note that at no time did I ever suspect a thing, and I was *looking* for reasons to distrust him. Even then, hopelessly in love, I was still skeptical and cynical and suspicious. But there was just…nothing. So, keep that in mind as I tell you the rest."

"Uh-oh."

"Yeah, uh-oh. I was out with Imogen and a few other girls. It was a time-apart night for Jared and I—I'd always insisted on regular nights out apart, me with my girls, he with his boys. I thought it was healthy, you know? Keep it fresh; keep my independence to some degree at least. So I was out with them, at a bar drinking, dancing, just girls being college girls. Well, the bar we were at started to feel stale, you know? So we bailed, headed for a different place. We had a few places we rotated regularly and, for some reason, none of us wanted to go to any of the usual spots. So, we picked a bar across town, way out of our usual stomping grounds. We rolled in, bought drinks; the single girls angled for the good-looking guys…you know the routine. There was this darker area near the back, behind the pool tables. There were a couple ratty couches, an arcade machine, and a coffee table kind of thing—a cool little hangout. I saw a few guys I knew from campus hanging out, some from the football team, some from the gym, but whatever, right?

None of them were in Jared's immediate crew, so I didn't even get a red flag when I saw them."

"Shit. This is making me queasy with anticipation," Franco says.

"Because you know what's coming, don't you?" I sigh, nodding. "Yeah. I went over and started talking to the guys. Just talking, not flirting or anything, just making conversation. And then I had to pee. I was laughing at something one of the guys said and not really paying attention as I headed for the bathrooms, which were right around the corner. So I went into the wrong one—quickly noticing, oops, those are urinals, and this is the boys' bathroom. No big deal, I haven't even closed the door behind me, so I'll just back out and pretend nothing happened...except I heard funny sounds coming from one of the stalls. And god, wouldn't you know—that grunt sounded *awfully* familiar? I peeked down, saw a pair of girl's knees on the floor, and a pair of jeans around a pair of very, very familiar, perfectly white Nike shoes. I knew those shoes—I'd watched him polish and clean them obsessively many times."

"Betrayed."

"I didn't freeze. Oh no, not me." I let out a breath. "I left the men's room, went to the ladies', did my thing, and went back out to the guys—all of whom were somewhat anxiously watching for my reaction.

I kept my shit together and acted like nothing was wrong. I hung around for a second, and then went to find my girls. I hid at the bar in the center of my group and kept watch. Sure enough, a few minutes later Jared comes out grinning like a fool, buckling his jeans, and this dumb little cheerleader bitch follows him out, wiping her mouth and hanging on him like he's Jesus. I mean, you should've seen the fawning look in her eyes. You'd think he was Justin Timberlake or something, the way she gazed adoringly at him."

"Yuck."

"Yeah. And he was...god, he was *gloating*. High-fiving his buddies, laughing, making rude gestures as he obviously detailed the blowjob he'd just gotten from Misty the cheerleader, or whatever her name was."

Franco snorts. "Damn, girl—you're still fired up about this."

I glare. "Yeah, I guess I am. So what?"

He holds up his hands, palms out. "So nothing. It's a long time ago, is all."

"And you're not still pissed at Maria for what she did?"

He sighs. "No, I guess I am."

"Exactly." I unroll and reroll the sleeve of my borrowed shirt. "I left, and started plotting my revenge."

"Oh dear." He sighs. "You didn't confront him there then?"

"Oh, hell no. I had bigger plans. I started following him. I was good at it too—he never knew I was there. I could've been a CIA agent, the way I tailed him. I took photographs like a private investigator and, bit by bit, I realized that he'd been playing me—elaborately, I might add—the whole time. It wasn't just one girl sucking him off in the bathroom of a campus bar. It was Shelley the med school major, in her dorm, after chemistry class on Mondays, and Abby the journalism student and marching band drum major on Tuesdays between European lit and Business Accounting. Wednesday was Rebecca, early in the morning, before his first class, and she was the most unlikely of his side pieces—she was a goth when goths were long-since passé, and he was literally everything she seemed to rail against. Thursday was Janelle late at night after he left my place; she was a drama nerd, library science major, and secret slut, apparently."

"Secret slut?" he asks, laughing.

"Oh man. In the process of all this, I discovered a lot of stuff about a lot of people. I was only stalking Jared, but I found out things about others just by accident. Such as that Janelle, who had this persona of nerdy innocence, complete with cat-eye glasses and sweaters and pleated skirts, and never swore or had boyfriends, was actually more active than I'd been before Jared. She had more guys than Jared did girls! She was just super tactful and quiet about it, and as organized as you'd imagine a library science major would be." I wave a hand. "Whatever. She was actually really cool, and we were friends for a while after college, until she moved to D.C. to work at the Library of Congress.

"Anyway. Where was I? Friday—Friday was Brit, bubbly, sprightly, giggly sorority girl majoring in sugar babying and high-end escorting. True story, actually—that's what she was, Jared was just her for-fun go-to. They met after lunch in her dorm. And all this was just his regular rotation girls. There were countless more random hookups, usually at night, at that bar."

Franco's eyebrows are raised. "Busy guy, Jesus. He must have had the stamina of a goddamn racehorse to keep up with that schedule."

I make a disgusted face. "I guess so, because he was with me regularly on top of all that." I shudder.

"How long did you stalk him?"

"It wasn't actually stalking, it was…revenge-driven research," I say, archly. "And for about three weeks. Until I had sufficient evidence collected. In the meantime, I pretended to be suffering from a long-term bout of the stomach bug, and buried in schoolwork, just so I didn't have to let him touch me."

"That was going to be my next question."

"Yeah, no—I never touched him again, sexually, after the day I caught him in the bathroom."

"So, what did you do with that research?"

I sigh. "I had a good friend who worked for the school newspaper."

"Uh-oh."

I nod. "Yeah. I got her to help me put the photographs into a spread, complete with a timeline of his activities. I didn't have anything against any of the girls, so I blurred their faces out, and used fake names, although anyone who knew them would know who it was. And then we published it as a front-page exclusive."

Franco rubs his jaw. "Let me guess—it backfired."

I nod. "Yeah. Turned me into the laughingstock of the entire fucking school—I guess everyone knew except me. Even the girls he was fucking in rotation knew there were others, just not who." I stand up, pace, and sit back down. "I worked out with a guy who knew Jared in high school, and he told me this was just his M.O.—a regular rotation of girls on the side, plus a clueless girlfriend. He had the system down pat, how to keep everyone separate, how to avoid suspicion and getting caught. He just didn't factor in me and my friends varying our routine, since we never did, except that one time."

"Was it the cheating that hurt the most, or the fact that you were the clueless girlfriend?"

"It was everything. The cheating, the obviousness of it all. I mean, he wasn't really hiding it—he'd walk around in public with these girls, he just wouldn't be publicly affectionate with them. But everyone saw them coming and going, and knew what was up, except me. And *I* saw him with them myself, I just prided myself on not being jealous, on trusting him to have female friends without going apeshit." I sigh, rubbing my face. "The fact that I was the clueless girlfriend? Yeah, that hurt. But so did the fallout of my stupid, naive revenge. I thought I was taking him down, you know? Like, tarnish the sterling rep of the school's golden boy. Apparently, his rep went deeper. Guys thought he was the man because he could haul down all this ass and not get caught by his girlfriend, and girls thought he was a pig, but they didn't care because he was hot and they just wanted him for his cock. Which was, honestly, pretty magnificent. And he was good with it, too. Which made it all the worse—because the stories about him were all true. Girls would spread stories about how great he was in bed and how big and amazing his cock was, and I just thought they were all jealous, like, how could they know? That was the one thing that should've clued me in earlier, but I just dismissed it as jealous gossip. But all the stories were true, which was what, for some reason, burned my ass almost more than anything. Stupid, but true."

I have to pause to gather myself, and Franco just listens, watches, and waits.

"Then, just as icing on the cake, after my revenge-reveal article published, my so-called friend who helped me publish the piece revealed in another op-ed that she knew all along that Jared was banging other girls, and she knew how everyone would react—laughing at me, and only cementing his rep on campus—*and* that she herself had fucked him several times in the library."

"Well fuck."

"So I only managed to burn myself. Everyone laughed at me. They'd always laughed at me, just behind my back, but after that it was to my face." I have to choke back a knot in my throat. "Ruined me at the school—and it's not like there was much to ruin, since I never really cared about my social status all that much...or so I told myself. But being Jared's girlfriend *had*, annoyingly enough, afforded me a popularity I couldn't have achieved on my own, and it *did* feel nice, even if was only because of him and not me."

"Fuck, Audra—that's brutal."

"The rest of my time at the school was utter agony. Just pure hell. He went open with everything—started flaunting his rotation. A few girls bailed, not wanting to be open about it, but he replaced them easily enough. He was like a…like a pimp, except all the sluts were selling themselves to him for free." I groan. "Stupid metaphor, but you get what I mean."

"That was a simile, actually," Franco points out with a smirk.

"You're seriously correcting my English right now?" I demand, half laughing. "Some nerve, asshole."

He just laughs. "I'm just messing with you."

"Not in the mood to be messed with, Franco."

"Sorry, sorry." He smiles, winking. "Anyway. So that was what cemented your hatred of love and relationships?"

I nod. "Yep. I spent the next ninety days after the story broke celibate, as in not a damn thing, not even with myself. And then…" I sigh. "And then, the month before graduation, I did something a little crazy."

"Uh-oh. Crazier than going Magnum PI on your boyfriend?"

I bob my head side to side. "That's debatable. I vowed I would erase Jared from my system, and get over him by getting under as many guys as I could, as further revenge. So, I slept with a different guy every single day for a month."

Franco whistles. "Wow. That's some interesting revenge."

I eye him sidelong, watching for his reaction. "Gross, huh?"

He shakes his head. "Nah. I'm in no position to judge. After my divorce from Maria was finalized and I had my own place, I sort of went nuts, too. Brought home a different girl every night, played the single Don Juan, until I got tired of the whole stupid game."

I nod. "Same here. It was fun for a while, then it was just exhausting and too much work. And then I graduated, got a job out here and started building my clientele."

Silence, then.

He says nothing, I say nothing—but something is boiling inside me, and I don't want to acknowledge it, or admit it into my thoughts, or past my lips.

No, no, no.

Don't say it, Audra.

"But I have one more thing to say, Franco. What we did, tonight, was more than just sex."

I can't believe I said it.

Franco sighs. Nods. "Yeah, I know."

"And not just because we forgot a condom."

"I know."

"And we just traded our deepest, darkest, most

painful secrets."

"We did."

I stare at him, waiting for him to say something more. "And?" I say, when he remains silent.

He sighs again. "And what, Audra?"

"What now?"

He shrugs, his face carefully blank. "And now... nothing."

I feel nothing at hearing those words. I refuse to feel anything. There's no punch to the chest at his words. No catch in my throat, or burn in my eyes. I feel nothing. I'm the ice bitch. Eat your heart out, Elsa.

How long do I sit in silence, refusing to feel? A whole minute? Longer? Definitely longer. An eternity, maybe. Or just a lifetime. I don't know. Long enough for the silence to develop a coating of hoarfrost.

"Okay." It's all I say for another long moment. But I have to say more, to keep the ice frozen solid. "And nothing. I just wondered where you stood about the whole thing...and now I know."

I rise from the stool and leave the garage workshop, exiting the comfort and warmth, and the familiar scent of wood and sawdust and age. I'm halfway to the house when I hear his voice ring out.

"Audra?"

I stop, turn, and see him in the warm incandescent

orange-yellow glow, shirtless and beautiful, with a carved eagle in one hand and a carving knife in the other, hair loose and golden around his shoulders, wood shavings on his thighs and the workbench and sawdust on the back of his hand.

"What?"

He pauses, swallows. "Did...did you want there to be something? I mean, did you want there to be a now?"

I think of Jared. Of Maria. Of the twenty years of one-night stands and hookups and quasi-not-really-but-almost relationships torched before they could become anything, and I think of the four-fuck rule, and the no-kissing rule; I think about how he felt in my bed, and how I felt in his; I think about the feel of his seed trickling out of me even now, and the protective curl of his arm around my shoulders, and feeling safe and small and vulnerable and protected there; I think about the stories we just traded, how it was so much easier to tell him than I thought it would be, how similar our stories are, how different we are yet how much the same; all of this passes through my mind in a Matrix-like scud and whirl and barrage of ideas and images and thoughts and feelings.

"No," I say, and my voice is steady, low, and not quite cold enough, but as cold as I can make it sound. "No, I didn't."

And then I go back inside, get dressed, grab my purse, and leave his house through the front door.

It's only a fifteen-minute walk over to my place from here, but I have no energy for it. I order a Lyft while I'm dressing, and in a stroke of dumb luck it's at the curb in less than five minutes. The driver says hello, and I summon enough to nod at him and smile tightly—the kind of smile that basically screams *fuck off and take me home*; or maybe it's my overall demeanor, or the obvious walk of shame. Ride of shame—whatever.

I see Franco in his driveway, fiddling with the eagle carving, watching me.

I thought about the bunny he'd carved, sitting on the workbench—dammit, I liked that little carving. It was cute.

And then...nothing.

Conceal, don't feel. Yeah, I identify, Elsa.

TWELVE

I BURY MYSELF IN WORK AND MY OWN WORKOUTS. IMOGEN is worried, but I assure her I'm fine. And that works for a while, at least on my end.

Sort of.

Okay, it doesn't work at all.

I still can't get my mojo back, as Austin Powers would say. I can't make myself care about guys—they're all lackluster and ugly and boring and lame, and I have no interest in pursuing any of them. I try, and I fail, multiple times—until I quit trying. Even alone, my sexuality is frozen. And I know why: it's safer this way. If I'm numb and frozen, I'm not feeling anything, especially whatever may be lurking below the thick layer of ice.

Finally, another three weeks after my ride of shame from Franco's house, there's a quiet, discreet knock at my door. It's late, almost midnight, and I'm in my robe eating Halo Top and drinking wine and binge watching a new Netflix comedy series.

Who would be at my door at this time without having pressed the buzzer? I check the peephole, and then open it.

"How'd you get past the buzzer?" I ask.

Imogen enters without answering, two bottles of wine in a bag in one hand, and a box of Enlightened ice cream bars in the other. "Somebody was coming in and I followed behind her."

"It's almost midnight," I point out, letting the door shut.

"And you're off tomorrow," she says, putting the box of ice cream bars in my freezer.

"How do you know my schedule?" I ask.

She rolls her eyes at me. "You're a creature of routine, Audra. No matter how busy you get, you always take the first Sunday of every month off. Always. It's your dedicated self-care day, and it has been since you started working as a personal trainer."

"Oh." I sigh, and snag glasses from the cabinet, pouring the rest of the bottle I started into our glasses. "Well, you're here, I assume, to drag the details out of me?"

She takes a seat on my couch, steals my spoon and the ice cream, and nods as she takes a bite. "You said when this whole thing with Franco first started that you two would either be incredible together, or you'd destroy each other. And, so far, it seems like the latter." She points at me with the spoon. "You've slept together, what? Three times? Meaning, three separate incidents? The day you met, at your place after your weird date-but-not-a-date, and the day of the barbecue. And in between those times, you threw yourself into ninety-hour work weeks, tore yourself apart with your own workouts, and have been totally ignoring me."

"I'm not ignoring you."

Her eyes well up, surprising me. "You are too!" She slams the ice cream down on the side table and scrubs at her face. "I barely see you anymore! You're always working, and even when I do see you, you're barely there. You're just...cold. Shut down. I know you see yourself as some ice queen, but I've never felt that from you toward me...until lately. Now? Yeah, you're ice-cold, all the time."

"I'm, look—"

"NO! *You* look! You're so fucking stupid, you know that?" She stands up, pacing away, and then stopping to face me from across the living room. "You and Franco are *made* for each other! Don't you see that? It's obvious to everyone else, except you! And him, too, apparently, because Jess is just as fed up as I am. I don't know what happened with you guys the day of the barbecue, but whatever it was, it must've

been big, because ever since then you've been just...
a block of ice. Like a statue of yourself carved out of
a glacier." She gestures at me. "And for someone who
brags about being so healthy and so fit, you're awfully
blind to the fact that you're overworking yourself—
you're ten seconds from burnout, Audra. You're thin-
ner than you've ever been, and at this point it's not a
good thing."

She pauses, blinks hard, staring at me even harder.

She's not done yet, it seems. "You're so fucking stubborn, you'd rather literally work yourself to
death than admit you're hurt, or that you want him,
or that you feel something for him, or whatever it is. I
don't know—god knows you sure as hell won't fucking tell *me*! I've tried to be understanding, tried to give
you your space, let you figure it out, tried to just be
your friend and love you no matter what, but I can't
just stand by and pretend it's fine anymore! It's not
fine, Audra. *You're* not fine. *He's* not fine. This whole
thing is absolutely bonkers, and it could be so simple
but you're both so goddamned stupid and stubborn,
so blindly clinging to decades-old hurt that you can't
see what's right in fucking front of you!"

You know Imogen is serious as a heart attack
when she swears like this.

"Imogen, it's not—"

"I'm not done!" she snaps. "It *is* that simple. It

is. It is absolutely without a doubt that simple." She sits back down. "I don't know what to tell you to do. I don't know what the answer is. If you can't let yourself love Franco, then maybe you need to leave, because you'll never get past this with him around. And if you don't figure it out, you're going to crash, and it's going to be messy. Ever heard of adrenal burn out? I know you have. That's where you're headed, babe, and I'm telling you so there's zero chance you're not aware of it."

I sigh. "I know, I know, I just—"

"Franco could be the best thing that's ever happened to you, Audra. I know Jesse is the best thing that ever happened to me, and I know they're different kinds of men, but they're cut from the same cloth." She sighs. "But you know this. I can tell just by looking at you that you know this. There's nothing I can say that you don't know."

I uncork a bottle of wine. "Can we just put this on pause for a minute, Imogen?"

She stares hard at me for a long time. "Honestly, Audra, I'm at a loss. Will you tell me what's going on? I know something happened with him, and I know you're compensating for it by icing yourself over."

I pour two glasses and hand her one, taking a long sip from mine. "We went to his house, and we had sex. Really, really, *really* intense sex. Unprotected sex. Emotional sex. We *connected*, Imogen. I felt it, he felt it. And then when I told him I was going to get a Plan B to cover all the bases even though I was on birth control, he freaked out. Something about the Plan B idea just freaked him out. So I went out and he told me about his parents and his ex, and why he's the way he is about sex and relationships—suffice it to say his story is enough like mine that I totally get it. So then I told him my story, about my shitty parents and fucking scummy-ass Jared and the whole thing. And then, on a—I don't know. A whim, maybe? Not a whim—it was…as close as I could get to putting myself out there, I guess—I asked him what we were going to do then. What now? That's what I asked him." I stop and swallow hard. "You know what his response was?"

She lets out a slow breath. "What?"

"And…nothing." I make a face and shrug. "That's exactly what he said, verbatim. So there it is. And nothing."

"And if he'd said something else, like 'and now we figure this out'—would you have been okay with that?"

I can only shrug. "I don't know. He didn't, and it seems futile to speculate."

"Ever consider maybe he's as unsure of what he wants and is as scared of being hurt as you?"

I think of his final question—*did you want there to be something? Did you want there to be a now-what?* I shrug it off, but with great difficulty.

"What's the point of any of it, Imogen?" I ask. "I'm not you, and he's not Jesse. It won't work and we both know it."

"But it could work, couldn't it?" Imogen asks, and her words echo the words I hear whispered deep inside me.

I can't reply. My throat is closed, knotted tightly. I don't dare let it out—not even in front of Imogen. It's too much, too dear, too deep.

She waits for a long time, and when it becomes clear I have nothing to say, she rubs her face with both hands, and then stands up. "I'm not going to drink this one away with you, Audra. You're making a huge mistake in pretending there's nothing there, that there's no way to make it work, and no use in even trying." She hesitates, looking sadder than I've seen her in a long, long time. "You're my family, Audra. I love you with all my heart, always, no matter what, but I'm not on your side in this one. I mean, I *am* on your side, always, and I support you always. But you're making a mistake, and I can't just sit idly by and let you make it." Her usually warm and endearing green eyes are unusually distant. "This is one time where I can't and won't just sit here with you, enabling you by biting my tongue and helping you drink and fake your way past it."

God, my heart aches.

"Imogen, come on." I stand up and follow her, feeling panicky and desperate and wrought with emotion I can't choke down any longer. "We enable each other in everything. It's what we do. Don't bail on me now."

She's already at the door. "I've been enabling your refusal to get over Jared for almost twenty years, Audra. He fucked you over and hurt you and made you look stupid, and you made it a thousand times worse for yourself with that idiotic newspaper stunt you pulled—and don't forget you didn't consult *me* on that, because you *know* I wouldn't have let you do it. What happened *hurt*, Audra, and you had every right to lash out and be angry and whatever. But you've been hoarding that pain and letting it rule you ever since. You're like…you're like Smaug from *The Hobbit*, and that old pain is your treasure. Just let it *go*." She hugs me, holds on tight for a long time, and then pulls away, her hands on my shoulders, her eyes filled with tears, as are mine. "I'm not bailing on you, Aud. Neither of us have siblings, so we're the sisters neither of us have ever had. But I wouldn't be a good sister or a good friend if I didn't finally *do* something. Maybe you'll never forgive me for this, I don't know. I hope you will. But if you're going to keep acting like everything is fine, like you're fine, like you're so totally cool with being alone your whole life, like hooking up with every Tom, Dick, and Harry in metropolitan Chicago is okay, but never having anything real or meaningful or impactful with any of them is actually what you want in your life, then I can't be part of it. I *won't* be. Especially when there's a man living less than five minutes from here who could, possibly, love you in a way you've never known but have always secretly and desperately wanted and needed."

A part of me wants to be angry, wants to get defensive, wants to lash out at her and act like she's abandoning me. But I know better. I can no longer ignore the blatant truth in everything she said and, like everything else in this entire situation, I hate it.

The truth burns.

I blink hard, but hot salty tears drip down my cheeks anyway. "I really want to hate you right now," I whisper.

Imogen hugs me again, a tight, fierce embrace that lasts until I'm uncomfortable with it and start squirming.

"I know," she says, eventually letting go. "I wish I knew what else to do, here, Audra, but I just don't. I won't apologize, because I know I'm doing the right thing, but I will say I'm sorry I can't support you in the way you want me to."

"I get it," I say. "I don't know that I have a way past this right now, but I'll figure it out." I pause as I suck back a breath and try not to totally break down in inexplicable sobs. "Somehow."

"Audra, god—"

"You're right, Imogen," I cut in over her. "I *know* you're right. You've *been* right. I hate it, and I hate you for it, but you're right, and I love you, always and forever and no matter what."

"I hate leaving like this," she says, her voice thick.

"It's fine." I wipe at my eyes with the back of my wrist, and then open my door and shove her out. "Go. Wake Jesse up and fuck him senseless, because one of us has to be getting some."

She laughs. "That was the plan anyway, babe." She frowns. "So, wait—you're not—"

"I haven't been with anyone except Franco since the day I met him," I admit. "I just…*can't*. I've tried, too, and I just…can't."

Her green eyes lock on mine, and I see a spark and a sparkle, and a hint of a smirk on her lips.

"Don't you say a goddamn word, Imogen Catherine Irving!" I say, laughing.

She mimes zipping up her lips and throwing away the key. "Not a word. But I don't have to say it, do I? You know exactly what I'm thinking."

"Yeah, yeah. I told you—he's the one who shut it down, not me. I was on the verge of being willing to consider something, and he shut it down. So it's on him, not me."

"And since when do you sit idly by and wait for someone else to give you what you want, *especially* a man?"

"This is different, and you know it."

She sighs. "Yeah, I guess it is. You can't force him to want something."

"Exactly." I give her another gentle shove. "Go. Get out of here. You have a cock to suck."

She rolls her eyes at me. "You're so nasty and vulgar."

"Yep. And you love me for it."

She hesitates. "We're okay?"

I laugh, another abrupt, unexpected half-sob escaping, tangled up with a laugh. "Yes, we're fine. *I'm* not, but *we* are."

"Can I leave you alone?" she asks.

I nod. "Yeah. I'll be okay."

"Don't try to drink your way past this." She lets out a resigned breath. "We've both done way too much of that, and it's not healthy emotionally or physically."

"I'm going to bed," I tell her. "And you're right, yet again."

"Call me, okay? You're not dealing with this alone."

"I will, and I know."

She walks away, then, and I watch her go. When she's out of sight, I close the door, lock it, and turn back to my living room. The pint of ice cream is melting all over my side table, so I hurry to clean it up and throw away the melted remainder. There's Imogen's untouched glass of wine on the table and my partially finished glass, plus the partial bottle on the counter, the cork forgotten beside it. Not one to waste a perfectly good glass of wine, I set my resolve and find my funnel. I pour both glasses of wine back into the bottle, shove the cork into the bottle, and put the bottle aside.

And honestly, I feel a little better about myself for having done that.

I'll never admit this out loud, but wine and ice cream don't actually fix things. They make a hell of a temporary bandage, but they don't really fix things.

I shut the TV off, climb into bed, and try to fall asleep.

I can't, though.

I keep replaying that day at Franco's house—specifically the moment he asked me if I wanted a *now-what*. I'd lied to Imogen about that—or rather, withheld the truth. I feel like shit about that, but I feel even shittier because I lied to him. And to myself.

I *did* want that. I did then, and I do now.

I don't have the slightest clue what a *now-what* looks like or feels like, but I know I want a *now-what* with Franco. I want him bare inside me again, consequences be damned—and no Plan B the next morning either. I want him to kiss me. I want to go to sleep and wake up with him, and have more sex and have breakfast, and have more sex and watch TV and have more sex...

I find myself quietly crying, tears sliding down my cheeks as I try to picture what that would feel like. Normally, I'd ask myself why the fuck I'm crying, but I don't have to. I know exactly why.

Imogen said it: I have secretly and desperately wanted to be loved. My whole life. I never felt loved by my dad, or by my mom. I thought I was loved by Jared, and I'd hung all my hopes and dreams for a happily ever after in which I would ride off into the sunset on the back of a white charger, my arms around a golden knight in shining armor, and be loved and be happy.

And then he fucked me over and crushed the nascent little blossom of hope I had, the tiny seedling of belief in love and men.

After that, I salted the soil of hope and belief in love and men, killing any possibility of anything ever growing there again. And I clung to that barrenness, salting the soil again and again throughout the years, making sure nothing could ever grow there.

But somehow, something is growing.

Not even a seedling, yet. More of a germinated seed, a tender little tendril of something green under the soil, just barely poking up to reach for the sun.

I fall asleep, eventually, but it's to dreams of Franco, of hands, of lips, of breath—erotic dreams of wet warmth leaking out of me, sensual dreams of clinging to Franco through breathless spasms of mutual connection.

I wake in the middle of the night alone in my bed, and he's not there, and my eyes sting and my chest contracts, and I know I'm at the most serious moment of my entire life.

For once, I have absolutely no clue what to do.

I don't fall asleep again, and yet I can't seem to stop dreaming about Franco.

Each successive dream, whether erotic or tender or sensual, only makes my heart clench harder and my body yearn more desperately for something I fear I'll never have.

THIRTEEN

THREE ENDLESS, MISERABLE DAYS PASS. I DREAM OF Franco, and I'm absentminded at work, and even my own workouts suffer. Finally, I submit to the inevitable: I reschedule all my clients, pushing everyone back two weeks, citing personal health issues. For the first time since…ever, I have an entire two and a half weeks off—no clients, no meetings, no seminars or workshops…and no workouts.

I have no clue what I'm going to do, but like Imogen predicted—I'm burned out. Psychologically, emotionally, and physically I'm just…gassed. Smoked. Done.

My first day off, I sleep in until noon. I watch Netflix and indulge in some midweek healthy carbs, when I usually only allow them into my diet on the weekends.

The first day rolls slowly into two, and I don't work out, which is difficult. I don't drink, which is also difficult.

At the top of day three, I tell Imogen that I'm tak-ing time off from everything, and she squeals loudly over the phone, hangs up, and then calls me back ten minutes later—she's taken off three of her vacation days, got her shifts today and tomorrow covered; it's Monday so she has a full five days off, and she's head-ed my way with her bags packed.

I splutter. "Bags? Where are you going?"

She laughs. "Where am *I* going? You mean where are *we* going! I'm stealing you! We haven't had a va-cation together ever in our whole lives *ever* and we're taking one right now!"

"Um. Where are we going?"

She laughs again, a light, tinkling, giggle. "Oh, you'll see. I have plans in the works."

"Plans in the works? What does that mean?" I ask.

Another giggle, and I'm getting annoyed at the giggling—whenever Imogen has something up her sleeve, she gets the giggles, and it has always annoyed the ever-loving shit out of me. "Can you please just trust me? Please? Pack a bag with lots of bikinis and flip-flops and sundresses, and that's all I'll tell you."

"Imogen, you know I don't do well with surprises."

"Tough. Deal with it." I hear her muffle into the

phone and talk to Jesse, and then she's back to me. "I'm on the way. Go along with it, and just trust me."

"Okay, okay." I pause. "Bikinis, sundresses, and flip-flops, huh?"

"And maybe some nice stuff in case we want to go to a fancy dinner or something. I don't know! Just pack for everything, but especially for a lot of beach time."

And then she hangs up as I hear her getting into her car, with Jesse's voice rumbling in the background.

I go into whirlwind mode. I spend a few minutes trying to pick bikinis, and then just say fuck it and grab all them out of the drawer in a giant handful, toss them into my suitcase, and call it good. Bras and underwear, sundresses, skirts, tops, a few nicer dresses and a few pairs of heels, some flip-flops and some gladiator sandals, my to-go makeup and toiletries kit, and a few T-shirts to sleep in. Things I don't bring: workout gear, condoms, or vibrators. The only thing that got me past Jared was a period of total celibacy, and I'm already well into another one, with almost a full month under my chastity belt. Might as well keep it going, right? I haven't heard a word from Franco, Imogen hasn't brought him up, and I've avoided going anywhere he might be. If it's over, it's over. Fine. There's nothing to *be* over anyway. I'm not going to try to stop thinking about him; I'm not going to try to get over him by getting under someone else. I'm just going to…live my life, and figure it out one step at a time.

What I was doing clearly wasn't working, so I'm not going back to it. What's next? I have no idea.

Right now, I'm going to take a beach vacation with my best friend, and not worry about any of it.

By the time I'm done packing, Imogen is buzzing at the front door. I let her in and she's at my door in seconds. I barely have the door open when she shoves through, already chattering, literally vibrating with excitement. She's talking so fast I can barely keep up with her, and I don't even try. She's talking about drinks with umbrellas, and cabana boys, and should she have higher SPF with her, and Jesse is so jealous he's talking to James about scheduling a boys' trip for when we get back, and…

I let her talk, absorbing her joy. I'm still not okay, but I'm okay with not being okay. It's a weird kind of peaceful resignation. I know I'll figure it out, one way or another. This is a turning point in my life, I'm realizing, and I'm trying to just take it one step at a time and enjoy the process, even the not-being okay part, if that makes any sense.

She's pawing through my suitcase, checking my packing. She goes through it twice, and then stops chattering abruptly. "Audra, there's something missing."

I frown. "What? I've got clothes for nice dinners, bikinis, sandals, makeup, bras and underwear…what am I missing?"

"You don't have any…" and here she gestures vaguely at her hoo-ha. "You know."

I snort and roll my eyes. "Say what you mean and use big girl words, Imogen."

"You don't have a vibrator or condoms." She gives me a meaningful look. "I thought you never went anywhere without that stuff. I remember you telling me that a few years ago."

I sigh. "Yeah, I don't usually. But I'm…" Another sigh, and if I sigh again I'll turn into an accordion. "I'm on hiatus. From everything."

"Another ninety-day celibacy thing, like after Jared?"

I shrug, nod, and then shake my head. "Yes—no. I don't know. I told you I haven't been able to get with anyone since Franco, well…that hasn't changed. But I'm not with him either, and I *still* can't get with anyone else. Worse yet—I don't *want* to. He…he broke me. He ruined me for anyone else, and now he doesn't want me. Which is what I was worried about in the first fucking place. Worst of all, Imogen—I can't even give myself relief. I've tried that too, and I've just got no…mojo, for lack of a better word. I'm frustrated as fuck and I can get close, right to the edge even, but I can't get myself over it. I can't bring myself to orgasm, Imogen! It's utter hell! The asshole didn't just ruin me for other men, he ruined me for myself! It's not fair." I groan, and wave both hands toward the door. "Which is why this beach vacation sounds fucking phenomenal, so let's quit yammering about my bullshit and get out of here!"

A brief but significant pause, and then Imogen brightens. "Beaches and drinks with umbrellas, and cute cabana boys, here we come!" she sings, zipping my suitcase and handing it to me.

On the way out, I glance at her. "Why are you so excited about cabana boys when you have a guy like Jesse at home?"

She rolls her eyes as we head out to my parking lot. "I love Jesse with all my heart, and I'm one hundred percent devoted to him, and if he doesn't ask me to marry him soon I'm going to end up popping the question to him. But. I still like looking at cute guys. Doesn't mean I want them, or want to *do* anything with them, I just appreciate nice-looking things. Like art, and architecture, and flowers…and men."

I laugh. "Atta girl, Imogen."

When we get out to my parking lot, Jesse is parked in one of my guest spots, his giant truck rumbling with screeching, howling, death metal or whatever it is shrieking from his speakers. His window is open, one thick, tattooed arm hanging out, two fingers tapping to the beat. He has his phone up to his ear with his other hand, and he's alternately listening and talking. I can't make out what he's saying, much less figure out who he's talking to. But then Jesse sees me and Imogen, makes a quick end to the phone call, tossing the device into the console cubby under the dashboard as we approach. I have a niggling suspicion about who he was talking to, and about what.

I push that train of thought aside, because it doesn't matter. What happened, happened, and what is, is.

And now it's vacation time.

I open the rear passenger door, shove my little suitcase across the bench seat beside Imogen's and climb up and into the truck, buckling up as I close the door. "Hey, Jesse."

He twists to smile at me. "Imogen, what's up? Doing okay?"

I smile back; I don't have to force it, because a smile from Jesse is pretty infectious. "Excited for Imogen's little impromptu vacation plan."

He nods, and something unspoken ripples between us. I gather from his tense expression that Franco is on his mind, but I don't ask, and he doesn't offer. Instead, he plugs a cord into his phone, hunts through Spotify for a moment, and then switches the music to a yacht rock playlist—all fabulous and fun and lighthearted, which he must somehow know is a perennial favorite of Imogen's and mine—as long as it's not the overly synth-laden pop stuff. It starts off with a Bon Jovi tune, and my spirits immediately lift. Imogen is in the front seat, and after she closes the door and buckles in, she leans across and kisses Jesse on the cheekbone, and then claims his right hand, twining her fingers into his.

He grins at her as he puts his truck into gear and backs out. They immediately start bickering in an adorably earnest way about whether Bon Jovi, Guns 'N Roses, or Poison is better. I can't help a rush of hate/love at the way they are together. It's so sweet it's almost saccharine, but it's totally real and deep and true, and the hate just may be jealousy in disguise.

The drive isn't too long—we're headed to O'Hare. I settle in, listening to the music and watching the familiar scenery out the window, and half listening to Jesse and Imogen's quiet, easy, ever-shifting conversation.

We reach the airport departure line, where Jesse pulls to a stop, parks, hops out, grabs both of our suitcases and props them upright on the sidewalk. Then, without warning, he grabs Imogen around the waist, yanks her up against his body, and kisses the shit out of her. By the time he lets her go, she's clearly breathless, horny, and a little shaken.

"Ohhh—okay," she mumbles, touching her lips with two fingers. "Um. Hi? Wow."

Jesse just grins at her. "Had to make sure you remember me while you're gone. Don't want you leaving me for any of those cute cabana boys."

"You heard that, huh?"

He grabs her by the ass and clutches her up against him again. "I eat cabana boys for breakfast, and don't you forget it."

She giggles breathily. "You eat *me* for breakfast, or have you forgotten already?"

He growls. "Forget? Why do you think I didn't brush my teeth this morning? I can still taste you."

"OKAY!" I shout, and walk away, grabbing both rolling suitcase handles. "AWAY WE GO!"

"You're not *jealous*, are you?" Imogen says, her voice full of teasing humor.

"You bet your fine ass I'm jealous."

"Jesse, you know I'm just being silly. Don't be insecure."

He rumbles again. "Ain't insecure. You're mine, and I know it, and I'm fine with you going and having the time of your life. But I'm jealous as fuck, and I'm not apologizing for it."

"I don't expect you to apologize." She reaches between them and rubs against him. "Remember how

I woke you up? That was me reminding you who *you* belong to—*me*."

I would be sick if it wasn't hot and sweet at the same time. "Hey, lovebirds. Remember me?"

"I'll be thinking of how you woke me up the entire time you're gone," Jesse says, and I know I'm being ignored.

Imogen lifts up on her toes and touches her lips to Jesse's, quickly, tenderly. "I have to go." She glances at me, grins, and then turns back to Jesse. "I think we're going to make poor Audra vomit in a second."

I sigh, waving a hand. "It's sweet. Just don't get carried away. I'd tell you to get a room, but that'd take too long, and I need like four sugar-free mojitos, stat."

"Plus, our flight leaves in an hour." She pecks him one last time. "Bye. I'll call you."

"How about you FaceTime me naked from the hotel room instead?" Jesse mutters.

Imogen rolls her eyes as she pulls away. "I'll see what I can do."

Imogen gets two steps away when his voice stops her. "Hey, Im—guess what?"

She pauses, turns around. "What?"

"I love you."

She sighs, visibly and audibly melting. "I love you, too."

"You're going to be apart less than a week," I

huff. "Get a grip."

Imogen shoves me playfully. "Don't be hating on our honeymoon phase."

"I'm not hating," I say as we head to check-in. "You're just being ridiculous."

"Yeah, well…" She shrugs, and her smile back at me is…weird. "Love is ridiculous, sometimes."

Both our suitcases are carry-on size, so all we have to do is check-in and go through security. Imogen gives the clerk both our boarding passes, which she printed out at home it seems, and I give her my ID. The clerk is bored and listless, checking our IDs, scrawling something on both boarding passes, and then repeating our gate assignment in a monotone voice as she hands the passes back to Imogen.

At no point is there a hint of where we're going. Once we're in the security line, I fix Imogen with a hard stare. "Where are we going? You *have* to tell me!"

"Do not!" she singsongs. "It's a surprise."

"How much were the tickets? I can reimburse you."

She blows a raspberry at me as we move forward, approaching the front of the line. "Nope! I'm so proud of you for taking this time off, and taking care of yourself, and this my way of showing it. Plus, I got promoted at work, so I'm celebrating that for myself."

"You're *proud* of me?"

She nods. "Yes, Audra, I'm proud of you. That's not condescension, either. You take care of your body in terms of nutrition and fitness better than anyone I know, but psychologically and emotionally, you're a disaster. You're like a diabetic person about to go blind, emotionally. You *need* this time off, and if you spent it all just languishing alone at home, you'd go even crazier, because I know you're also not working out or drinking—both of which are good. But you need a distraction, and it is my absolute pleasure to provide it."

"Oh," I say. I do have to take time to think. "Guess that makes sense." I give her a quick side hug. "Thank you, in that case."

Just then, we're called up to the next open security guy, who glances at us, looks us up at down appreciatively, and then turns his eyes on me as I hand him my ID. "Where are you two lovely ladies going?"

Imogen answers. "I'm surprising her with a vacation because she's never taken one, so she doesn't know where we're going."

The security guy, who clearly is wishing he was going with us, eyes me in surprise. "You've never taken a vacation?"

"Nope. Lots of working trips, but never a real vacation with zero work and all play."

"What kinda play you planning on, huh?" he asks with a broad, playful grin.

I wink at him. "Wouldn't you like to know?"

He just laughs good-naturedly. "I sure would. You're all set. Have a good flight." He makes a big show of handing the boarding passes back to Imogen without letting me see them, and then we get our bags and shoes and purses on the conveyer belt, go through the scanner, collect our stuff, and head for the gate. It didn't take us long to go through security, and Imogen checks our boarding passes for flight time, and announces that we have plenty of time for a preflight drink. So we find seats at a bar not too far from our gate, order a glass of wine, and settle in, our bags at our feet.

"So. You got promoted?" I ask.

"I sure did! I'm a shift supervisor, now."

"Congratulations. It seems like you're really thriving at that hospital, huh?"

"I really am," Imogen says with a happy sigh. "I love it so much, and it's all thanks to Jesse. I can't even begin to explain all the ways he's made my life better."

"I know I'm kind of a joy-kill about it sometimes, but I really am super amazing, sparkly-hearts, happy for you."

Imogen bumps me with her shoulder. "You're not a joy-kill, Audra. And I don't want this vacation to turn into an endless discussion of your…stuff. It's a distraction. It's about fun and relaxation and that's *it*."

I sigh in relief. "God, thank you. I just want to have fun and relax and not think about anything."

"What did you do for your first couple days off?" she asks.

"Not much, and it was everything I thought it could be." I laugh. "Honestly, it was great. I slept in later than I've ever slept in, in my whole life, ate a bunch of garbage—well, garbage for me, at least. I also watched two whole seasons of a show on Netflix, and that's about all I did, and it was awesome."

"Good for you," Imogen says. "And about damn time."

We chat more about the kind of random crap two lifelong best friends gab about over a glass of wine, and then I pay for the wine and we head for our gate. And just in time: I see the gate number we've been assigned, and the attendant at the desk is on the loudspeaker:

"Now boarding zone two, now boarding zone two. Once again, flight D-L one-two-three-four, departing at one-twenty for St. Barth's is now boarding zone two."

I stop, gaping. "Are you for fucking real?" I grab her by the shoulders. "St. Barth's?"

She grins at me, leaning in to kiss me on the cheek. "St. Barth's, for fucking real!"

"How?"

"Let's get our seats and I'll tell you on the plane."

We board, get our bags in the overhead compartment, find our seats and buckle in. By some mutual but unspoken agreement we decline a drink as the attendant comes around, and I turn to Imogen, who has the aisle seat, leaving me the window.

"So. How did you swing St. Barth's? And where are we staying? I know things are pretty good for you with the new job and the promotion, but…"

She just laughs. "Oh god, no. I couldn't afford an outhouse on St. Barth's. It's Dr. Waverley—both of them. I was in Dr. Waverly's office, my boss, not her husband. She was discussing the responsibilities of my new position, you know, the usual rundown. And then Dr. Waverley, her husband, comes in. Apparently they'd been planning a vacation for a while, but a big thing came up for him, and then something came up for her, and I guess they'd been discussing via email their options for postponing, and he got sick of emails and decided to drop by and let her know that he thought it'd be best to put it off a few more months."

I lift an eyebrow at her. "Sounds like a fascinating conversation."

She snickers. "It was, actually. They've been married so long they have their own, like, shorthand in conversations." She shrugs. "Anyway, after Mr. Dr.

Waverley left, my boss Mrs. Dr. Waverley gave me a funny look and asked me if I'd ever taken a vacation, and I said not really, not for a long time. And she told me she and her husband have a place down in St. Barth's that sits empty most of the year, and if I ever want to take some vacation days, I could hike myself down there and stay, free of charge."

I blink at her. "Oh my god. That's...absurdly generous."

Imogen laughs. "Oh yes, it sure is. But I've gotten to be pretty good friends with Dr. Waverley since I started working for her, and she and her husband are basically just those kinds of people—they'll do pretty much anything for anyone without even blinking. So, when you called me and told me you'd taken some time off, I called her, asked if I could bring you down for a BFF getaway, and could I also have some time off. She arranged for me to have the days off, and I got Michelle to cover my next two shifts, and here we are."

"Well, I'll have to thank Dr. Waverley and Dr. Waverley, then."

"They like red wine," she suggests. "Particularly a nice, dry 2012 Napa Valley cabernet sauvignon."

"Who doesn't?" I say, laughing, but make a mental note to bring them a bottle when we get back. "How do you even know that?"

She laughed with me. "Oh, well, when I told her I'd have to find a meaningful way of saying thank you, she suggested that."

The flight was long, but we spent it watching comedies on the in-flight entertainment, laughing together and acting like teenagers, even though we didn't have anything else to drink. We transferred in Atlanta, had a short stopover in Saint Maarten, where we finally indulged in a couple more drinks, and then we transferred to our final, and smallest, flight to Saint Barthélemy.

We arrive at the Waverley's condo at almost two in the morning after something like eleven hours of travel, including the stopover in Saint Maarten—and we're both absolutely exhausted. The entire time we were en route, I'd been entertaining this notion of getting to the condo, changing into a bikini, and going right out to the beach for a starlight swim. But… no. We trudge through the doorway, set our bags down just inside, spend a few minutes marveling, and oohing and aahhing about the condo…and then pass out, together, side by side on the bed.

I'm stiff, foggy, bleary-eyed, and disoriented when I wake up. For the first few minutes of being awake, I think I'm back home in my bed. I don't want to wake up—I'm comfy, sleepy, and the sun is bright on my face and there's a warm body next to me. Some instinct has me curling around the body, wrapping my arm around it. A soft murmur rises at my touch.

I clutch, squeeze...why is it soft? I think I was expecting a male body—a certain, specific male body. I'd been dreaming, but the dreams are hazy and mostly forgotten already. What—who—am I spooning? I'm starting to wake up even more, gradually becoming more aware of my surroundings.

"Audra?" The voice is soft, quiet, puzzled, and female.

"Mmmm." Mine is scratchy and vaguely irritated at being spoken to, at having to think.

"That's my boob."

I squeeze again, exploring, and realize I've got a big handful of Imogen's breast. I laugh, not letting go; instead, I spoon closer up behind her and squeeze harder. "I see why guys like them so much. They make great handholds for spooning."

Imogen is cackling, wiggling her butt against me. "At least neither of us is waking up with a sausage between our buns."

I let go, rolling away as I snort in laughter. "Hey, I personally don't mind waking up like that."

"Oh, like you've *ever* spent the entire night with a guy," Imogen says, sitting up.

"I have too...once...by accident." I sit up, as well. We'd both fallen asleep fully clothed, and

Imogen is scratching and tugging at her bra straps and underwire.

She glances at me, holding up a finger. "Quick interruption—if I don't get this bra off right the hell now, I'm going to lose my mind. Just fair warning, I'm letting the girls loose, and I might even give them a good rub down."

I laugh, already ripping my shirt off and fumbling with my own bra strap. "Last one topless buys the first round at the beach."

Within seconds, we're both bare from the waist up, sighing in relief as we rub at the itchy, achy points of compression and friction where our bras had been.

Imogen flops back to the bed with a sigh, still massaging herself. "So. You once woke up with a sausage between your buns. What'd you do?"

I lie beside her, glancing past her at the doorway, marveling at the view from the balcony: sparkling, glittering azure water, white sand beaches, not a cloud in the sky, seagulls wheeling and cawing. "What do you think I did? I grabbed the condom we'd opened and never used, woke him up, told him to put it on, and we fucked, laying down on our sides, still drunk enough that that was about all we could manage. And then we passed out again and I woke up, snuck out, and met you for breakfast." I laugh. "I never knew his name, and never even looked at his face. When I woke up and snuck out, he was turned away and had the blanket over his head. He could have looked like a cave troll for all I know. He had a nice dick, though, I can tell you that much."

Imogen is laughing and shaking her head at me. "You're terrible. You never even saw his face?"

I shrug. "I mean, at the bar, but I was honestly so wasted I barely remember that night. I remember the next morning just fine, though," I say, laughing.

"I bet you do." She shakes her head. "I just can't fathom having sex with someone whose name I don't know, and someone I have never even seen naked."

"It was a hell of a thrill, actually. Kind of...naughty, in a way."

"Don't you ever just want...something a little deeper?"

I wink at her lasciviously. "I *always* want something a little deeper."

She groans, laughing. "Oh my god, you slut. That's not what I meant and you know it."

I leave the bed, going to the doorway, clad in yoga pants and nothing else. There are probably people down there who could see me if they wanted, as the beach is mere yards away, but it's kind of fun taking that risk. "Anyway, I thought we weren't having this kind of conversation?"

"Don't you care that anyone could look up here

and see you topless?" Imogen asks.

"Yeah, I do care a little, but it's also fun. Plus, I'll probably make some old rich guy's day." I shoot a glance at her. "Come over and try it."

She yanks the sheet up to cover herself. "NO!"

"Why? You worried about what Jesse would say?"

She snorts. "No!" A hesitation. "Well, yeah. I wouldn't want him wagging his dick at the entire beach, so I'm not going to shake my tits at the entire beach."

"I have no such impediments," I say, propping the girls up in both hands and shaking them at the window. Far down the beach, near the water, I see a male silhouette turn this way, glance up as he's walking, do a double-take, and trip over someone lying on the beach on a towel. I turn away, laughing, spluttering, and covering myself with both hands.

"I just made some guy trip over another person," I say, backing away from the window out of sight.

Imogen wraps the towel around herself and tiptoes to the edge of the door, peeking out. "Oh my god! They're arguing! Like, they're going to start punching each other in a second. The guy is gesturing at the window—now they're both looking this way."

"Should I give them a show?" I say, tiptoeing closer.

Imogen snaps the blinds closed and pushes me

backward. "No! You definitely should not give random guys on the beach a free boob show. Bad plan."

"Why?" I ask. "It's not like they can see details of what I look like, and it's not like I'll ever see them again."

She stands in front of me, resolute. "You're compensating, Audra."

I sigh, blowing her a raspberry. "Fine, spoilsport." I head for the bathroom. "I'm gonna take a shower, and then we should go get breakfast and hit the beach."

"Sounds good to me," Imogen says, watching me carefully.

I stop in the doorway to the bathroom. "I'm *not* compensating, *by* the way. I have nothing to compensate for."

"This is about relaxing and having fun, so I'm not going to argue with you," Imogen says, after a moment, "but no more boob shows at open windows, okay? I don't want gaggles of horny tourist dudes lining up over there with binoculars hoping for another peep at the hot older lady who likes to flash people."

I flip her the bird. "I'm not an older lady."

"Yeah, but you're not twenty-five anymore, and this isn't Mardi Gras."

"No, but my tits look almost as good now as they did then, so that's a win."

"Can we stop talking about your tits?" Imogen says, grabbing her suitcase and opening it on the bed.

We both shower, change into bikinis and cover-up dresses and find a place within walking distance to eat some food—it's well past lunch, but we have omelets and bacon and sausage and a bowl of berries and endless cups of coffee.

Eventually, I look at the time and toss down enough cash to cover the meal. I stand up and announce, "Time to find a cabana, and a cute cabana boy."

She nods, adds cash for a tip, and we head out for a few hours of lying in the sun, swimming, and drinking way too many gin-and-soda-waters.

And that is how we spend the week. One day drifts into the next, pleasantly, slowly, but also way too quickly. We shop, go to fancy dinners in the evenings and linger over extended breakfasts in the morning, and order food to our cabana in the afternoons. We collect shells and tease the guys on the beach around us with elaborate shows of rubbing sunscreen on each other, laughing as they all but trip over themselves trying to get a better look.

I leave my phone turned off and stuffed in a pocket in my purse, forgotten. I don't think about anyone, or anyone in particular. I don't work out. I eat food I haven't eaten in years—and while I know I'll have gained a bunch of weight when I return to reality, I honestly don't care. I know I can strip it away again, and the sense of peace and relaxation is totally worth it.

I can't shake the lingering weight of sadness, though. It's not overbearing, it's not a crushing cloud of depression, its just...sadness. Like I'm missing something.

Someone.

I don't let it bog me down, and I don't let it show, but it's there.

As the week wears on, though, and we get closer and closer to having to go back home, the heavier the sadness gets, and the harder it is to push it away. True to her word, Imogen never pushes the conversation to anything heavy, and I'm grateful for it.

It's early evening on Saturday, the last full day of our trip. We've been at the beach most of the day, and I'm trying to pull myself out of the funk of sadness, trying desperately to convince myself it's just end-of-vacation melancholy that's not about anyone in particular.

Imogen is beside me, on her belly on the cabana mattress, sunglasses pushed up on top of her head to hold her hair back, texting Jesse. Abruptly, she pops her head up and swivels it around as if looking for someone, and then casually lowers it back down again, a strange expression on her face.

I eye her. "What was that about?"

She tugs her glasses back down over her eyes. "Nothing." She's not good at lying, and worse at pretending she's not. "Thought I saw someone I knew, but it was just a lookalike."

I frown at her, rolling to my side and tugging my top up so I'm not spilling out of it. "Imogen, you suck at lying. What's going on?"

She clicks her phone to sleep and clutches it in her fist, staring at me through her bug-eye sunglasses. "You know I love you, right?"

All my suspicions are on high alert. "Yes?" I say, drawling the word into a question.

She glances past me, lets out a breath, and then moves to a sitting position, gathering her purse and cover-up. "So...you're here through Tuesday. I changed your flight and stole your phone while you were sleeping to reschedule your Monday and Tuesday appointments."

"Why would you do that?" I frown harder. "What do you mean, *I'm* here till Tuesday? Just me? Where will you be?"

"In St. Pete's with Jesse."

"You're ditching me here, alone, to spend time with Jesse?" I sigh, shrugging. "Okay, I get it. We've had a great week and I'm super thankful we've had this time together. I really needed it."

She's smirking, sort of, but hiding it. "This is where you just need to trust me."

"Trust you?"

She leans over me, and I sit up to hug her. "Yes, Audra. Trust me. I have my reasons for doing this beyond wanting time alone with Jesse on a beach."

I stare at her, examining her—she's up to something. "And you're leaving right now?"

She nods. "Yup. I need to pack and catch my flight."

"Just like that?" I frown. "This is really weird, Imogen. And what am I supposed to do alone for two days? It's not the same being on a beach by yourself."

She just shakes her head. "It'll make sense eventually."

I sigh, throwing my hands in the air and then hug her again. "Fine, fine. I'll just trust you—but it's hard, I hope you realize that." I pull away, holding her arms and blinking away sudden tears. "For real, though— thank you, Imogen. I needed this more than you'll ever know."

She kisses my forehead. "I love you, Audra. And…" She bites her lip. "Open mind, open heart. Okay?"

Oh dear—I really don't like the sound of that. "Imogen? What did you do?"

She just pats me on the cheek as she stands up and backs away. "Open mind, open heart. Just remember that, okay?"

I roll my eyes and wave her off. "Okay, Yoda." I blow her a kiss. "Love you. Say hi to Jesse for me."

"Oh, I'll do more than say hi."

I laugh as she walks away across the beach back to the condo, already texting Jesse again. I stay in the cabana for a while longer, and then decide to go for one last swim before heading in to find some kind of dinner.

I toss my sunglasses into my purse, tighten the knots on my halter-top bikini, and head for the water. The sun is starting to set, a giant bright orange-red ball just barely touching the horizon, setting the whole ocean on fire. The waves are gentle and noisy, tugging at my ankles and then my calves as I wade in. The seagulls dart and wheel on wingtips and caw at each other. There are other beachgoers all around, but I feel totally alone, like I'm in a bubble of solitude.

Finally, I let the sadness bubble up, let it breathe.

I wade in up to my waist, and then to my chest, letting the waves crash up against my breastbone and chin, and then dunk under, taking a few long strokes under the water and surface, spluttering as I come up for air. I scrape my hair back and wipe my face.

Let the sadness rise, let it percolate through me.

And finally, finally, I let myself admit what it's really about—the sadness is about Franco.

I miss Franco.

I want Franco.

Not just the sex, not just his body, but *him*. His laugh, his blue eyes. His humor, his deep, smooth voice. His soothing presence. The way he can turn me on with a look, a glance.

The sadness is about my missed opportunity with him.

"Did…did you want there to be something? I mean, did you want there to be a now-what?"

I should have said yes. I should have told him yes, I wanted a *now-what*. I wanted more. I should have admitted that feeling him bare inside me was the scariest thing I've ever experienced, not because of the risk of pregnancy, but because of the intimacy of it. The realness of it. The *rightness* of it. It terrified me because it had been so right. So perfect. It had been… *home*.

He had taken the risk—he'd asked if I wanted something else. I'd known what he meant, but I was scared and stubborn, and I shut him down. Blew my one chance at…whatever could have been between us.

I suck down a sob.

I should have said yes.

I hear splashing around me, but it doesn't register—nothing can penetrate my bubble of solitude.

And then...

I feel it.

A tingle.

It's ephemeral at first, but it's a familiar feeling.

An awareness of something...someone.

A knowledge, in my bones and blood and soul.

I splash water on my face, scrape my dripping wet hair back over my scalp, and then I slowly turn around.

He's ten feet away, up to his waist in the water behind me. He's shirtless and gloriously beautiful. Breathtaking. His hair is down, loose around his broad, hard shoulders. He has on a pair of cheap airport-kiosk plastic sunglasses instead of his usual Oakleys.

He's just standing there, waiting. Staring at me.

I choke. "Franco?"

He closes the space between us, until mere inches separate us. He stares down at me, his chest rising and falling deeply, rapidly. The water laps at us, licks between us; the sun sets beyond us, bathing everything in a red-orange glowing fire, staining the sea and our skin and his eyes.

His hands wrap around my waist, and he pulls me up against him. "I decided you were lying."

"Lying?" I whisper. "About what?"

"About not wanting a *now-what*."

I laugh, or sob, or some tangled mix of the two. "I was," I manage, trying furiously to catch my breath, which has mysteriously disappeared. "I *was* lying. I admit it."

"Why?"

"Because I'm scared of getting hurt again. Of being hurt worse than before, because you—you could…" I shrug, unable to finish the thought coherently.

"I'm scared, too," he says. "I've spent the last month trying to convince myself otherwise, but…I couldn't do it."

"Ask me again," I say, my voice a murmur as I run my hands up his chest to clutch his shoulders.

He knows what I mean. "Audra…do you want there to be a *now-what* with us?"

I rest my ear against his chest, listen to his heartbeat and his breathing. I nod, my chin brushing his pec. "Yes, Franco. I want a *now-what* between us."

His arms encircle me, and I feel safe and protected and the weight of sadness is gone.

"Me too," he says, relief in his voice.

FOURTEEN

NEITHER OF US SAY IT, BUT WE'RE BOTH TEMPTED TO hide in the condo for the next two days, doing you know what until the last possible moment. Instead, we do something neither of us is quite ready for, but know is the most responsible thing: we just… talk.

We stay in the water as the sun sets, and we hold hands, rest palms on waists, steal sensual touches, exchange small, secret smiles. And we talk. I tell him more about my childhood, my eternal sense of loneliness, how I always felt more at home in the gym with the football guys and wrestlers than with other girls, and how that often translated into assumptions about my gender identity or sexual preference, especially since I've hated how I look with long hair since I was six, and have insisted on short hair ever since. And how those assumptions and rumors probably fueled the way I approach sexuality.

He tells me about his grandfather, about his carpentry apprenticeship, about his first girlfriend—who was, in his words, the most stereotypical Catholic schoolgirl there's ever been, down to the pleated skirt hiked a bit too high and the white button-down unbuttoned a bit too far, and the behaviors and predilections that were anything but Catholic.

We talk about everything. Movies, sports, cars, music. We talk as the sunset disappears at the approach of nightfall; we transition back to the cabana long after the rest of the beach is deserted. When the cabana boys start closing down, I gather my purse and cover-up, and Franco collects his phone and wallet from where he had them rolled up into his shirt, tucks the T-shirt in the back pocket of now-dry board shorts, and we walk hand in hand along the beach, letting the moon-tinged surf lick at our ankles.

We talk about our exes, and our parents, and trade horror stories of growing up in our respective familial disasters. We talk about run-ins with disgruntled ex-hookups, awkward morning-afters, comical bedroom mishaps, close calls with crazy almost-lovers whom we realized were crazy in the nick of time. We talk about sex in an almost clinical way—discussing favorite positions and least favorite positions, foreplay tactics, exit strategies; this is a strange part of the conversation, because you'd think talking sex would lead to doing it, but somehow, it's intimate and informational and personal rather than erotic or sensual.

At some point we realize we've wandered so far down the beach that we have no idea how far we've gone, and that it's deep in the night.

We stop, turn around, and keep talking.

He tells me hysterical stories of the various hijinks he and the other guys got into over the years, and I tell him some of the wild and weird trouble I'd get Imogen and myself into, which she would then have to sweet-talk us out of. We talk about the future—how he wants to eventually make furniture full-time, but that he loves working with the guys too much to ever quit. I tell him about my dream of eventually owning my own gym.

The stars twinkle and blink overhead, and the moon is huge and bright. We're alone on the beach, except for the occasional couple passing by on their own late-night wander.

You hear about "long walks on the beach," but the reality? It's more magical than you'd believe.

I *know* this man.

He knows me.

I know that he cried when his grandfather died. He knows I got my first period at thirteen, and that I cried out of fear because my mom hadn't prepared me for it, and I thought I was going to bleed to death.

I know that he was scared stupid when he moved into that shitty basement apartment in Chicago, terrified that he'd get shot just for living there as a white man. He knows I chose the shot for birth control in defiance of my own needle phobia, which I force myself to face every few months when I get a new shot.

He even knows things Imogen doesn't—that I've always been low-key jealous of her body, the extra layer of softness and curve she has that I don't, but that my addiction to exercise is greater than my jealousy, so I stay lean and shredded.

Finally, as we start to get back to the area of beach that's familiar to me, with the condo building approaching in the distance, we seem to run out of things to talk about. Except for a few topics, which somehow seem fragile and delicate, and we whisper to one another about things past, present, and future.

Franco stops, toes dragging through the wet sand, his eyes going to mine, to the sand, and then back to mine. "I know I may not have any right to ask you this, and I may regret it, but…has there been anyone else?"

"If there's a *now-what* with us," I tell him, "then I think you do have a right to ask."

He nods. "I guess that makes sense. I think I'm just nervous to hear the answer."

"Why?"

He shrugs. Chews on his lip, and then meets my eyes. "Because I don't want there to have been anyone else. Honestly, the thought of you with anyone else makes me queasy. That's part of what got me to admit that I want this with you, and that I needed to do whatever I had to, to get to you."

"No." And in that moment, I'm pathetically relieved I can say that with honesty. "There's been no one since you. Not since that first time we were together."

"Really?"

I nod. "I couldn't." I laugh awkwardly, nervously. "I tried, actually. Quite a few times. Went out and tried all the usual tricks to pick up a guy, and succeeded at that part. But when it came time to start doing anything, I just…couldn't."

"Why not?" he asks.

I shake my head and shrug. "None of them were you." I meet his eyes. "That's all I can really say. They weren't you, and I knew they'd never be…enough. They'd never be you, and there never would be another you. And I just *couldn't*."

"I couldn't either," he murmurs; he looks away for a moment, and then back down at me. "I know it might sound shitty, but…I didn't want this."

I laugh, a quiet huff. "I thought I didn't either."

"That night at my house…" He licks his lips. "I

ran to the garage because what happened—the sex, I mean...being bare inside you. It was...too much. It was..." he trails off, swallowing hard. "It was the most perfect thing I've ever felt in my entire fucking life, and it felt so right it scared the absolute bejesus out of me."

I'm having trouble breathing, catching my breath, swallowing, seeing anything but his eyes, his lips. "Me too," I whisper.

Franco stares down at me, and I can't pierce his expression, can't fathom what he's thinking.

And I desperately need to know.

"Franco..." I step closer; the sea is behind him, the condo behind me; stars and moon bathe us in silver, the surf crashes quietly, and my heartbeat is the loudest sound around. "Tell me what you're thinking. What you're feeling. Sometimes I look at you and I just know what you're thinking and feeling, and other times I can't read you at all."

"I've got a hell of a poker face," he says. "I'm thinking...I'm super conflicted right now."

"About what?"

"I want you. I need you." He rests a hand on my waist, and his touch is gentle and warm and soothing and arousing. "I need to kiss you, I need to feel you...I need to be inside you. I need to connect with you like we did that night in my bedroom." He swallows hard again. "But I'm also just so fucking exhausted and overwhelmed and emotionally just…" He shakes his head, words failing him. "And I also just want to lay down with you and…and hold you. And just sleep."

"Franco," I interrupt.

He stops short. "Yeah?"

"That honestly sounds like the most amazing plan I've ever heard."

"It does?"

I trail my fingers through his hair, let my hands caress his shoulders in a possessive sort of affectionate way that I've never allowed myself to show anyone before. "You, holding me. Just sleeping together." He starts to talk, and I touch his lips to quiet him. "There will be all the time in the world for other stuff, Franco. You know as well as I do that you and I have the most ridiculously combustible chemistry on the planet, and I know you want me, and you know I want you, and I think it's fine for us to explore other areas of a physical relationship."

"I actually think it's important, you know? Neither of us are familiar or comfortable with this whole emotional component thing, and…we need to explore that together, not just get caught up in sex all the time."

"We agree, then," I say.

I take his hand in mine and we walk up to the

condo together. It's dark in the condo, lit only by the stars and moon, and the green glow of the digital clock on the microwave. I close and lock the door behind us, set my purse down on the counter, and we just stand there in the silence for a moment.

I can feel the sexual tension rippling and crackling between us.

Franco groans, pivoting to hold me against him, my breasts crushed against his chest, my head against his breastbone, his hands on my waist. "You're killing me in that fucking bikini, Audra."

I murmur a laugh. "Glad you like it. I have a few others that are way sexier."

"Holy fuck. Well, don't show me those right now."

"No, why?" I say, laughing.

"Because I really do just want to hold you. I need to sleep—I've been up for almost forty-eight hours at this point. But you're so fucking sexy I'm not sure I'll be able to help myself if you don't cover up somehow."

"You're so weak-willed," I tease.

"You're telling me if I took off my board shorts right and showed you a monster fucking hard-on, that you'd be totally cool, tell me, nah, let's just chill?"

I sucked in a harsh breath. "No," I whisper. "I'm just as weak-willed as you are."

"Exactly." He laughs. "So put a shirt on, at least."

I pull away and go to my suitcase, find one of the T-shirts I brought to sleep in, and shrug into it. "There, is that better?"

He sighs. "Better enough that I can think straight without the urge to throw you onto the floor and fuck you senseless."

I moan in frustration. "You can't say shit like that, Franco." I suck in a deep, steadying breath. "You talk like that, you'll find yourself on your back, balls deep in my mouth."

"Fucking hell, Audra."

I laugh. "You started it."

"Truce," he grumbles, closing his eyes and breathing slowly. "I surrender. I'm not strong enough to resist temptation."

I laugh, wrapping my arms around his neck. "Fine, truce." I pull back, eying him. "Did you bring any luggage?"

He chuckles. "Nope. I have the clothes on my back and that's it. Showing up here was...somewhat last minute."

"What happened?" I ask.

He juts his chin at the bedroom door. "Let's lay down. I'm seriously bushed beyond all comprehension right now."

"Lead the way," I tell him.

He precedes me into the bedroom, his hand tangled in mine. My heart is thrumming madly in my chest, nerves singing in my veins, an aviary fluttering in my belly. Why am I so nervous? We're just going to sleep.

But it's more than that.

So much more.

Talking is easy—even as hard as it was to admit I wanted something with Franco, talk is easy. Crossing the line into action—allowing affection and touch that is nonsexual and emotionally intimate…that's taking this *now-what* scenario into reality. And that's scary.

I'm actually shaking all over. My hands are quaking, my breath is coming in short pulses, and part of me wants to run as far away as fast as I can. I'm tempted to call on my old friends sarcasm and vitriol, and to redirect everything into what I know so well—the distraction of sex. But my heart, and that tender little seedling of hope deep down is begging me to let this happen. Be brave. See it through. Let him in.

He seems just as unsure. His palm in mine is clammy, and his hands are usually dry and warm. He moves slowly toward the bed, tugging the blanket and sheet back, letting go of my hand to rub his palms on the front his board shorts.

He laughs, a nervous huff. "It's stupid and embarrassing to admit this, but I'm actually kind of—"

"I'm scared out of my mind right now," I tell him. "Or, not scared, just…"

"Nervous?"

I nod, laughing. "It's stupid, because nothing is happening—"

"But that's what's scary about it," he finishes.

"Exactly."

A tense, silent moment, and then he slides into the bed, moves to the far side, and glances at me. "Come here, Audra."

I swallow, let out a breath, and then shakily crawl into the bed. My instinct, once again, is to flop on my back as far from him as possible and lie there like a stiff log. Instead, I push through the nerves—I recall what it felt like in that brief moment of comfort in his arms, in the afterglow, that night in his bedroom.

His warmth envelops me as I slowly, gingerly settle into the cradle of his outstretched arm. I rest my head on his arm, where bicep, shoulder, and chest all meet—it feels like a nook created specifically for me, meant solely for my comfort. I find myself holding my breath as I shift this way and that, getting comfortable. I settle my hand on his chest, as far from the danger zone as possible, and end up with my palm over his heart, and I feel his heart beating, something that is so damned intimate that I feel like I'm going to cry. He curls his arm around me, his hand coming to rest on my hip.

Now that I'm within the shelter of his arms, I let out the breath I've been holding. This feels amazing.

I have to swallow hard against the onslaught of emotions I feel, a bizarre and overwhelming welter of things: comfort, fear, doubt, need, security, insecurity, arousal, exhaustion.

I blink and swallow, but the bite of emotion in my throat is too hot and thick and too insistent. I find tears in my eyes, inexplicable and stupid.

"Franco, I—" My voice is thick. "I'm sorry. I don't know why I'm like this. I just feel overwhelmed…in a good way."

His voice is so close, low and quiet. "Audra, don't apologize. Feel what you feel. Let yourself feel it. Let it out, all of it, whatever it is."

"I'm not usually emotional like this—" I shake my head, tears trickling. "I feel silly."

His hold on me tightens. "I know. Me too."

"Really?"

He nods, grunting an affirmative noise. "I feel… fuck. Overwhelmed. Confused by…by how comforting it is to just…be here. Like this. With you."

Tears fall and I can't stop them. "It's like…" I untangle my fingers from his and wipe at my face, tasting salt. "Like I'm coming to a home I never had, and never knew I was missing, and now that I'm home,

I'm missing it for all the years I never had it."

"Exactly."

I cry, and he doesn't make me feel stupid or weak. I feel the emotion in him, and though he's not crying, I can tell he's just affected. I don't even have to look at his face—I just...*feel* it radiating from him in palpable waves.

"What made you come here?" I ask, eventually. "Because the last thing that happened at your house... you asked about a *now-what*, and I lied. And I thought that was it...it was over."

"I knew you were lying. I knew then that you were lying, and that I was a coward for letting you get away with it, for letting you go."

"We both knew, then," I admit.

"But we were both too fucking scared." He sighs. "So what happened? I was a miserable jackass, and impossible to work with, and a pain in the ass to be around. Eventually, James all but kicked my door in, poured about six shots of Buffalo Trace down my throat, and then flat out asked me what the fuck was wrong with me."

I laugh. "I'd hate to be on the receiving end of scary James."

Franco snickers. "You don't have the slightest clue. I don't scare easily, and I've known James almost as long as Jesse has, but when he gets riled up like that, I don't care who you are, you get scared."

"So what'd you say?"

He sighs. "I asked him what he was talking about. Lame, I know. That really got him going and he threatened to knock my block off if I didn't quit pussyfooting around and man up. So, I asked for clarification." A pause. "He told me, and I quote, 'that woman is stupid in love with you, and if you don't grow a pair of balls and tell her you feel the same way, you're the dumbest dumbshit that's ever walked the earth.'"

"Wow, wasn't holding back, was he?" I say, laughing.

"Not at all, no. But he wasn't finished. He asked what my problem was, and if I didn't tell him the god-damn truth the first time, he'd beat the truth out of me."

"Do you think he would have?"

Franco shrugs. "Would you be willing to find out?"

I shake my head, eyes wide. "Hell no."

"Exactly. So I told him flat out that I was scared of getting hurt, and that what Maria did had fucked me up, leaving me scarred and untrusting. I told him I didn't know *how* to tell you what I was feeling, or if I was even capable of it."

I re-twine our hands. "What'd he say?"

"He didn't say anything for a long time." Franco's voice drops to almost a whisper. "I'll never forget what he finally said." A long, long pause. "'Franco,' he said, 'I had a once-in-a-lifetime love. Renée was my everything. The only woman I've ever loved. I've never, ever touched another woman. She was my first kiss and my last, my first fuck and my last. And I lost her. I watched her die.'"

"Jesus," I whisper.

"Yeah," Franco murmurs. "He wasn't done, though. He said, 'and you want to know something? I wouldn't trade a single second of it for the world.'"

"Incredible. I guess that's the definition of true love."

Franco was silent a moment. "James said he held her hand as she died, and that Renée knew she was dying, and...nobody could stop it. It happened so fast, you know? The hospital staff tried to keep him from the OR, but he knew something was going wrong and he bulldozed his way in to see her. He grabbed her hand, and she looked up at him, and she told him... her last breath, her last words were to promise her he wouldn't be alone forever."

My eyes stung again. "Oh my god."

"Yeah. He promised her, and he told me that night that if the right woman ever comes along, he'd keep that promise. And if he can keep *that* promise, then I can get the fuck over a betrayal that happened twenty years ago."

I think of Nova, and the intense conversation I'd witnessed in his kitchen the night of the barbecue, and I wonder if anything ever came of it.

Which leads me to thinking of Ryder and Laurel, and their date, and whether anything came of it…and all these wonderings led me to realize how self-absorbed and blind to the rest of the world and my own friends I'd been during the last few months.

I laugh, a bitter bark. "I've been a shitty friend."

I don't have to elaborate—Franco understands what I'm saying. "Yeah, me too."

"You know if anything happened with Ryder and Laurel?"

He shakes his head. "No idea. I've been too much of a selfish bastard lately, too focused on my own miserable bullshit."

"We suck," I say, laughing. "We need to fix that."

"Yeah, we do."

I laugh again. "Why was I so nervous?" I say. "Being with you like this…it feels like…"

"Like we've always been together like this?"

"Yeah," I whisper. "Exactly."

Franco is silent a long time, and I feel his breathing slow. "Audra?" I hear him murmur, as I start to drift off myself.

"Hmmm?"

"You'll still be here in the morning, right?"

"Yeah, I will." A pause. "Will you?"

"Yeah. I will."

And then, for the first time in my life, I fall asleep in the arms of a man.

FIFTEEN

I WAKE UP SLOWLY, ONLY VAGUELY AWARE OF MY surroundings, or myself. All I know is that I'm warm and comfortable, and deeply and wildly content. I feel sunshine on my face. Something solid and warm and protective surrounds me, and I'm so comfortable that sleep pulls me back under.

I wake up a second time, but this time more fully, and I'm more immediately alert. I'm on my left side and Franco, huge and broad and hard and warm is in front of me, so close my nose is pressed against him. I'm too sleepy, drowsy, and content to open my eyes, but a rush of happiness floods through me like a bolt of adrenaline:

This is Franco. We're in bed together. Cuddling. We slept together, and we're both still here.

I murmur sleepily, happily. If this is how it's going to be, then I'm all about it.

Ugh. I have to pee; as soon as I'm aware of the

sensation, it intensifies, until I'm aware that my bladder is full-on screaming, aching. Reluctantly, I roll away and get out of bed, go to the bathroom, wash my hands, and head back to the bed—I do it all on autopilot, still half asleep and hoping to get back in bed and get back to the cozy, drowsy, happiness.

When I get to the bed, Franco has rolled over onto his back and, judging by his breathing, is still sound asleep. The blanket is rucked around his hips, leaving his upper torso bare, and a bolt of desire and need shoots through me at the sight of his naked, muscular body. I slide back into bed, turn my back to his front, and close my eyes. I feel Franco stir, hear him make a wordless, sleepy sound. His arm drapes heavily over my waist, and his breath huffs hot on the back of my neck.

I'm drowsy, but I know I won't be going back to sleep; I'm too hyperaware of Franco, now.

I feel a change in the air, though. His breathing is different. I remain still, not pretending to be asleep but not really letting him know I know he's awake, either. His hand flattens against my belly, and I feel him take a deep breath, hold it, and then let it out slowly.

"You're here," he mumbles, his voice thick and groggy with drowsiness.

"So are you," I say.

"Best night of sleep in my life." He runs his hand

to my hip, and his fingers catch almost accidentally at the string of my bikini bottom.

"Waking up with you…waking up in your arms…" I hear myself, and my voice is so small, so quiet, so fragile. So unlike me, but a more true version of me—the hidden, secret, delicate Audra who's always lived deep inside, way down behind my walls, within the shell of strength and athleticism and take-no-shit-don't-give-a-shit attitude. "It's…I love it." The final three words are so quiet I can barely hear myself say it.

His lips touch the back of my neck, just above my shoulder blades. "I love it, too," he murmurs.

His nose nuzzles against my nape, and his hand cups my hipbone. I press my butt back against him, and I feel the hard, thick evidence of his arousal against me. I'm in no hurry, though. Let this take as long as it takes—let it go slow. Let it take all morning.

I arch my back, baring more of my neck to his kisses, and his lips explore around the knot of my halter bikini top, peeking above my sleep shirt. He moves to my hairline, and down to my shoulder blade, and across to the base of my neck again, each kiss soft and slow and gentle. I breathe in deeply, inhaling the affection in those kisses. I push my ass harder against him, and he pushes forward against me, nestling the ridge of his erection hidden behind his board shorts more firmly between the globes of my ass, which is hidden by the thin fabric of my bathing suit bottom.

Too much fabric. I want it all off. I want to be bare with him.

But even more, I want to explore this with him as slowly and deeply and openly and deliberately as possible. This will be not just sex—this will be so, so much more. This will be the beginning of love, and I know it, and he knows it. It thrums and throbs between us, pulses in the air, hangs thick in the atmosphere between us.

He's in no hurry either.

His palm skates up my waist, over my belly, slides across my diaphragm, and then glides just beneath my breasts; I arch my back, needing his hands on them. He clutches me just beneath my breasts, and I almost groan in frustration but hold it back. I'm fraught with need, but I want to draw out each particular second of this experience, so I don't miss a single sensation or emotion.

I'm waiting for him.

Letting him guide me.

Succumbing to his pace.

Giving myself to him, rather than taking what I want as I want it. I'm trusting him to take us where we want to be.

It's total surrender, and I'm breathless with it.

I feel his lips touching and kissing across my nape again and, at the same time he tugs my T-shirt off. Then he pauses, and I feel a tug at the knot of my bikini top—he's using his teeth to free the knot. A moment later, I feel the strings fall free, and the top sags loose. He lowers himself, kissing his way down the centerline of my spine to the second, lowermost knot. And again, his teeth tug at the loose strings, and the knot falls apart, and his kisses skate and dance and slide up my bare back, and his hand gathers the bikini top between my breasts, tugs once, and then he tosses the top aside, and I'm bare to his touch. Oh, god. God. Yes, god. His palm descends on my bare flesh, my nipple puckering in anticipation of the roughness of his strong hand, and he's clutching me, kneading, caressing, tweaking my nipple. God, this is so incredible. Arousal slams through me, and I feel myself clench, heat throbbing in me, essence of need making me slippery and damp.

I lose myself in his touch, then. He kisses my neck and shoulder, my back, hairline, behind my jaw. Around my ear. I twist, needing more of his kisses, and fall onto my back. He rolls into me, and I twist my head toward him, and our lips meet, almost by accident. He groans, a ragged sound of ecstasy, and his hands toy with and tease and caress my breasts, tweaking my nipples until I'm aching with arousal.

And then, our lips locked, tongues tangling, his fingers dance downward. He's growing impatient, now. He tugs at the elastic of the bikini bottom, his fingers hooked in just below my navel. I lift my hips, and he yanks the tiny collection of string and fabric off and then his touch begins to explore between my thighs, and *fuck*, I need him. I need to touch him.

I can't help myself. It's been so long and I can't make myself hold out anymore, I can't wait for him.

I untie his board shorts, loosen the front and he lifts up and I yank them off, impatiently.

I grasp him, moaning at the feel of him.

He catches his breath, his hips lifting at my touch. "Fuck, Audra. I haven't come in so long."

"Me either."

"You touch me like that much longer, and I'm done. I won't last a second with your hand on me like that."

"Good," I whisper against his lips, grinning. "I'm in no hurry. I just need to touch you. Feel you. Be here with you, connect with you." I stroke him slowly. "I just need you, all of you, in every way there is."

His fingers are busy, exploring me, touching me. "I feel like a damn teenager. Seriously, I'm ten goddamn seconds from coming all over your hands."

I gasp at his touch, writhing my hips upward. "I'm in no better shape, Franco." I lose my breath.

"Jesus, ohhh god, yes, the way you touch me, Franco, it's so perfect."

I grasp his arousal, squeezing, halting in my strokes as his fingers find my ecstasy and drag it out of me, making me writhe, making me whimper, taking me to the edge within seconds and flinging me over, throwing me screaming his name into the throes of climax.

And then, once the waves of orgasm have subsided a bit, I'm stroking him again. I know how close he is, and I'm watching eagerly. I keep my strokes slow and lazy, but he's losing it, groaning, thrusting.

"Oh god, Audra," he growls. He tries to get up, tries to move. "I need you, Audra."

I move downward, sliding my face across his chest and down his belly, and I taste him. Feel him slide between my lips, stretching my jaw. I taste him, flick my tongue against him, swirling, licking. He knots his fingers in my hair and his breathing catches, and he's moaning low in his throat.

And then, abruptly, he pulls away. Rolls up onto his knees, staring down at me, breathing raggedly, chest heaving, saliva-coated erection bobbing and swaying and glistening.

"Franco, I wanted to—"

"Later," he murmurs. "That's not how I want this one to go."

He lowers himself over me, and I spread my legs wide and reach for his face, guiding his mouth to mine, and as his body moves to cover mine and I feel his weight on me, I caress his cheek and bury my fingers in his hair. His lips slash across mine and I'm breathing him, tasting his tongue, and then I feel him against me, nudging, sliding against my entrance.

There is absolutely no hesitation. I know exactly what I'm doing, this time. I'm not lost in a haze of lust, and I know the potential risks and I don't care.

I need him.

All of him.

Bare.

Now.

I notch him between my lips and thrust my hips up against him. I cry out as he fills me in a slow, burning, sensual slide. His moan matches mine, and then his mouth devours mine and I'm whimpering...sobbing, as we find our rhythm together.

I wrap myself around him, my arms clinging to his shoulders, fingers clawing into his muscle, my legs hooked tight around his waist, my face buried in the side of his neck, the salt of his skin on my tongue. I'm writhing, he's pulsing deep, and we're matching thrust for thrust and whimper for moans.

There's nothing but him and me, and we are lost in a whirlwind of union, and all of our senses are tangled together. I feel only him, taste only him, hear only him, smell only him. I open my eyes and see his back arched and flexing, his buttocks tensing and releasing as he thrusts, and my own ankles locked together at the small of his back.

I seek him, and I find his mouth, and I kiss him as he comes. I swallow his desperate grunts, and kiss him through his cursing and I devour my name as it falls from his lips.

When he's finished, he goes limp on me, but only for a moment, and then he tries to roll off me.

I cling to him and refuse to let go. "Stay," I whisper. "I love the way you crush me like this."

He pulls away enough to kiss me, and this time, the kiss has no end. It moves, it morphs into more than a kiss. He's softening inside me as we kiss, and he's leaking through me and I don't care. I want all the mess we can make.

We kiss, and we kiss.

I could kiss him forever, until I'm breathless and my lips are swollen and I can't breathe.

Then we roll together so he's on his back and I'm straddling him. He's flaccid, slick and sticky, and I take him into my hand and toy with him and play with him and tease him and stroke him, and he watches as I bring him back to life, stroking him to full hardness, and then I lift up and take him into me once more.

He palms my breasts as they sway above him and I brace one hand against his chest as I ride him slowly, and with my other fingers I touch myself. His thumb takes over at some point, but I've lost all sense, only aware of the aching slide of him, at the throb of my orgasm as it rises through me. I roll my hips slowly, taking him in deep, long grinding thrusts. And then he's grunting and moving and I'm whimpering and thrashing, and then I feel him throb inside me and he's crying out my name and I'm screaming his as I come, and I feel him unleash inside me in a hot wet rush and I'm coming around him and he's coming inside me and we're lost in this together.

After a too-brief eternity, it's over and I collapse onto him, and I feel his breath ragged on my scalp, and his heart beating wildly in his chest.

I lay on him, and he holds me, and we're content like that for who knows how long.

Eventually, I lift up, prop my elbows on his chest, and gaze at him. "Clean me, feed me, and fuck me again, in that order."

He rumbles a laugh. "How about we take a shower together and I take care of two of the three at the same time?"

"Oh, I was planning on that," I say, smirking. "I'll just need you all over again as soon as we're done eating."

"How long can we stay in this condo?" Franco asks.

"I have to be back for work day after tomorrow."

"Good, so we have all of today and most of tomorrow to stay in bed?"

"And then, when we're home, we can take turns between my place and yours, fucking until we're exhausted."

He cups my face in his palm. "Audra…this isn't fucking anymore, and we both know it."

I wrinkle my nose. "Do we have to call it that other thing? Can't we call it something different?"

"Yeah, we can, but just once we need to acknowledge, out loud, what this is."

I huff, pretending to be irritated by his insistence. "Fine." I kiss his lips again, a quick peck. "Franco, carry me into the shower and *make love* to me up against the wall."

He rolls out of bed with me in his arms, getting to his feet without putting me down, carries me into the bathroom and sets me on the closed toilet seat lid. Turns on the shower, and then bends over me and kisses me as the water runs hot.

We don't make love in the shower, though.

We take turns washing each other clean, rinsing off, and then I press him up against the wall and sink to my knees and…well, I make love him with my mouth. Slowly. I grasp his hips and use only my tongue and mouth, and I take so long the water runs lukewarm, and I swallow every last drop of him and wash him all over again…and then he carries me into the bedroom, throws me, dripping wet, onto the bed, pulls me to the edge, goes to his knees, and makes love to me with his mouth in return, making me scream and thrash and come so many times I lose count.

And then, clean, momentarily sated, we spend hours eating and talking and watching Netflix, and then we go out to the beach and swim and tease each other with dirty words and promises, and then he takes me to dinner and plies me with wine and sweet words and sweeter promises, and we spend the whole night through making good on every single one of those promises.

We don't come up for air until well past dawn the next day, and then we sleep till afternoon, only to wake up and do it all over again until we have to scramble, flustered and smelling of sex, to the airport to catch our flight home.

Unbeknownst to me, Imogen had conspired with Jesse to change my return flight home so Franco and I could sit together. I spend the entire trip, including the layover, passed out on Franco's shoulder.

Hours later, I stumble bleary-eyed and bedraggled to Franco's truck, and fall promptly asleep on the drive home. Which becomes a true drive *home*, as he takes me to his place.

He carries me in to his room and cradles me in his arms in his bed.

I wake up as he climbs in behind me.

I twist, blinking sleepily at him over my shoulder. "Hey, Franco?"

He smiles at me, a tired curve of his lips. "Yeah, babe?"

"I don't think I've said this yet, but...I'm in love with you."

He twists me so I'm on my side, facing him, chin against his chest and gazing up at him. "Audra, I am so hopelessly in love with you it's actually kind of stupid."

"You're stupid for me?"

He nods. "Completely."

A long silence; neither of us fall asleep, and I can feel Franco thinking.

I nip at his chest with my teeth, playfully. "Say whatever you're thinking, Franco."

"You're sure? It's kind of crazy."

"Hit me with all of your crazy."

"Sell your condo. Live here with me." I don't answer for a long time, and I feel Franco getting antsy. "Too soon?"

I shake my head. "No, not too soon." I smirk up

at him. "While you were sleeping on the flight from Atlanta, I emailed a friend who's a realtor."

He blinks. "You did? Why?"

"To tell him I'm interested in listing it."

He blinks again. "You...did?"

I laugh. "There's an open house in two weeks." I hesitate. "My realtor anticipates it selling in a matter of days."

He sighs and laughs at the same time. "You knew I'd ask."

"I knew if you didn't, I'd just...move in." I push a strand of hair away from his eye. "I don't ever want to spend another night apart from you."

"Good," he says. "I wasn't planning on letting you."

A long, easy quiet settles between us.

"Franco?"

"Hmmm?"

"Are we taking this from zero to a hundred way too fast?"

"Yeah. But this has been developing between us for months." He's so sleepy, now. He only slept a few hours on the leg from Atlanta to Chicago, while I slept the whole time.

I feel him falling asleep, and I drowse with him, content, happy, in love...and not at all scared of it anymore.

EPILOGUE

O NCE IT WAS CLEAR THAT FRANCO WAS ASLEEP AND I wasn't going to sleep again anytime soon, I hold him, his head cradled against my breast, and sort through emails from the last week and a half, mostly updates and questions from my clients. Then I answer a barrage of texts from Imogen, asking for updates. I text her a photo of us right now, Franco's head on my chest, his hand on my breast.

I include a message beneath the photo: *I'm selling my condo and moving in with him.*

Imogen sends a shocked face emoji, and then an all-caps text: *OMG!! ARE YOU F-ING SERIOUS??!!*

I send back the same shocked face. *Totally legit. Should be moved in here within a month, max.*

Imogen: *You're sure? I mean, that's fast, Audra.*

Me: *Never been more sure of anything in my life. It's just...right.*

Me: *And, Imogen? Thank you. More than I can say.*

Imogen: *We just gave you a little nudge. Me, Jesse, and James*.

At that moment, my phone rings: LAUREL MADISON.

I answer the phone, using the quietest whisper possible. "Hey, Laurel. I was thinking about you, actually. I've been a shitty friend lately, and I'm sorry. I said we'd stay in contact, but I sort of fell off the face of the earth."

She responds, but it's distorted, tangled in sobs. "I—he—we—"

"Laurel, Laurel, breathe. Calm down. Talk to me, tell me what's wrong."

She takes a few steadying breaths. "It wasn't supposed to happen like this."

"What wasn't?"

"Him. Us. This whole thing."

"Who?"

"RYDER!" she wails. "Oh god, I'm so stupid."

"Laurel—*what happened*?"

"I'm so, so stupid. I knew it was a dumb idea, and I did it anyway."

"Did what? Dammit, woman, talk sense."

She laughs. "Sorry, sorry. I'm just distraught."

"You *think*?"

"I went on a date with him, and it was great. We went on another date, and it was great. Three dates, then a fourth."

"Laurel."

"What?"

"What did you do?"

"I fell for him."

"And?"

She sighs. "You of all people should understand, Audra! He's not the kind of guy you fall for. He said so himself, right before he stopped answering my texts and calls."

"Oh." I pause, because what I'd normally, instinctively tell her doesn't jibe with my newfound state of being. "I mean, he can't be that hard to track down, can he?"

"Probably not, but..."

"But what, Laurel."

"Do I *want* to track him down? What would I say if I did?" She sighs yet again. "I knew better than to let myself like Ryder, but I couldn't help it."

"Do you need a girls' night? You, Nova, Imogen, and me?"

"Yes!" She sounds pathetically grateful. "And then you guys can talk me out of liking him."

"Well, I can't guarantee that will happen. That part might be tricky."

"I was afraid you'd say that," she says, laughing. "But you can try."

"Tomorrow, or today, whatever. How about after work—say seven. There's this great Mexican place Imogen and I have been going to for years. You guys will love it. We'll get hammered on margaritas and eat too many corn chips and you can tell us about Ryder."

"I don't want to tell you about him, I want to forget him!"

"If he's anything like Franco, then good luck, honey."

She groans. "That's what I'm afraid of."

Want more of Ryder and Laurel's story, and the
world of Dad Bod Contracting?

Book Three: *Nailed*

Coming soon!

Jasinda Wilder

Visit me at my website: **www.jasindawilder.com**
Email me: **jasindawilder@gmail.com**

If you enjoyed this book, you can help others enjoy it as well by recommending it to friends and family, or by mentioning it in reading and discussion groups and online forums. You can also review it on the site from which you purchased it. But, whether you recommend it to anyone else or not, thank you *so much* for taking the time to read my book! Your support means the world to me!

My other titles:

The Preacher's Son:
Unbound
Unleashed
Unbroken

Biker Billionaire:
Wild Ride

Big Girls Do It:
Better (#1), Wetter (#2), Wilder (#3), On Top (#4)
Married (#5)
On Christmas (#5.5)
Pregnant (#6)
Boxed Set

Rock Stars Do It:
Harder
Dirty
Forever
Boxed Set

From the world of *Big Girls* and *Rock Stars*:
Big Love Abroad

Delilah's Diary:
A Sexy Journey
La Vita Sexy
A Sexy Surrender

The Falling Series:
Falling Into You
Falling Into Us
Falling Under
Falling Away
Falling for Colton

The Ever Trilogy:
Forever & Always
After Forever
Saving Forever

The world of *Alpha*:
Alpha
Beta
Omega
Harris: Alpha One Security Book 1
Thresh: Alpha One Security Book 2
Duke: Alpha One Security Book 3
Puck: Alpha One Security Book 4

The world of Stripped:
Stripped
Trashed

The world of *Wounded*:
Wounded
Captured

The Houri Legends:
Jack and Djinn
Djinn and Tonic

The Madame X Series:

Madame X

Exposed

Exiled

The One Series

The Long Way Home

Where the Heart Is

There's No Place Like Home

Badd Brothers:

Badd Motherf*cker

Badd Ass

Badd to the Bone

Good Girl Gone Badd

Badd Luck

Badd Mojo

Big Badd Wolf

Badd Boy

Badd Kitty

Dad Bod Contracting

Hammered

Drilled

The Black Room
(With Jade London):
Door One
Door Two
Door Three
Door Four
Door Five
Door Six
Door Seven
Door Eight
Deleted Door

Standalone titles:
Yours

Non-Fiction titles:
You Can Do It
You Can Do It: Strength
You Can Do It: Fasting

Jack Wilder Titles:
The Missionary

To be informed of new releases and special offers,
sign up for
Jasinda's email newsletter.